Blackballed!

For Alexis
Good Luck with
Your Book!

Leo A Murray

Blackballed!

Leo A. Murray

Library of Congress Control Number:		2011962248
ISBN:	Hardcover	978-1-4691-3435-2
	Softcover	978-1-4691-3434-5
	Ebook	978-1-4691-3436-9

blackballedthenovel@yahoo.com

This book was printed in the United States of America.

To order additional copies of this book, contact:
Xlibris Corporation
1-888-795-4274
www.Xlibris.com
Orders@Xlibris.com
107824

This piece of fiction is dedicated to the memory of Ann Pica: Without "Annie's" nudging, prodding, and sometimes outright nagging, Blackballed would have never seen the light of day. I will be forever in your debt, "Annie." At the time of her passing, this wonderful woman was simultaneously reading two books, a pastime she enjoyed for most of her 89 years. We love you and miss you, "Annie."

ACKNOWLEDGEMENTS

Thanks to Jackie Ernst and Steve Petruso for their individual contributions to this novel.

A very special thank you to Lackawanna County, Pennsylvania, Discovery Court Judge Henry Burke.

PROLOGUE

He had managed to secure—strong-arm really—enough votes to get elected. But it was difficult, if not outright impossible, to find anyone who actually liked Archville mayor Albert Jenkins. The thirty-five-year-old bastard, born into old coal money, was a backstabbing manipulator who knew no bounds when it came to obtaining what he wanted. He used and abused people as if it were sport. But when he was found in his office lying in a pool of blood, having been clubbed to death with a baseball bat, it touched off an investigation that would eventually expose a wealthy family's decades-old secret and carve a path to corruption at the highest levels of the county's legal system.

CHAPTER ONE

THE ARCHVILLE LITTLE League all-stars had not won an opening-round game in a World Series tournament for two decades. Those in the rural, former coal town nestled in Pennsylvania's Pocono Mountains knew that for the last nine years, the town's team had been beaten by only one run in each game of the opening round—with four of those losses coming in extra innings.

This year was going to be different. For the first time ever, the all-star team was loaded with talent. League sponsors, coaches, and managers alike had high hopes for the team with twelve-year-olds Danny Fitzgerald, Tommy "Three Fingers" Snook, and Vince Anders in the lineup. All three could play every position on the diamond with admirable skill and agility. It was a miracle that Three Fingers—who had just two fingers and a thumb on his right hand—could even throw the ball.

Two summers earlier, Tommy Snook suffered the misfortune of holding on to a quarter-stick firework a few seconds too long. In the local emergency room, doctors did all they could to save the thumb, index, and middle fingers of his right hand. With the ring and pinky fingers missing, Three Fingers—as he quickly became known—worked very hard to make do with what he had left.

Of course, there were intense occupational hand therapy sessions, which at times, took a toll on the then ten-year-old son of former major leaguer Jack "Snuff" Snook. The elder Snook was an often flamboyant pitcher whose trophy case included three Cy Young Awards and two championship rings—all won with different teams.

Snook's reputation in the major league was that he kept his bags packed at all times because he was traded often. He was a notorious brawler and had a rap sheet of minor convictions ranging from pot possession and drunken driving to minor assaults on women.

Snook's talents were desirable, but teams signing the powerful left hander did so with trepidation. Once, while at spring training with the Indians, he was charged with felony assault, a charge later dropped when the woman he was accused of assaulting refused to testify against him. The baseball world was shocked two weeks later when the announcement was made that Snook and the alleged victim, Gloria Rapkin, planned to wed.

Three Fingers looked up to his father. The kid was practically born with a baseball in his hand. But now that hand was incomplete, so not much hope was harbored in the Snook family for Three Fingers to play pro baseball, never mind being a standout star like his father. But the seventh grader surprised almost everyone when he not only adapted to throwing a baseball with only two fingers and a thumb but excelled. Tommy had a blazing fastball that was once clocked by a local high school coach at speeds of more than eighty miles per hour—no small feat considering his digit deficit.

Having dipped deep enough into the gene pool to inherit his father's aptitude for baseball, Three Fingers also picked up his father's knack for trouble. Like Jack, Tommy was ready to brawl at the drop of a bat and, several times, was ejected from games for mouthing off to umpires. He was even known to challenge some to a fight.

In fact, it was Three Fingers's feisty behavior that was used against him when the league coaches gathered in June to vote on the all-star selections. There were eleven teams in Archville, all sponsored by local businesses for the "good of the community." The balloting that took place in the backroom at Marty's Café was pretty much uneventful—until Three Fingers's name was placed in nomination.

"I nominate Tommy Snook," uttered Sam Cortino.

Cortino had been a standout athlete in high school, lettering in three sports, and he had been heavily recruited by division one colleges for his football talents. However, a knee injury on the last day of football season ended his chances for scholarships. He ended up attending a community college for two years and studying accounting.

Surprisingly, there was no second made for Tommy Snook. The room fell quiet as eleven coaches glanced back and forth at one another.

Jeff McCracken, the coach of the league's winning team, finally spoke up. "Tommy Snook does not deserve to be on this team. He doesn't possess the qualities that exemplify the true character of an all-star."

McCracken loved baseball, had played for years, and was in excellent physical shape at fifty. He'd been an all-state first baseman in high school and had been drafted by the Tigers right out of school. There wasn't much money involved in playing Triple A ball, and McCracken called it quits when he was traded to a Florida team.

Sam Cortino was shocked. "Without Snook," he said, "we may not win the opening game *again* this year." Cortino stood up and pointed his finger at the other coaches. "The kid is a natural talent and he's just that—a kid." Cortino's voice grew louder. "I can't believe you guys are not going to put a kid who throws an eighty-mile-an-hour fastball on this team."

Next to speak was Al Jenkins, Archville's mayor. "Sure, he may be a good ballplayer," the mayor said, "but he certainly brings nothing else to the table." The mayor went on to say that the town's police had had a number of problems with the twelve-year-old. Actually, the mayor was manipulating things a bit. Three times in recent months, the Archville police investigated complaints that Three Fingers was bullying kids on the playground. None of the allegations, however, were ever founded. And academically, Three Fingers was about average.

"I'm placing Tommy Snook's name in nomination again," Cortino said. "If you guys are loony enough to leave such talent off the roster when this town has a chance to make history, I say you'll live to regret it."

There was still no second for Three Fingers however.

*   *   *

At the Snook home on Laurel Street, the family was preparing to celebrate. Close friends and business associates of Jack Snook were mingling in the yard, awaiting word that the child who overcame a horrible accident would be one of the twelve boys representing Archville in its quest for a championship title.

Perhaps the most revered guest that night was Sally Powderly. She was the occupational hand therapist whose work with Tommy had greatly aided his recovery. Often working seven days a week with him, she helped strengthen what was left of his badly injured hand. Even Sally was surprised at the way her work paid off. "Quitters never win and winners never quit" was the catchphrase she would use to push Tommy when he needed motivation. Ms. Powderly was very attractive and turned heads wherever she went. She didn't dress the part of a vamp, choosing instead to leave something to the imagination. In fact, many people told her she looked like Heather Locklear, a compliment she never got tired of hearing.

A white stretch limousine rolled up in front of the modest Snook home. Everyone knew the limo belonged to a local used-car dealer by the name of Charlie Wetzel. Sleazy he may have been, but Charlie Wetzel was a salesman, for he turned a used-car business he acquired through an inheritance into a gold mine. Rumors abounded in the northeastern part of the state that he was worth millions. People said Wetzel was so cunning he could sell a condom to the pope.

The relationship between Charlie Wetzel and Jack Snook was purely business. Soon after word got out that the famous Jack Snook was moving to Archville, Wetzel seized the opportunity to sign him as a television pitchman. Wetzel advertised his business exclusively on late-night cable and was sure that a former baseball player with three Cy Young Awards and a pair of championship rings would sell cars.

Charlie Wetzel's beliefs were not far off the mark. "The paperwork on every car we sell is signed by Jack 'Snuff' Snook," Wetzel proclaimed in his ads. Then he would add, "If you're buying a used car, don't get thrown a curveball." The television spots would always end with Jack Snook signing papers and congratulating people who had just purchased a used car from Wetzel's lot.

Charlie Wetzel had just gotten out of his limo when Sam Cortino's Chevy pickup truck pulled up across the street. "How's the truck running, Sam?" Wetzel chuckled. "I still say you stole it from me."

Sam Cortino could not find it within himself to laugh at Charlie Wetzel's humor, though he had laughed at that same line at least a hundred times before. He crossed the street without looking and was damn near hit by a car.

"What the hell is the matter with you?" asked Wetzel. "Are you drunk?"

"I'm as sober as a judge," replied Cortino. "The coaches left Three Fingers off the all-star roster," he added, hanging his head as they walked toward the Snook front yard.

"You *must* be drunk, or crazy," said Wetzel.

"I'm neither, and they did."

"What was the vote?"

"Let's put it this way, I couldn't get a single coach to second my nomination."

"Those bastards," replied Wetzel.

Cortino shook his head. "That scumbag Jenkins was behind it. I know he was."

"He's still mad because Jack Snook beat him in the last Democrat primary," Wetzel declared.

Beat Jenkins in the primary Snook did. However, Jenkins ran a write-in campaign for the Republican nomination and forced a general election race. By a mere four votes, Jenkins was elected to a second term in November. He threatened everybody he could: "You pull my lever, or I pull the skeletons out of your closet!"

"I spent a ton of money on that election," said Wetzel.

Cortino nodded. "I know. That's why Jenkins doesn't like you either."

"Fuck him," said Wetzel, growing more agitated.

Jack Snook came out on the porch and motioned to Cortino and Wetzel to come inside. "The drinks are on me."

Both men joined the elder Snook at his basement bar, which was nicely decorated with keepsakes from the major leaguer's baseball days, the centerpiece of which was a glass case holding a pair of World Series rings.

"Tommy's not on the all-star team," uttered Cortino.

Jack Snook jerked backward like he had just taken a bullet. "What do you mean he's not on the all-star team?"

"The coaches didn't select him. The only vote he had was mine."

Snook sneered venomously. "Let me guess. Jenkins was behind it."

"You could say that," said Cortino.

Just then, Three Fingers walked into the basement. "Hey, Coach, Mr. Wetzel," Tommy said with a big grin. "When's the first all-star practice?"

Charlie and Sam made an excuse to get some fresh air, leaving the father and son to talk.

Three Fingers was alarmed. "What's going on, Dad?"

Jack Snook took a deep breath. "Son, I have bad news. The coaches didn't put you on the all-star team. I'm sorry, I know how hard you worked to get on the team."

Three Fingers fought back tears. "But, Dad, why?"

"I don't know, son. But I will find out."

At that, Tommy erupted, grabbed one of the barstools and threw it across the room.

In that moment, Jack Snook saw himself in Tommy's tirade. He put his arms around him and reminded him that acting out would not change anything. "I learned that the hard way, son. What is, is."

Tommy breathed heavily and began to calm down.

When Tommy, his only child, was born, Jack developed a new outlook on things. His son's birth was his proudest moment after which he made a vow to never again let his temper get the best of him. Now, however, that vow's memory was clouded by his fury. He could not, however, let Tommy see how angry he was. He had to teach his son how to overcome his own worst enemy: a hot temper.

Once Tommy had cooled off, Jack reluctantly went outside to inform his guests that his son would not be on the all-star team.

"You're such a kidder," said Sally Powderly. "Everyone in town knows that Tommy is the best player in the league, and probably the state."

"I'm not kidding, and I would like it if everyone left. My family and I would like to be alone."

Saddened by the news, the crowd slowly departed, all except Sally. She lingered behind, hugged Tommy, and whispered in his ear, "Don't worry, right now, you're the best, and you will show them some day. Remember, a winner never quits and a quitter never wins."

Tommy gave her a weak smile and hung his head as he trudged upstairs.

Alone in the basement, Snook poured a shot of Jack Daniel's, something he had not done in a very long time. Just as he was raising the glass to his lips, Gloria came up behind him. "Honey, you don't want to do that. You promised."

He set the shot glass down on the bar. "This is my fault. If I hadn't listened to Wetzel telling me I could win the mayor's race, Tommy would be on the all-star team."

"What's the mayor's race got to do with it?" Gloria quietly asked. She was petite, barely measuring five feet in height, with red hair that wisped her shoulders when she walked. Gloria was loved by everyone. Her easygoing personality allowed her to find good in everyone. And there was plenty of good to be found in her own generous spirit. Gloria was famous for baking batches of her famous chocolate chip cookies to sell at the refreshment stand at Tommy's home games. The cookies were usually gone before the first inning was over.

Gloria taught first grade at Washington Elementary in a nearby school district. Twice in recent years, she had been nominated by her peers for Teacher of the Year.

Now, she called upon her better self as she leaned against her husband. "Well?"

"Sam said Jenkins was behind keeping Tommy off the team. I ought to go up to the mansion right now and bust his pretty-boy face up for him. He's taking his dislike for me out on Tommy. Typical politician."

"That's exactly what he and his rich friends are expecting you to do," said Gloria. "Then they'll say, 'I told you he never changed.'"

Snook sighed. "You're right, as always." He kissed her on the cheek and told her he loved her.

"Now what do we do with our lad?"

"Let's talk to him."

When they went upstairs, Tommy was nowhere to be found.

"I know where he is," said Jack.

Sure enough, Three Fingers was working off some of his anger in a nearby field, where years ago, his father had hung a tire from a tree so Tommy could perfect his pitching. At first, it was a car tire, but as Tommy's deadly accuracy developed, they needed a smaller target—the thirteen-inch tire from a lawn tractor. Recently, Tommy had thrown 33 for 33 through the small tire. This from the major league distance of sixty-feet six-inches.

Jack and Gloria gathered up their son and headed out for ice cream and some talk. The Snooks had no way of knowing that night their lives were about to be turned inside out.

CHAPTER TWO

T HE NEXT MORNING, all of Archville awakened to startling news.

Mayor Al Jenkins had been found savagely beaten to death in his office. Authorities were not revealing much information other than that the murder weapon was believed to have been a baseball bat.

The county coroner removed the body from the building at noon—just in time for the live midday news on local television.

The state police mobile crime lab was parked all day in front of the municipal building where Jenkins's body was discovered in a pool of blood by janitorial aide Fred Saunders. Saunders had worked at the municipal building for as long as anyone could remember. During the school year, he doubled as a crossing guard.

All three local television stations held "exclusive" interviews with the custodian during which he told viewers of his bloody early-morning discovery. Crossing Guard Fred, as the children knew him, was indeed having his fifteen minutes of fame.

The patrons over at Marty's Café meanwhile were tuned into the local CBS affiliate. The station broke into the middle of an interview with Tim Richards, Archville's council president and the man likely to replace Mayor Jenkins, to report that police had identified a person of interest in the brutal slaying.

Reporter Tim Kearns, who could make a PTA meeting sound like an investigative report, came on the screen. "WPNA has learned that former major leaguer Jack 'Snuff' Snook has been taken to the state police barracks in Drewmore for questioning about the homicide."

Marty's Café was unnaturally quiet. Among the patrons was Jeff McCracken, the coach of this year's all-star team. "Doesn't surprise me one bit," said McCracken. "Mayor Jenkins slipped Snook's kid the 'blackball' last night right back there." He pointed to Marty's back room.

This sparked a loud murmur among the stunned patrons.

McCracken, an electrical contractor by trade, finished his sandwich and got up from his stool. "Gotta go," he announced. "First all-star practice is in twenty minutes at the Complex."

The Complex was a beautiful facility made possible when Archville obtained a federal recreation grant two years earlier. Upon its completion, Archville was able to host nighttime baseball. There were three well-manicured fields—one for Little League, one for Teen League, and a multipurpose softball diamond where men's and women's teams played.

Jeff McCracken's Corvette rolled to a stop in the parking area at the Complex. Much to his surprise, there was only one member of the all-star roster waiting for him. He was puzzled.

Vince Anders, a stocky kid who was big for his twelve years, was sitting on the bleachers in the home team section. He braced his head in his hands, elbows on knees.

"Hi, Coach," said Anders as Jeff McCracken walked in his direction.

"Where is everybody, Vince?"

Anders took a deep breath. "They're not coming," he said.

"Why?"

"Well, Coach, we sorta had a team meeting this morning. The other guys and I decided by vote. We don't want to play in the all-stars this year."

"What?" Jeff McCracken yelled.

Anders shrugged and stared at his sneakers. "We don't want to play."

"Why?"

"Because everyone feels that Three Fingers should be on the team. He's better than all of us. And he worked hard for this." Anders crossed his arms in growing defiance. "If he's not on the team, we don't play."

"We'll see about this," McCracken said and pulled out his cell phone to call Jerry Fitzgerald, father of Danny Fitzgerald and president of the Archville Little League.

"Jerry," he said into the phone. "We have a problem."

"I know." Jerry's surprisingly calm voice cackled through the line. "Danny already told me about the team's decision."

"What are you going to do about it?"

"I'm going to back the players 100 percent. It's their decision."

"Are you serious?" McCracken snapped, ignoring Anders standing a few feet away.

"Look, Jeff, we let that asshole Jenkins bully us into not putting Tommy on the team, just because the mayor hated the kid's father. Jenkins's politics and his vendettas do not belong in the Archville Little League's decisions. Jenkins bullied us and twisted arms to get his way. I regret even listening to him." Fitzgerald paused, "By the way, Jeff, if you don't mind my asking, how did the mayor twist your arm?"

"He didn't twist my arm," McCracken growled.

Fitzgerald shot back, "Oh, really? Because rumor has it the mayor helped you get the contract for the town's new fire sirens in order to get you on board with his little blackball plot."

McCracken fell silent.

"Let's face it, Jeff. Jenkins had something on us all. I hope the bastard burns in hell."

McCracken glanced at Anders and lowered his voice. "What did he have on you?"

"He told me if I didn't support him in banning Three Fingers from the team, he could make my wife's municipal job a nightmare. The guy was a prick!"

The two continued the conversation twenty minutes later at Dunnigan's Tavern, where they sat at the end of the bar, nursing beers.

"It would be a shame not to have a team in the tournament this year, especially with the talent we have," said McCracken, staring into beer foam.

"We can right this mess," said Fitzgerald. "Let's call the coaches together for another meeting."

"Can't," said McCracken, and he went on to explain that the roster had already been submitted to the district commissioner.

Fitzgerald reached into his shirt pocket, pulling out an envelope. As league president, Fitzgerald had the responsibility of mailing the roster in to district officials. "With all of the commotion this morning, I forgot to mail it."

"Well, that still leaves one more issue," said McCracken. "We have already named twelve players to the roster. If Three Fingers gets on, somebody has to come off."

Fitzgerald shrugged. "We'll deal with it."

They set a coaches-only meeting for 7:30 that evening.

*   *   *

McCracken was the last to arrive at Marty's for the meeting. All the other coaches knew about the team's earlier decision not to play in the tournament.

"Gentlemen," said McCracken, "we called you here tonight in hopes that we can right a wrong. As you know, our all-stars have unanimously decided not to play in the tournament this year unless Tommy 'Three Fingers' Snook is on the roster. It was their decision."

"We already picked a team," shouted Barney Clarkson, coach of the team with the worst league record this season.

"Nevertheless," said McCracken, "all of our votes last night were cast in the shadow of intimidation by the departed Jenkins. Tonight we vote according to our conscience."

"Who's going to be deleted from the roster?" asked Clarkson.

Before McCracken could address the question, however, Ed Gardener, whose landscaping business sponsored a team in the league, stood up and declared that his eleven-year-old son, Eddie Junior, wanted to be taken off the roster.

"That scumbag mayor twisted my arm for my vote and threatened to revoke my municipal contract if I didn't go along with him. He's dead now, and we don't have to be afraid," said Gardener.

As Gardener was addressing his fellow coaches, McCracken could not help remembering the first time the two met. "Let me get this right," McCracken had said, "your name is Gardener, and you're a landscaper?"

"I get that all the time," Gardener had replied wearily.

Tonight, however, Gardener was adamant about his son's name being removed from the roster. "He's only eleven, and he'll be eligible to play next year. This is the year for Archville."

Gardener received thunderous applause from his fellow coaches. The clapping and cheering was so loud, people from the bar at Marty's poked their heads through the doorway to see what was going on.

The roster was redone and promptly placed in the nearest mailbox. Because Sam Cortino was close to the Snook family, it was decided he should be the one to tell Three Fingers.

Cortino set out while the other coaches stayed at Marty's guzzling beer and talking about the great team Archville would be fielding for the tournament.

*   *   *

Cortino steered his Chevy truck on to Laurel Street. Dozens of news people were gathered in front of the Snook residence, a Cape Cod-style house with a well-manicured lawn. What stood out about the modest home were the beautiful flowers in the garden. Gloria Snook found peace and relaxation working in her garden. It was the envy of the neighborhood.

The street had gotten so congested with the media that the local police had arrived to maintain control of the situation.

As Cortino made his way to the Snook porch, he was greeted by Charlie Wetzel. "They charged Snuff with first-degree murder about a half-hour ago. It's been like this ever since," said Wetzel.

"Where's Tommy?" asked Cortino.

"He's inside with his mom and Sally Powderly."

Cortino told Wetzel of the meeting and the coaches' decision to add Tommy to the roster.

"Shoulda done that yesterday," he snarled. "Maybe all of this wouldn't be going on."

Cortino and Wetzel entered the house.

Three Fingers and his mother were on the couch, crying. Sally Powderly was sitting in a recliner. Gloria and Sally had become good friends over the past two years, bonding over their shared but very unique love for Tommy.

"I don't know if this is a good time or not, but Tommy has been added to the all-star roster," declared Cortino.

Gloria was numb with shock. Cortino's words did not register with her. "I'm sorry," she said. "Did you just say something?"

Cortino repeated himself. "Look," he added, "we all know that Jack did not kill Jenkins. God knows with Jenkins's reputation, there will be more than enough suspects by tomorrow morning."

"They say Jack did it," said Gloria, wiping away tears. "I doubt they'll be looking for any more suspects."

Suddenly, there was a knock at the door. Sally Powderly rose to answer it. "If it's another reporter, I might forget that I'm a lady," she added.

However, when she opened the door she was shocked to see the hulking frame of John Lovello—a man widely recognized as one of the nation's top criminal defense attorneys—standing before her. She welcomed in the six-foot two-inch Lovello. He kept himself in good shape, but lately, he'd been neglecting his exercise regimen and was tipping the scales at 210 pounds. Nevertheless, he made an imposing presence. Judges knew that when John Lovello was defending a client, sparks would be flying in the courtroom. Over the years, Lovello had accumulated so many contempt-of-court citations, he could wallpaper a room with them. Lovello was often told he looked like actor Brian Dennehy.

"It took you long enough to get here," declared Charlie Wetzel. "At a grand an hour, you must have taken a slow bus from New York to find us."

Lovello shot back, "Just make sure the $500,000 retainer check doesn't bounce."

"We can't afford you," said Gloria, shaking her head.

Before she could utter another word, Charlie Wetzel chimed in. "I'm paying him. It's the least I can do. Jack Snook has helped me sell cars for the past twelve years."

"I'd like to talk to the Snooks alone," announced Lovello.

Wetzel headed out with a nod to all. "Good luck."

"See you at practice tomorrow, Tommy," said Cortino as he departed.

"Not sure I'll be there, with all this going on," Tommy replied downheartedly.

Lovello, a huge baseball fan himself, said that it would be good for Three Fingers to have the distraction of baseball. "I think your dad would want you to play."

Gloria nodded, but Tommy just shrugged.

"Tommy, you look tired," said Lovello. "Why don't you go get some rest so your mom and I can talk?"

Tommy said good night and ambled away to the staircase.

When the room had emptied, Lovello clasped his hands together and demanded to be told everything. He already knew most of it from talking to Wetzel, but he listened with rapt attention.

Gloria quickly recapped the last two days for the attorney.

"Gloria, I want you to tell me about last night and give me as much detail as you can remember," Lovello urged gently. "Was Jack here all night?"

"After we found out Tommy had been blackballed from the team, we went for ice cream and came back here at about 10:30. Jack wasn't sleepy and decided to take his Mustang out for a drive. He got back around 2:30. I heard the car pull into the garage. He came upstairs, took a shower, and came to bed."

"Are you sure about the time?" Lovello asked.

"Yes. I know it's important."

"Very," he said. "The coroner has fixed the time of the mayor's death at between midnight and one thirty a.m."

Gloria shuddered.

"Did you talk to Jack this morning?" Lovello asked.

"He was still sleeping when I got up. I took my Girl Scout troop to the museum in Scranton this morning. I got home shortly after noon, just in time to see the police taking Jack away in handcuffs. They wouldn't let me talk to him."

Lovello nodded with sympathy. "Well, I've made arrangements to meet with Jack in the morning. I think it will serve us all well to get a good night's sleep."

"Where will you be staying?"

"I'm booked at the Holiday Inn in Drewmore."

Before he departed, Lovello cautioned Gloria not to talk to the news hounds outside. "I'll see what I can do about getting rid of them in the morning. Please, tell Tommy not to talk to them either. They twist every word you say."

Lovello was indeed the coveted interview the press was waiting for. It was 10:00 p.m. when he stepped outside. Immediately cameras and microphones were stuck in his face.

"I will possibly have a statement at three a.m. outside the murder scene," he said as he made his way to his car. Of course, he had no plans whatsoever of being in front of the municipal building at 3:00 a.m. He chuckled to himself as he knew that the place would be a circus inside of twenty minutes, with reporters and photographers jockeying for position. *Let the cops deal with it,* he thought. At the very least, the Snooks deserved a few hours of peace.

CHAPTER THREE

A S THE NATION'S top criminal defense attorney sped away from Laurel Street, he kept a keen eye on his rearview mirror. Sure enough, he was being followed. "Damn reporters," he mumbled.

Lovello turned on his cell phone's GPS device to get a fix on his location. Then he clicked open his numbers directory and tapped in Jake Barclay's number. Barclay answered instantly.

"Are you in Archville yet?" Lovello asked.

"Yep, got here two hours ago."

Jake Barclay was a former Secret Service agent now in the private investigation business. He was one of only a handful of PIs licensed in all fifty states. He had served two presidents and trained at the FBI's Quantico facility before deciding to join the Secret Service. His reputation was known almost as widely as Lovello's. The two had served together in the Marine Corps during Vietnam and had been friends ever since.

"I have a buzzard on my tail," Lovello told him. "I need you to run some interference for me."

"No problem, what's your location?"

They swapped information, and soon they were pulling into a parking lot midway between Archville and Drewmore. As soon as the buzzard's car made its way into the lot with its lights off, Barclay knew what to do. Lovello sped out of the exit like a bat out of hell. Barclay waited until the last possible moment and strategically used his car to block the reporter's hasty exit.

The reporter was Charlie Mars, the crime beat guy from the local daily, the *Gazette-Times*. Mars had won numerous awards for investigative reporting and was known for going to outrageous lengths for a good story. Right now he was ticked off that he lost Lovello. He got out of his car and started shouting at Barclay.

"Blow it out your ass," snapped Barclay. "You're wasting your time following Lovello."

Mars was stunned. Questions ran through his mind: How did they know? Who was this guy running interference for a top-notch LA defense attorney in Northeastern Pennsylvania?

"Who are you?" Mars asked.

"Jake Barclay," he snarled. The detective stepped out of his Jaguar. His size—six-feet three-inches—dwarfed Mars's five feet, eight inches. As Barclay stretched, Mars noticed the Walther PPK handgun in his belt. Mars knew exactly who Barclay was. He'd read about him dozens of times in the LA and New York papers. Barclay was known to have a short fuse. Mars made a mental note not to fuck with the detective.

Charlie Mars was an award-winning reporter who had worked the local paper since receiving his degree in journalism from Penn State University in the seventies. Typically, Mars was dressed like a reporter: golf shirt with the paper's logo on it and dress jeans. He had a reputation for sniffing out stories and not taking no for an answer. However, he was a wildcard, and his editors carefully scrutinized every word he wrote.

"You're here on the Snook case with Lovello," Mars stated.

Barclay eyed Mars and gave him a once-over. "You might say that. I would guess that a reporter with enough balls to follow an attorney to see where he's staying likes to be on top of his game. Right now, I have nothing on this Snook matter. If you tell me what you know now, you could be paid back later in spades when I sink my teeth into this."

Mars thought for a moment. "Deal. I know an all-night diner about six miles from here. Go for coffee?"

Barclay agreed. "I'll follow you."

Mars, however, pointed out that he had to be back in Archville by 3:00 a.m. for Lovello's statement in front of the municipal building.

"Trust me," said Barclay. "There will be no statement at three. Lovello doesn't care much for the media. He's just messing with you guys."

Mars chuckled good naturedly. "Lawyers can be so cute."

At Chick's Diner, the two men took a booth in back. The diner was empty, save for a burly truck driver at the counter. They were approached by a middle-aged waitress wearing a stained apron and a hairnet. After they ordered coffee, Mars took the lead. "So, who's paying for Lovello? The Snooks can't afford talent like that."

"Off the record for now?" asked Barclay.

Mars raised both hands in a gesture of innocence. "Off the record."

Barclay leaned forward and lowered his voice. "Charlie Wetzel's writing the checks. They're longtime acquaintances, and of course, Snook works for him. Wetzel likes the guy."

Mars nodded. "It was rumored in the district attorney's office today that Wetzel might, if you pardon the pun, step up to the plate for Snook."

Barclay raised his eyebrows at Mars. "What else have you heard about the case?"

"Well," said Mars, "most of what they have is circumstantial. The autographed Louisville Slugger used to beat the mayor to death was a gift from Snook to the community. The guys went bonkers when they found out an ex-major leaguer had moved to town. They made a plaque out of the bat, along with one of Snook's gloves."

Mars went on to say the DA believed the motive for the murder was Mayor Jenkins's role in blackballing Snook's kid from the all-star team. Couple that with the fact that Snook did not have an alibi for where he was at the time of the murder, and there's the DA's case in a nutshell.

"Any other suspects?"

"Tons," said Mars. "Nobody liked Jenkins. He was trounced by Snook in the Democrat primary last May by a two-to-one margin. However, he managed to get the Republican write-in vote and won the general election in November by four votes. Jenkins brutalized Snook with TV ads about his well-publicized marijuana arrests."

Mars took a long sip of coffee and continued. "It took the county board of elections six weeks to dispose of all the challenges and vote recounts. Nevertheless, he was declared the winner just in time to be sworn in to a second term in January.

"Rumor has it that Jenkins was preparing to enter the Democratic primary next year in a bid for the state senate. His family is loaded with money from back when the coal industry was thriving. But party officials saw him as weak when he lost to Snook in his own primary in Podunk Archville. The party hierarchy was not likely to gamble on a candidate like that.

"Couple all of that with the fact that Jenkins was ruthless in any pursuit that was self-beneficial and you could name dozens of suspects. Of course, none of them are immediately visible." Mars rubbed his eyes. "You have your work cut out for you, Mr. Barclay."

Barclay collected his thoughts as he sipped his coffee. "What do you know about this all-star thing?"

"Apparently, Jenkins strong-armed and threatened the coaches of the Archville Little League, intimidating them into blackballing the kid from making the team. He wielded influence like it was a blunt instrument."

"Jenkins had that much sway?"

"Sure. According to my sources, the only coach Jenkins could not compromise was Sam Cortino. He and Snook have been friends for years. Cortino served as treasurer of Snook's mayoral campaign."

Barclay fiddled with his coffee cup. The waitress came by and asked if they wanted refills.

"Might as well," said Mars.

The waitress sighed as she poured warm coffee into their white porcelain cups.

"Do you think Cortino could be considered a suspect? Would he kill for his friend?" quizzed Barclay.

"Not likely," said the newspaperman. "Cortino's a pretty straight shooter. He's married, no children, active in community sports programs for more than ten years. He's been the coach of the midget football program's A team since its inception. Last year, he chartered buses to take anyone in Archville who wanted to see the championship game in Harrisburg, a game his team won by twenty-one points."

Barclay nodded slowly, but his mind raced as he simultaneously processed information and tried to conjure up another suspect to ask Mars about.

"Hey," Mars said. "I thought this was a two-way street. When do I get to ask questions?"

"When I have some answers," Barclay replied. He scribbled his cell phone number on a napkin. The reporter returned the favor. The two men parted company in the parking lot.

Barclay flipped open his phone and dialed Lovello once he was inside his car. "I just left the buzzard. He'll be manageable."

"Good," said Lovello. "See you for breakfast at 7:30?"

"Sure, why not?"

Barclay's drive from his Upstate New York vacation home and the two cups of coffee he downed at Chick's had left him jittery. Sleep was not in the cards. He decided to acquaint himself with Northeastern Pennsylvania. Barclay drove back to Archville using the route he took with the reporter. He noticed that most of the homes were older but well taken care of. He tried to imagine what the area was like when coal mining drove the economy. He also noticed many empty buildings that were in a state of decay. The empty buildings reminded him of the empty steel mills that once dotted the banks of the Monongahela River outside Pittsburgh.

*   *   *

Lovello and Barclay met for breakfast in the Holiday Inn. The defense attorney was holding a copy of the morning paper in his hand. A banner headline on page 1 proclaimed: TOMMY SNOOK ADDED TO ALL-STAR TEAM. The story detailed how the team had been defeated in the first round of the tournament for the past twenty years. The coaches interviewed for the story all agreed that this year's team was the best they had ever assembled, and they predicted that the first round would take on a life of its own. An entire town was preparing to embrace this team, the story said.

Lovello didn't bother with a greeting as Barclay sat down, and he dove headfirst into the case. "I've made arrangements to see my client at nine fifteen," he said. "The arraignment's at ten. In the meantime, I want you to go to Archville and pick up Snook's wife and kid and bring them to the courthouse."

"No problem. What's up?"

"Apparently, after the kids on the all-star team learned that Tommy Snook was not on the roster, they decided they would not play in the tournament. With Jenkins dead, the coaches reshuffled the cards and put the kid on the team. His mother just told me Tommy doesn't want to play." Lovello continued, "I need his father to talk to him. I think he should play. It will keep him occupied while we sort this thing out."

"Got it." Barclay nodded and took a bite of toast. He was looking forward to meeting the Snooks and beginning the arduous task of untangling what appeared already to be a baffling case.

At the courthouse, the press was assembled en masse. Lovello parked his rental car and worked his way through the crowd. ESPN had even sent a stringer to cover the arraignment.

"That was some statement you gave at three a.m. in front of the municipal building," yelled a reporter from nearby Luzerne County's *Valley Voice*.

Lovello looked in the reporter's direction and quipped, "Look up the word *possibly* in the dictionary. I said I *possibly* would have a statement."

"That's no way to win friends in the Fourth Estate," said District Attorney Morgan Thomas, who had just arrived on Lovello's heels.

The DA was in his second four-year term and was widely speculated to run for an open judge's seat next year. He looked like the consummate politician: early fifties, with thinning brown hair. Lovello made note of the fact that DA Thomas was shaking the hands of the assembled media. *What a suck up,* he thought. He did not like the DA's smug attitude.

Lovello and Thomas shook hands. "Come on to my office," Thomas said.

In the office, Lovello made his pitch to let his client meet with his son and his wife.

"It's an out-of-the-ordinary request, but I think we can handle it," said Thomas. He looked Lovello square in the eyes. "You know, there is no bail for capital murder in Pennsylvania."

Lovello acknowledged Thomas's statement and reminded the DA that he was licensed to practice in the Pennsylvania courts and thus knew the law. "I didn't talk to my client yet, but I think we'll waive the preliminary hearing."

"I figured you would." Thomas smiled. "Come on," he said. "I'll take you downstairs and make arrangements for your client to see his family."

"Thanks."

Tommy and Gloria were seated in a basement room, waiting for Jack Snook to be brought in. As a decent gesture, the DA ordered that Snook's handcuffs be removed before he entered the room. The sheriff's deputies reminded Thomas about court protocol, but the DA quickly assured them that he was assuming all responsibility if anything happened.

"Thank you," Lovello said as the deputies removed the handcuffs from his client's wrists.

Snook was wearing the usual prison jumpsuit. His unshaved face and circles under his eyes told Lovello his client had a rough night. "Jack, I'm going to be your attorney. Charlie Wetzel retained me for your defense. Tommy and Gloria are waiting on the other side of that door." Lovello then told his client he would do whatever it takes to free him.

There was no reaction from Snook, who hung his head as though he had already been convicted.

"Come on, Jack, let's go see your family." Lovello did his best to sound encouraging and hopeful.

Together Lovello and Snook entered the room. Tommy dashed to his father's side, casting his arms around him. Lovello himself was moved by the moment. But the criminal defense attorney knew their time together was short. Lovello wasted none of it explaining to the former baseball player that things had now changed in Archville and that Tommy was now on the all-star roster. However, the lawyer told Jack, his son did not want to play.

Jack stood up and walked over to his son. "Tommy, we as a family are going to get through this. I did not do what they say I have done. In the meantime, son, I want you to do what you do best—play baseball. You may not realize it now, Tommy, but you're special. Most kids who have accidents like yours just give up. I don't want you to give up. Remember, a winner never quits and a quitter never wins. Promise me you'll play and do your very best for the team and for Archville. Promise me."

Tommy hugged his father again. "I promise," he said as tears streaked down his young face. Gloria too was crying. It was a sad moment for all in the room, especially for Jack.

After Tommy and Gloria left, Lovello explained to Snook that he was charged with first-degree murder, and there was no bail in a capital case in Pennsylvania. Lovello's experience in capital cases was extensive. "Jack, I am not going to come right out and ask you if you killed Mayor Jenkins. If I thought you did, I wouldn't be here."

Snook was still drying his eyes. "I swear on the lives of my family," he said. "As much as I wanted to confront him about blackballing Tommy, I did not kill that prick."

Lovello then told the ex-major leaguer they would talk more sometime after the arraignment. "I will do everything I can to prove your innocence," promised Lovello.

The room they were in had a damp musty smell to it, and Lovello's allergies were starting to bother him. He was relieved when the knock came to the door.

"We're ready for the arraignment," the DA announced.

The deputies put the handcuffs back on Jack's wrists and led him to the elevator that would take them to the second-floor courtroom of Magistrate Russell Morris, who was once a star in Triple A baseball.

The room was packed with press and spectators. Order came quickly when Magistrate Morris entered the courtroom. He was a no-nonsense kind of guy who lacked tolerance for those who ignored court decorum.

"You have been charged with first-degree murder, Mr. Snook," the magistrate stated. "Do you wish to enter a plea at this time?"

"We will enter a plea of *not guilty*, Your Honor, and ask that the charges be waived to the Court of Common Pleas," Lovello said for the record.

"So ordered," the magistrate declared.

The magistrate then stated for the record that the charges were of a nature where no bail was allowed. He ordered the defendant returned to the county lockup until his next court appearance.

Tommy and Gloria Snook wept as the sheriff's deputies led Jack away.

Lovello then told Tommy to remember his promise to his father.

Tommy's tear-stained face wore a fierce expression. "I will," he said.

CHAPTER FOUR

A T 4:00 P.M. that day, Archville would get its first glimpse of the team the town had been talking about for months. The all-stars were set for their first practice session at the Complex. It was unusually warm for a late-June afternoon, but the humidity was low, and the heat was not a bother. Coach McCracken was amazed at the turnout of townspeople for a mere practice, but he welcomed it. He knew, however, that the Snook arraignment had much to do with it.

Earlier in the day, McCracken became upset with the television coverage of the arraignment. The upcoming practice session had somehow eked its way into the so-called news on the local stations, but there was little he could do about it.

Joining the coaching staff with McCracken were Sam Cortino and Eddie Gardener, the father of the boy who had stepped aside to make room on the roster for Tommy "Three Fingers."

Unbeknownst to McCracken and his staff, Jake Barclay was in the crowd. Without any leads to follow, Barclay figured the practice session might reveal something. If not, he reasoned, rationed, it would be interesting to see a kid with two fingers and a thumb throw an eighty-mile-an-hour fastball.

McCracken took the four youths who would be sharing the pitching assignments to right field and told them to get loose with each other. The four boys—Tommy Snook, Danny Fitzgerald, Pete Carlson and Patrick Williams—began throwing the ball back and forth between them.

Looking from behind the right field fence, watching the pitchers, was janitor Fred Saunders. He had a very thin frame and a weather-beaten face. Barclay estimated his age to be about sixty. He was poorly dressed, and his work boots were just about worn out. Barclay figured Saunders did not make much more than minimum wage. The detective could tell just by looking at the man that he was not going to be much of a conversationalist. He decided to wait a while before approaching Saunders.

Saunders loved to watch the kids play ball. He never missed a regular season game nor had he missed a single one of the league's all-star games in the past. He was always in the bleachers cheering. Fred supported the league's fund-raising events too. During the league's carwash earlier that year, he was adept at flagging down motorists. He supported the teams with all his heart.

After about forty-five minutes, McCracken called his coaches together. "I find this crowd to be a distraction," he said. "What do you guys think?"

Both coaches nodded in agreement. "From now on, let's keep the practice times a secret." He had no sooner said that when a television crew from the local ABC affiliate pulled into the parking area.

"Here we go," said Cortino.

"They have every right to be here," said McCracken. "Let's just get through this session."

As batting practice started, McCracken delegated the pitching responsibilities to Danny Fitzgerald. As expected, the crowed started yelling, "We want Three Fingers! We want Three Fingers!"

McCracken quieted the crowd when he announced, "If I had a player capable of hitting an eighty-mile-an-hour fastball, I'd put Tommy on the mound. But since I don't have one, we will be saving Tommy for when it counts—the tournament."

Things couldn't have worked out better. The news that Tommy Three Fingers wouldn't be taking the mound was enough to chase the news crew away.

Tommy was the last to take batting practice. While he threw righty, the twelve-year-old batted from the left side of the plate. The first pitch tossed by Carlson, who was now on the mound, was in the dirt. "Come on, Pete, give me something I can swing at," Tommy yelled.

He got what he wanted, a fastball at the knees. With one huge swing, he crushed the pitch twenty feet beyond the right field fence. He put the next three pitches in about the same place, much to the approval of the remaining crowd.

"Mighty impressive," said John Barclay in a faint whisper to Fred Saunders.

"Who the hell are you?" croaked Saunders.

"I'm a private investigator who works for Jack Snook's lawyer. I recognized you from your picture in the paper. You're Fred Saunders, the man who found Mayor Jenkins's body."

"Yep, that's me."

"Mind if I ask you a few questions?"

"Look, I already told the police and the detectives everything. But go ahead."

"What time did you find the body?"

"Half past six. That's what time I start." The crossing guard kept his eyes turned away like he wanted to be somewhere else.

"Did you notice anything unusual that morning?"

"Sure did." Again, Saunders looked away.

"Mind if I ask you what?" The detective was getting a little bored with the vague answers, but this wasn't a good time to press it.

Just then, the pair heard the crack of the bat again. This time, Tommy had drilled a pitch over the centerfield fence. The crowd loved it.

"He's quite a kid," said Saunders. He showed sincere emotion for the kids.

Barclay thought for a minute before he threw out the next question. "What was it that you found to be unusual?"

"The mayor's keys were still in the door," replied Saunders as he fidgeted with the chain-link fence.

Barclay's ears perked up. "How did you know they were his keys?"

"Jenkins was so full of himself he had a custom-made key ring that said 'Mayor'." Then Saunders added with shake of his head, "He also had a plate for his Cadillac that said 'Mayor'."

From Saunders's body language alone, Barclay could tell that he didn't care much for Jenkins.

"Here's my card," said Barclay. "If you can think of anything else that might help Jack Snook, give me a call."

Practice had ended, and the team was having a meeting in the dugout.

"Boys, we have only eight days to prepare for the first game of the tournament," McCracken said. "We have to make the most of those days. You all know there will be some distractions. Distractions are not good. From now on, we will be keeping our practice times a secret. Only tell your parents and no one else. Is that clear?"

"Yes, Coach McCracken," they said in unison.

"Tomorrow is Saturday. Be here at 9:30 in the morning."

With that, the team collectively assembled in a huddle outside the dugout and placed their hands on top of each other. "Go team!" they yelled at the top of their lungs. They left little doubt that they were on a mission.

When the huddle broke, Danny Fitzgerald noticed Eddie Gardener standing outside the fence. "Wait a minute, guys!" he yelled. They huddled up again, and Fitzgerald beckoned, "Come on, Eddie, get in this huddle with us."

Eddie charged to join the team. When the huddle broke the second time, Fitzgerald called out, "All in favor of Eddie being our batboy raise their right hand." All the boys raised their hand except Pete Carlson. Needless to say, this drew a stare from the other team members.

"Just kidding, Eddie," Carlson said. "We all know what you did, and we will be honored to have you in the dugout."

Still observing, Barclay shook his head and marveled at the scene he was witnessing. "These kids are winners already," he said to himself.

CHAPTER FIVE

E ARLY SATURDAY MORNING, John Lovello arrived at the county prison for a meeting with his client. The charge guard led him to the attorney's meeting room to wait. The guard twisted the key in the lock and came right out and asked Lovello who was covering his fee for the "big-time defense."

Lovello was put off by the guard's question and answered it with the expression on his face. Nothing further had to be said.

Another guard delivered prisoner Y36A4009 to the meeting room.

"How are they treating you, Jack?" asked Lovello.

"Okay, I guess." Snook too was a big man. His six-foot four-inch frame was draped over a steel chair in the prison room.

Lovello could tell Snook had not slept much since he saw him the day before. "I saw you pitch that shutout against the Dodgers in 1999," he said.

Snook remained motionless and appeared to be distracted. Lovello repeated his statement.

"I was lucky that day," he said. "The umpire gave me the benefit of the doubt more times than he should have. But a shutout is a shutout."

They talked baseball for a few more minutes, and Lovello loosened the ex-major leaguer up. He could see Snook beginning to trust him and repeated his question. "How are they treating you, Jack?"

Snook shrugged; it hardly mattered how he was being treated, and he knew it.

Lovello removed a legal pad from his briefcase, took off his suit coat, and rolled up his sleeves. "Well, we have some pressing matters to attend to. If I'm going to defend you, you have to tell me what you did after you and the family returned from getting ice cream the night of the murder."

"I got the Mustang out, dropped the top, and went for a ride to sort things out. I stopped at the Dunkin' Donuts out on the highway and bought an iced coffee and drove into the Endless Mountains. I must have driven around for hours."

"You didn't see anyone or talk to anyone?"

"No."

"What time did you get back home?"

"About two-thirty. I took a quick shower and went straight to bed." Lovello noticed that Snook remained calm, even robotic, as he spit out the details of his evening. It was clear he was weary with repeating the same details again and again in the futile hope that the right people would believe them.

"That's exactly what your wife told me." Lovello scratched his head. "Do you know anyone who would have wanted to kill Jenkins?"

"Do you want the names in alphabetical order?" replied Snook dryly.

"I see. That many, huh?"

Snook composed himself. "Well," he said, "I know there was some bad blood between the mayor and the council president, Tim Richards. Little league registrations are always held at the municipal building. This year, Tommy and I were running late on the last night of registration. It was seven fifty-five when we got to the municipal building. As Tommy was being registered, the mayor and Richards were in the mayor's office. They were yelling and screaming at each other. Their voices were a bit muffled behind the closed door, but it was an argument all right."

"How did you know it was Richards?" Lovello shot back, writing furiously.

"I didn't until he stormed out of the mayor's office. His face was beet red, and he slammed the door behind him."

"Anyone else?"

"Sure. After what I read in today's paper, you could list ten coaches from the meeting two nights ago. That son-of-a-bitch thought he could manipulate everybody."

Lovello nodded and continued scribbling. "We'll talk again soon," he said. He was anxious to start investigating the Tim Richards lead. He needed this lead, any lead, desperately. "In the meantime, see if you can think of anybody else who could be a suspect."

"Aren't you going to ask me if I did it?"

"Not really. Like I told you before, if I thought you did it, I wouldn't be here." This drew a wide genuine smile from Jack Snook. "But we have to find out who did—and soon."

Lovello knocked on the door, and the guard let him out and returned Snook to his cell.

As Lovello exited the prison, DA Thomas was on his way in to interview a prisoner. He paused long enough to ask Lovello to join him for dinner that evening.

"Why not," said Lovello. "Where?"

"Russell's on Ash Street, say about eight thirty."

"I'll be there. Mind if I bring my detective?"

"Not at all," replied Thomas. "I'd like to meet the famous Jake Barclay. See you tonight."

Lovello reached for his cell phone to touch base with Barclay. When he flipped it open, he saw there were three missed calls from the detective. Lovello's call to Barclay went straight through to voice mail. "Jake, it's John, give me a call."

No sooner had Lovello put the phone in his pocket than Barclay was ringing in. "What's up?"

"Meet me in the parking lot where we ditched the reporter the other night," Lovelo came back. "It's important."

Lovello and Barclay arrived at the same time in the shopping center's parking lot. The detective got out of his car and went to the driver's side of Lovello's car. As the lawyer rolled the window down, Barclay said, "I'm famished. Let's get something to eat while we talk."

There was a hoagie/pizza place right there in the plaza. "Let's try this joint," said Barclay. The detective's face said he hadn't had much sleep.

"You all right?" asked Lovello. "You look tired."

"I am. I was up for the past two nights researching our dead mayor's family. Boy, talk about disasters. The Jenkins family has certainly had its share."

They ordered roast beef hoagies with french fries and sodas and sat down in a booth with a grimy orange tabletop.

"What's happening?" asked Lovello

Barclay bit into his sandwich, chewed, swallowed, took a sip of his drink, then he began his tale. "Well, for starters, our dead mayor was one of two remaining members of the Jenkins family. There was only him and his grandmother, Bessie Jenkins. The old lady is said to be in such poor health her doctors advised that she not be told that her grandson is dead. They figure the news might finish her off. She hasn't been out of the mansion on the hill for almost five years.

"According to what I have been able to dig up, the old lady and her husband, Archibald Jenkins III, had three children—two boys and a girl. The two boys were exceptional athletes, bright, ambitious, and very well liked.

"All was well until 1968 when the boys were killed in a snowmobile accident. They were home for Christmas. Archibald Jenkins IV, or Archie as he liked to be called, was out of law school and was clerking for a federal judge in Washington. Reginald, who was thirteen months younger than

Archie, was in his last year of law school at Dickinson. They decided to go snowmobiling on Archville Mountain one afternoon. Unfortunately for them, it started snowing. From what I was able to dig up on the Internet and from newspapers at the county library, the Jenkins brothers went off a 100-foot cliff on the mountain in what authorities called whiteout conditions.

"The newspaper accounts I read said search parties looked for the pair for several days. The storm was so fierce, searchers couldn't even find a snowmobile track on the mountain. Their bodies weren't discovered until the following spring by a Boy Scout troop on a weekend hike.

"The old man was devastated by the boys' deaths. He had high hopes for both of them and apparently had confided in close friends that he believed Archibald would someday be a US congressman or maybe even a senator. He had similar plans for Reginald.

"People I talked to said the old Archie never was the same after the boys were killed. Two years later, the old man, who just happened to be the mayor at the time, killed himself in the very same office where his grandson was murdered the other night. Kind of ironic, huh?"

Lovello whistled softly and shook his head. "I'll say. What about the daughter?"

"Another tragedy," said Barclay. "The old man didn't have much love for Rebecca because she was female, only good for producing male grandchildren. Rebecca and the old man were estranged by the time she was fifteen or so. Unlike her two brothers who had the benefit of private schools, Rebecca was sent off to public schools and did not receive any of the perks he bestowed upon his boys.

"According to Rachel Ormsby, the town's unofficial historian, Rebecca had gotten herself knocked up in 1974 when she was twenty-four years old. Bessie Jenkins, the matriarch, if you could call her that, was furious and attempted to force Rebecca to have an abortion.

"Rebecca, however, wanted the kid. She refused to identify the father until the kid was born and in her arms. But she never had the opportunity to tell Bessie the father's name because she died giving birth to a baby boy—our dead mayor.

"Bessie did her best to conceal the fact that the father of the boy was unknown by concocting a story for public consumption. That he was a soldier who was killed in action in the final days of Vietnam. Nevertheless, Bessie Jenkins decided to raise the boy with the Jenkins's name, an effort she regretted many times over in his youth."

Lovello took it all in and nodded thoughtfully. "Good job, Jake," he said. "Got anything else?"

"Well, according to my Internet research, Bessie is worth anywhere between forty and fifty million dollars. She funds scholarships at the local prep school and full-ride scholarships at Dickinson Law School in memory of Archibald IV and Reginald. Not much is known about who benefits from the money when the old lady croaks."

"We have to find out," said Lovello. "Fifty million dollars would be a nifty motive for murder, wouldn't you say?" Lovello then told Barclay he wanted to get a subpoena for the mayor's cell phone and landline records for the last six months. "Find out if he had a municipal phone. If he did, get a subpoena for that too."

"I'll get on it first thing Monday morning."

Lovello then informed Barclay that they were having dinner that night with DA Thomas.

"I pass," said Barclay. "I want to see if I can talk to this Sam Cortino guy from the Archville Little League. I've got a serious hunch."

"The last 'serious hunch' you had almost got you thrown in jail, remember?"

"I'm still trying to forget it," Barclay said with a grin.

In fact, Barclay remembered it well. Never again would he bring a drug-sniffing dog into a courtroom without first asking the judge's permission. While the dog sniffed drugs on the person Barclay believed to be guilty, the dog got a hit on the judge too. It was an embarrassing situation, but it got Lovello's client acquitted.

The two men went their separate ways.

It was only 11:30, and Barclay decided to see if there was any activity at the Complex. He was still waiting to see Tommy "Three Fingers" throw an eighty-mile-an-hour fastball.

He pulled into the Complex only to see practice coming to a close. Once again Crossing Guard Fred was holding up the right field fence as the boys were huddling up outside the dugout for their ritual. This time, however, Eddie Gardener, Jr., was in the middle of the pack.

Assistant Coach Sam Cortino was gathering up the team's equipment—helmets, bats and balls. Barclay approached him. "Excuse me, Mr. Cortino, my name is Jake Barclay. I work for John Lovello, the attorney representing Jack Snook."

Cortino turned around and extended his hand for Barclay to shake. "I know who you are. This is a small town. Word gets out."

Barclay asked Cortino if he had some time to talk.

"Sure. Let me finish up here and I'll let you buy me a beer at Marty's Café."

*　　*　　*

It was noon on a Saturday and Marty's was packed. The pub had been in Archville for as long as anyone could remember. It had gone through many facelifts over the years and now was a sports bar with mostly a local clientele. When coal was king, Marty's was called the Bank of Archville because the miners could get their checks cashed there.

Now, there were a few relics of the bygone days of coal, but those antiques were eclipsed by all the sports memorabilia, which included an autographed uniform shirt in a frame given to Marty by Jack Snook. The pub had a good lunch clientele and was famous for its hot wings. Of course, the topic on almost everyone's lips was the all-star team and the upcoming tournament. It seemed like everyone in the place knew Coach Cortino. "Hey, Coach, who are we going to be playing in the first round?" asked a man at the end of the bar.

"Don't know yet," replied Cortino. "Coach McCracken is on his way to Scranton right now to get the brackets."

"Hope we get Drewmore," the man said.

With no seats available at the bar, Cortino and Barclay grabbed a table. "What'll you have?" asked Barclay.

"A Yuengling Lager."

"I'm not from around here," said Barclay. "Do you recommend it?"

"Try it, I think you'll like it," said Cortino.

Barclay returned to the table with a pitcher and a pair of mugs. As he poured the golden liquid into Cortino's glass, he asked the coach about the Drewmore remark the man at the bar made.

"Drewmore is a borough outside Scranton," he said. "They constantly have a good team, but rumor has it that they cheat."

"How the hell do you cheat in little league?" asked the detective.

"Ineligible players," said Cortino. "They doctor birth certificates so older kids can play. It happened at the Little League World Series a couple of years ago."

Barclay admitted hearing something about it but said he did not think it was a widespread problem.

"Oh, it is," said Cortino.

Cortino went on to say that he already had heard rumors that a big kid on the Drewmore team was thirteen but that his father was well connected and league officials were hoping they could get away with turning a blind eye. Cortino explained eligible players had to be twelve years of age by April 30. "This kid is rumored to have turned thirteen in January," said Cortino.

"What's the kid's name?"

"The name I heard is Vinnie Bonito."

Barclay filed the name away in his memory. He then asked Cortino the obvious question, "Do you think Jack Snook murdered Mayor Jenkins?"

"Of course not," Cortino answered dismissively. "I was the one who carried the news to Jack that night about Tommy not making the roster for the tournament. Jack was upset, and sure, he had a history with Jenkins. But kill the mayor over it? Not likely. Jack knows his kid has talent and doors of opportunity will open up for him, whether or not he plays on the all-star team."

Barclay then asked the coach, who was pouring his second beer, how well he knew the mayor.

"I knew him all my life. We were the same age. We just grew up differently," Cortino said wryly. "He was a spoiled rich kid and figured he could get his grandmother to buy him out of anything." Cortino added that he couldn't stand the boy Albert or the man Albert.

The detective sipped his beer and thanked Cortino for turning him on to the Lager. "Pretty good stuff. Don't think we have it in LA." Then he asked Cortino to fill him in on the mayor's background.

"Jenkins was not afraid to flaunt his grandmother's money. The kid got everything he wanted. He had full-time nannies from day 1. You know, silver spoon in the mouth and all that. Typical rich kid. He was always getting into trouble of some sort, but Granny's money always got him out of it. When he was ten or eleven, he torched the old train station. Granny had to dig deep on that one. It was rumored that she paid the police chief off and agreed to pack the kid off to a military school somewhere in New England."

Barclay sipped his beer, listening intently.

"That was the last we heard of him until he showed up back here with an MBA from Harvard. The old lady's money probably bought that for him too." Cortino fidgeted with the coaster under his beer. He was slowly picking the cardboard apart. "In all honesty, I can't say I'm sorry he's dead."

The pitcher was now empty, and Cortino grabbed it from the table. "I'll get this one," he said.

However, Barclay insisted on getting the beer. "I'm on an expense account."

Just as Barclay returned with the beer, the front door of Marty's opened, and Coach McCracken walked in. He was excited as he waved the playoff schedule in the air. "We'll be playing Drewmore in the opening round of the tournament, and we will be hosting at the Complex."

A rousing cheer erupted throughout the bar.

McCracken spotted his assistant coach at the table and walked over. "Can you imagine, Drewmore in the first round," he said. "This should make things interesting." Then he paused and looked at Barclay. "Who's your friend, Sam?"

Barclay stood up and introduced himself.

"Pleasure to meet you," said McCracken as he shook the detective's hand.

"We were just discussing our dead mayor," said Cortino.

"Oh, that asshole," said McCracken.

"Coach McCracken and I both knew the mayor when he was a kid, before he went to military school," said Cortino.

"We didn't, as they say, travel in the same circles, but I knew him," said McCracken. "Can you imagine that asshole saying he had an MBA and was running for Congress?"

"He ran for Congress?"

"Certainly did," said McCracken. "Got his ass drilled too. The prick actually thought he could beat a nine-term incumbent who was squeaky clean in the political world."

Barclay then asked the two coaches how Jenkins ended up being mayor.

"That's a funny story too," said Cortino. "He came in and out of town on occasion after he lost the congressional election to visit his grandmother. She had become somewhat of a recluse. Anyway, Al Jenkins moved back here supposedly to be close to the old lady. The next thing we know, he entered the mayoral primary. That was five years ago."

Barclay was making mental notes as he downed the beer.

"He actually had zero chances to win the primary," Cortino went on. "But fate intervened. The three-term incumbent mayor who worked as the business manager in the local school district was indicted by a federal grand jury for stealing federal monies two weeks before the primary. Needless to say, Al Jenkins became mayor of Archville."

McCracken chimed in, "He practiced the kind of old politics from his grandfather's generation. He would manipulate, threaten, and even use blackmail to get what he wanted. He was a prick."

"I trust you two won't be at the funeral on Monday," said Barclay.

They both chuckled.

"Look, I have to go. What time is practice tomorrow?"

"We decided to keep the starting times a secret for now," said McCracken. "Because of the Three Fingers situation. It's too much of a distraction for the team with all those people and media milling around. But if you want to come, we'll be at the Complex tomorrow at four thirty."

"I'll be there" said Barclay. "By the way, what was the name of the kid from Drewmore again?"

"Vinnie Bonito," replied Cortino.

"Got it. See you guys later," said Barclay and strode away.

Barclay was tired. He decided it was time to grab some sleep. With the three lagers he had consumed, he knew he could sleep for hours. He arrived at the Holiday Inn in Drewmore and went straight to his room.

Before passing out, however, he took out his cell phone and called his associate.

The phone rang but once before a cheery voice uttered, "Hello, you great big handsome man."

"Hello to you too, sweetheart. Look, it's rare that I call you on Saturday, but I need something ASAP."

"Anything for you, big guy."

He told her he wanted a complete Internet search on a kid from Drewmore, Pennsylvania, by the name of Vincent Bonito. "Check everywhere you can. I want chapter and verse on this kid. I've been told he is between twelve and fifteen."

"Is he connected to the Snook case?" she asked.

"Sort of, I think."

He terminated the call and fell immediately to sleep.

CHAPTER SIX

JOHN LOVELLO PUT the address to Russell's restaurant into the GPS system and sped out of the hotel parking lot. "Take me to Russell's, Nancy," he said. Nancy was the name given to his GPS system by an old girlfriend. The girlfriend was history, but Lovello saw no reason to dump Nancy.

Russell's was one of the area's best restaurants, frequented by the area's well to do. It was widely known for its Italian cuisine, delicious steaks, and seafood. Lovello wasn't surprised to find the parking lot crowded. He sauntered inside.

The district attorney was already seated at a table covered in cream-colored linen. Immediately, Lovello noticed that the DA was not alone. Seated beside him was a beautiful redhead, conservatively dressed, easy on the eyes.

Thomas gestured to Lovello to join them, then stood up, and greeted him with a firm handshake. He introduced the redhead as Barbara Grochowski, first-assistant district attorney.

Ms. Grochowski started to rise, but Lovello stopped her. "No need to get up," he said, extending his hand across the table. He was surprised; her grip was stronger than the DA's.

"Barbara is going to be prosecuting the Snook case," Thomas said. "We hope to have it listed for trial on the September docket. The case has been assigned to Judge Mooney."

Lovello was barely paying attention to Thomas. He was taken with Barbara Grochowski's looks. "What did you say your last name is again?" he asked her.

"Grochowski. G-R-O-C-H-O-W-S-K-I," she responded.

"Any relation to a Mitch Grochowski?" he asked.

"Afraid not," she replied.

"How on earth do you know Mitch Grochowski?" DA Thomas inquired.

"He was the reporter assigned to cover a criminal trial I was defense counsel on twenty years ago in Scranton. He was a decent reporter. Is he still around?"

"Selling real estate," replied Thomas.

The pleasantries were now dispensed with. The waitress took the trio's order, and Lovello was the first to speak. "My client tells me he didn't kill the mayor."

Thomas snidely said, "They're all innocent, aren't they?"

"From what I understand, the only forensic evidence you have is a bloody baseball bat with no fingerprints and a corpse. What else have you got?"

"How about the sworn testimony of a police officer that your client asserted he wanted to kill the mayor, mere hours before the murder occurred?" asked Grochowski.

Lovello nodded silently. Snook had left that bit of information out of their conversation at the prison. He felt like leaving right then and there but knew the two prosecutors might have more to share. He decided this was as good a place as any for some discovery.

"An Archville police officer, Joe Sampson, was working the night shift," Grochowski said. "He claims he saw your client at the Dunkin' Donuts out on the highway at about eleven last night. Sampson and Snook had a conversation about the coaches leaving Three Fingers off the all-star roster. During that conversation, Sampson said Jack Snook angrily informed him that he wanted to, quote, 'kill Mayor Jenkins'."

"Come on, the guy was mad and just blowing off steam," said Lovello. "You really think he would go kill the mayor after that conversation with a cop?"

"Doesn't matter," said Grochowski. "Snook said it, and Jenkins is dead, symbolically beaten to death with a baseball bat, we believe. That's what the jury is going to hear anyway."

This was one of the few times in his life that John Lovello was lost for words. *A statement like that made to a cop only a few hours before the mayor was killed is almost as good as an eyewitness,* he thought.

"We're prepared to offer your client a plea," said Grochowski. "Under the circumstances, the state will accept a guilty plea to second-degree murder with life in prison and no chance for parole. Your client avoids the death penalty and the state saves the expense of a trial."

"You know I have to take a deal like that to my client," said Lovello.

"I know," said Grochowski. "That's why we've made arrangements for you to visit him at the prison tomorrow morning. They'll be expecting you around nine."

The meals came, and the conversation shifted to other topics. Lovello was glad to pick up the tab and get the hell out of Russell's.

Back at the Holiday Inn, Lovello called Barclay and dropped the bombshell on him. The two agreed to meet in the hotel bar for a drink. "Be there in fifteen minutes," said Barclay.

It was Saturday night, and the lounge was packed. The music was being provided by a trio playing hits from the '80s.

"We may have a losing hand here, my friend," said Lovello.

"Before you go thinking like that," said Barclay, "you ought to give your client the benefit of the doubt, at least until you talk to him."

"Yeah, you're right. It's still innocent until proven guilty, isn't it?"

"*Semper fi*, pal," replied Barclay.

The bartender, whose nameplate read Kathy, was wiping down the bar in front of them. Somewhere in her midthirties, she had on a short black skirt and a low-cut blouse that revealed the top of her ample breasts. "What are you fellows having?"

"A couple of Dewar's, neat, and your phone number," said Barclay. He threw a $50 bill on the bar.

She returned with the drinks and a big smile.

"What about the phone number?"

She grinned and flashed her wedding ring. "Sorry, my husband gets mad when I get calls at the house."

"Damn," said Barclay. "Another one gets away."

* * *

At 7:30 Sunday morning, John Barclay's cell phone woke him. On the caller ID he could see that it was Charlie Mars. "What now," he wondered as he fumbled with the phone.

"Good morning, Charlie," he grunted out. "What's up?"

"Is Snook looking to cop a plea?"

Barclay just shook his head and wondered which DA had fed the plea deal to Charlie. *Probably the broad,* he thought. "Look, Charlie, if that were the case, I would have called you."

"Well, I heard that the deal has not yet been presented to Snook. That's all I know."

Barclay then told Mars he was working on something the reporter could sink his teeth into. "I should have it for you by tonight, Monday the latest."

CHAPTER SEVEN

JOHN LOVELLO ARRIVED at the prison at nine o'clock and was greeted by Captain Caswell. The corrections officer at the gate was ready to run the electronic wand over the attorney, but Caswell intervened. "That won't be necessary," he said. "I'll take responsibility for the counselor."

"Thank you, Captain."

"They're bringing your client up now," said Caswell. "Want some coffee?"

"I'll pass," said Lovello, "but thanks anyway."

The captain let Lovello into the locked meeting room. When Snook was brought in, Caswell ordered the handcuffs removed.

"I'm glad you came back," said Snook. "I forgot to tell you something yesterday. It completely slipped my mind." Snook was pale in color and looked like a beaten man.

Lovello looked his client in the eyes: "What did you forget to tell me—that you told a cop you wanted to kill the mayor?"

"You know?"

"Yes, I know. The assistant DA laid it out for me last night. It's the lynchpin of their prosecution."

"Look," said Snook. "I know Joe Sampson for a long time. I told him what had happened to Tommy with the coaches. I was pissed. I mouthed off, but I didn't mean any of it. I was just as shocked as everyone else when I heard . . ." Snook had a perplexed and pained expression. "The idea of Sampson turning around and using that information against me just doesn't make sense. He was the first person on the scene when Tommy got half of his hand blown off. The guy even rushed me over to the hospital with the siren on."

Lovello believed his client and was aggrieved witnessing his heartfelt confusion. "He's a cop," Lovello said. "He had to report what you said when the mayor was found murdered." He stretched his arms. "Boy, we need another suspect, and we need one bad. Is there anything else you *forgot* to tell me?"

"No, that's it," Snook said, shaking his head distractedly.

"All right, let me work with this, and I'll see you later."

Lovello knocked at the door. The guard put the handcuffs back on the prisoner and began walking him back to his cell.

Snook called out, "Tell Gloria and Tommy I love them."

Caswell was waiting for Lovello at the gate and asked if he had a minute to spare.

"Sure, Captain."

"I live in Archville. My kids grew up in Archville. The only reason Mayor Jenkins associated himself with baseball is because he thought it was a voting base for him. That asshole didn't know which end of the bat to use. He hired a retired high school coach to run his team for him. He fixed the team lotteries so he always ended up with the best players. He was strictly no-good. Period."

"Why are you telling me this?" Lovello asked.

Caswell eyed him carefully. "Because I don't like having an innocent man in my lockup."

"Thank you, Captain. I'll do my very best to find out who is guilty here. You can count on it." Sensing an ally, Lovello reached into his pocket and pulled out a $50 bill. He handed the crisp bill to Caswell and asked him to see to it that Jack Snook gets whatever he needs from the commissary.

"Glad to," the captain said. "Glad to."

Lovello called Barclay once he was outside. "We will be going forward with our defense," he said. "Jack Snook is an innocent man. I'll call the first assistant DA in the morning and tell her there will be no plea."

Barclay interrupted. "Watch her, John. Charlie Mars called me early this morning. He knew about the plea offer already. Thomas or the lady DA is a snake with an agenda."

"Thanks, pal," said Lovello. "Call me if anything comes up."

Next on Barclay's agenda was a conversation with Tim Richards, the council president. Fortunately, Richards's number was listed. He dialed it and a deep, terse voice answered on the third ring. "This is Tim Richards."

"My name is Jack Barclay. I work for Jack Snook's lawyer. I would like to talk to you. The sooner the better."

Richards agreed to a meeting at his home at 2:00 p.m. that day.

"That was easy," Barclay said to himself as he hung up the prone.

*   *   *

At 2:00 p.m. on the dot, Barclay's Jag rolled up in front of the Richards's house on Gravity Street. Richards was dressed in work clothes and was just finishing up mowing the lawn. Barclay opened the gate and let himself into the freshly cut yard. He took a whiff of the air; he loved the smell of freshly cut grass.

The council president invited the detective in for a cold drink. He was a little overweight, and his tee shirt didn't completely cover his pot belly. Richards was chewing on a little cigar. "It keeps the bugs away when I cut grass," he explained.

Even though they'd never met before, Richards was prepared to tell the detective anything he wanted to know as he was sure Jack Snook could not have killed the mayor or anyone for that matter. "What's on your mind?" asked Richards.

"It is my understanding that you had words with Al Jenkins in his office at the end of April. Mind telling me what that was all about?"

Richards thought for a minute. "Look," said the council president, "this is not for public consumption yet, but the council here has been approached by a Texas company that wants to build an experimental facility on the west side of Archville to turn coal into diesel fuel. Purely experimental, mind you."

Richards went on to tell Barclay that he and three other members of council—the majority—were in favor of approving a zoning change for the land where the experimental plant would be built. "Between permits, land preparation, construction jobs, and permanent jobs," said Richards, "the town stands to benefit greatly."

Richards pointed out that the council had been approached about the experimental plant solely because the Town of Archville was recently discovered to have millions of tons of coal still beneath its surface. "All of our neighboring towns have similar situations," he added.

According to high-tech satellite geological studies, Richards explained, "There are large veins of coal running beneath our existing mines, too deep for the coal barons to have tapped years ago." Billions of dollars were at stake.

"That son-of-a-bitch Jenkins wanted the council to reject the land use change sought by the Texas company and instead steer the company toward land he and his grandmother own on the east side. Greedy bastard. Hope he's rotting in hell."

Barclay repressed a smirk. Hearing the various townspeople rant and rage against the mayor was becoming amusing. And ironic as it seemed the killer they were in such hot pursuit of had done everyone a favor by eliminating the much-abhorred man.

The council president was passionate in his desire to make his town a better place with more jobs and a more prosperous future. It was ironic, the shift back to coal—which had put the place on the map decades ago. However, the detective did not view Richards as a suspect in the mayor's murder.

Richards said Jenkins had three votes for his plan. "I assume he had already paid the minority off. Either that or he had something on them. But there were big bucks at stake no matter how you slice it."

Barclay was more than fascinated by these "not for public consumption" revelations.

"That night in the municipal building, Jenkins offered me $150,000 and scholarships for my two kids at the prep school his grandmother supports in exchange for shifting my position on the land use issue. I told him to shove the bribe up his ass and to start thinking about the community instead of himself."

"I'm no expert," said Barclay, "but was coal mining going to make a return to the region?"

"Quite the contrary," said Richards. "The point man for the Texas firm said the company had discovered a way to liquefy the coal veins and pump it out in a way very similar to the way oil is pumped out. Then it would be transported by tankers to the plant for processing.

"We initially were worried about leaving underground voids after the extraction," continued Richards. "However, the company had already solved that problem by developing a cheap way to fill the voids with a liquid that turns to stone after each day's extraction."

Richards said the company was finalizing the patent on the liquid process developed by some whiz kid out of Texas A&M, and a September announcement to the public was planned.

"What's the name of this company?" Barclay asked.

"Can't tell you," said Richards. "We all signed confidentiality documents when we were approached with the plan. The company lawyer insisted upon it. I probably told you too much already."

Just then, Barclay's cell phone rang. "Excuse me, I have to take this call." He stepped outside and said, "Talk to me, sweetheart." It was Monica, his secretary in LA.

"I got everything you wanted on Vinnie Bonito," she said cheerfully into the phone. "He was thirteen on his last birthday. The kid's a computer junkie. He's all over Facebook and has four MySpace pages featuring all kinds of accolades for his baseball talents. But, Jake, there's something weird about this assignment. I went back to see the web pages again after I printed them out. They were gone, taken down."

I'm not surprised, Barclay thought. "Be a sweetie, will you, and e-mail me everything you've got."

"Will do, chief."

He thanked her and clicked off.

Returning to Richards's den, Barclay thanked him for his cooperation and an "enlightening conversation." He gave the council president his card. "I'm at the Holiday Inn in Drewmore, room 312, if you think of anything else. Thanks again."

CHAPTER EIGHT

BARCLAY'S JAGUAR ROLLED into the Complex. Much to his surprise, the lot was filled. Cars were starting to park out on the streets. "Some secret practice," he mumbled. He ended up parking blocks away from the Complex. Walking over, he used the time to call Lovello and fill him in on what he had learned from Richards.

"We have to find out the name of that company in Texas," Lovello said.

"I'm willing to bet that Jenkins's phone records will lead us in that direction. I'll get the subpoena in the morning, right after the mayor's funeral," said Barclay. "I want to see who shows up for the asshole's farewell and, more importantly, who does not show up."

"Excellent idea," said Lovello.

By the time Barclay reached the Complex, Fred Saunders was already at his usual spot. "Mind if I join you, Fred?"

"Not at all," he replied. He pointed to the bleachers and said, "There're certainly no seats available. This is the biggest crowd I have ever seen here. And this is only practice."

Coach McCracken was hitting grounders to the infield and fly balls to the outfield. Barclay watched intently as Three Fingers chased down a fly ball that looked like it was going to be impossible to catch. The boy snagged the ball and threw it to Anders, who was behind home plate. The throw, all the way from center field, was right on the money.

"That kid's got a hell of an arm," muttered Fred Saunders. "And to think he almost didn't play."

"So I hear," said Barclay. The detective then asked Saunders how long he had been employed by the municipal government.

"It will be forty years come October," he said. "Started right after I got out of the army in 1970. Only job I've ever had."

Barclay started doing the math in his head. "Were you working there when Archibald Jenkins III committed suicide?" asked Barclay.

"Know about that, do you?" asked Saunders. "Yes, I was working there. Found him right there in the mayor's office. Weird, same spot I found his grandson two days ago. Only the old man was slumped over his desk with a .38 caliber revolver on the floor. The police and the coroner ruled it a suicide."

What a coincidence, Barclay thought. For the time being, he changed the subject. "What unit did you serve with in the army, Fred?"

"Airborne," he replied.

"Any tours in 'Nam?"

"Two." Saunders looked Barclay in the eyes. "You know," he said, "you ask too many questions."

Barclay knew he should back off. "I was there twice myself," he said.

This softened Saunders up somewhat. "What branch?" the janitor asked.

"The Corps," he replied.

"Bad memories," Saunders said. "Don't like to think about it."

Just then, the television crew from the ABC affiliate came walking into the complex, cameras in tow.

The skinny blonde reporter asked Barclay and Saunders which kid was Tommy Snook.

Barclay pointed at the players on the field and said, "I think he's the one wearing the baseball cap."

Barclay's remark drew a grin out of Saunders; the first time the detective had seen any kind of emotion on the man's face.

"They're all wearing baseball caps," the blonde said.

"Wow, you must be a good reporter," said Barclay. "Nothing gets by you."

She was pissed and flipped an erect middle finger, then beckoned her photographer to follow. However, it appeared as though they were too late for a story. Coach McCracken had just summoned the team into the dugout to talk.

Barclay told Saunders he would like to talk again sometime if that was okay with him.

"I'll be here," he said as he put forth a halfhearted semi-smile.

The detective wanted to see Coach Cortino, so he walked up to the dugout. The blonde reporter was standing just outside. "No news here," he heard McCracken say. The coach then told the reporter he was having a *private* meeting with his team. He asked her to leave.

Barclay waited for the team meeting to break up. Once again he witnessed the boys gather together and perform their ritual huddle, with Eddie Gardener standing proudly in the middle.

Cortino set about picking up the equipment as Barclay yelled to him, "Sam, got some time to talk?"

"Marty's in about twenty minutes," Cortino shot back.

The bar was packed. On several of the television screens in the sports bar, the Yankees were playing the Red Sox. The other screens showed the Mets and the Phillies. Archville really liked its baseball.

Barclay managed to get the same table he and Cortino had shared a day earlier. He got a pitcher of the preferred beer and two glasses. He was joined by Cortino a few minutes later.

"Some crowd up there today," said Cortino.

"How does the word leak out?" asked Barclay.

"Probably the parents. Tomorrow we're taking the team over to Jefferson Township to practice. League officials there understand our plight, and they said we could use one of their fields. That should cut down on some of the distractions." Cortino filled his glass and smiled. "But I think the kids are actually enjoying the attention. At least they won't be spooked by the crowd come game day."

"You do have a point there." The detective took a sip of his beer. "By the way, you were right about that Bonito kid, Sam. He's thirteen. Are you sure Drewmore is going to play him?"

"That's what I've been told. How do you know how old he is?"

"I have a great staff," Barclay replied.

"There's nothing we can do about it until Bonito is announced in the lineup."

"I figured that. I haven't reviewed the evidence my secretary sent me yet, but she told me that the information she had found on some websites has vanished. Mighty suspicious. Once I review the evidence, I'll figure out my next step."

"What do you have to gain from this?" Cortino asked the detective, with curiosity and just a hint of mistrust.

"Absolutely nothing," said the detective. "I just like to see people play by the rules. If we teach kids that kind of bullshit is okay, they might grow up to be politicians. Scary."

They both laughed but knew it was true.

Barclay pointed at the television closest to them. "The Yankees and the Phillies are popular here, are they?" asked Barclay.

"Very," said Cortino. "What's your team?"

"I grew up in LA. I used to follow the Dodgers, but I'm on the road so much now I just follow them in the standings."

Just then, Cortino and Barclay were joined by Coach McCracken. Like the day before, McCracken was greeted by patrons the way Norm was greeted on that old sitcom, *Cheers*. It was easy to tell he enjoyed the attention.

The three men sat there for the next two hours as if they were old friends. During that time, Cortino and Barclay disclosed to McCracken the evidence Barclay's secretary had uncovered about the Bonito kid. The coaches gave their word they would not discuss the matter with anyone until the time was appropriate. As they enjoyed a beer together, Barclay quizzed them about Fred Saunders. "The guy seems a little strange to me."

Cortino and McCracken looked at each other with an expression on their face that told the detective he had struck a nerve.

After a long pause, Cortino said the janitor was a nice guy. However, the coach followed up with a remark that perked Barclay's ears up. "When he's drinking, he has a mean streak," said Cortino. "Not too long ago, Fred mixed it up with two guys outside the VFW. He put a pretty good beating on them too. He's been in and out of fights of various kinds—only when he's had too much to drink."

McCracken chimed in, "I don't know if it was ever diagnosed," he said, "but I think he may have that post-traumatic stress disorder from combat in Vietnam."

Cortino removed his baseball cap and scratched his head. "He's a strange person all right." He went on to say that Fred kept to himself. "He found the mayor's body a few days ago, *and* he found old Mayor Jenkins's body years ago. The guy must be pretty spooked out."

McCracken motioned to the barkeep to toss him a bag of pretzels. "He was always nice to my kids," said McCracken. "I heard he was jilted by a lover years ago, but I think that's just a rumor."

Barclay stopped beating around the bush. "Think he's capable of murder?"

Both men shook their heads. "Fred? Capable of murder? You've got to be kidding," said McCracken.

"If Fred Saunders killed the mayor, I would be the most surprised man on this planet," added Cortino. "But stranger things have happened."

"I had to ask," said Barclay. "I'm still looking for a suspect other than Jack Snook."

"You're in a tough business," said Cortino.

"At this early stage," said the detective, "I have to consider everyone."

Coach Cortino smiled. "Have you ruled us out as suspects yet?"

"Yes," replied the detective with a wink. "But I'm keeping an eye on you two."

They shared a hearty laugh, finished their beers, and called it a day.

CHAPTER NINE

EARLY MONDAY MORNING, Barclay got a call from Lovello. "Good morning, counselor," he said.

"Are you still going to the funeral?" asked Lovello.

"Wouldn't miss it for the world," said the detective.

"Listen, I have to fly back to LA tonight to handle a case for a client whose kid got busted on a cocaine possession charge. Think you can handle everything while I'm gone?"

"No problem," Barclay said. "I'll keep you informed. I'll stop by the courthouse today and get the subpoenas for the mayor's phone records. It'll probably take a week or so to get them. Be safe."

"*Semper Fi*," said Lovello.

*   *   *

The arrangements for Al Jenkins's funeral had been made by family friend and lawyer, one Clarence A. West, who had been practicing law in Archville for more than forty years. West was strictly old school when it came to the law. He ran three times unsuccessfully for a seat on the county bench, using his own money, he always boasted, and refusing to take contributions from anyone.

West had a remarkable disdain for his fellow members of the Bar Association who advertised on television and the back covers of phone books and commonly referred to those who did as "clowns." He was in his late seventies, but in remarkably good health. Early in his law career, he worked as an assistant US attorney in the Middle District of Pennsylvania, and prosecuted some big-time public corruption cases.

West's only son, Clarence Junior, was killed during Operation Desert Storm. West was crushed by the loss of his only child, and part of his frequent routine—no matter what the weather—was a trip to the cemetery for a visit with his son.

West was known far and wide for his fondness for veterans. He represented GIs with problems for free. Virtually every military organization in the county counted him as a member. He was the commander of the local American Legion Post, named the Clarence A. West, Jr., Post 696 to honor the attorney's fallen son.

The Jenkins funeral West had arranged would consist of a graveside service at the Protestant Cemetery in Archville. Barclay arrived at the cemetery about forty-five minutes early so he could get a good vantage point from which to watch the service without being seen.

He collected his spy equipment, as he called it, his binoculars and camera with good zoom-in capability, and headed for the woods on the western edge of the graveyard. There was only one freshly dug gravesite, thus making it easy for the detective to choose a good hiding place where he could view the service without being detected.

At 9:50, the funeral procession arrived at the cemetery. In all, there were five cars and, of course, the hearse. The pallbearers, one of whom was Clarence A. West, carried the coffin to the gravesite. About a dozen or so mourners got out of the other cars.

Barclay was watching everything through a telephoto lens attached to his Canon digital camera, all the while snapping pictures for later review. Curiously, no one got out of the last car in the funeral procession, a late-model Mercedes with darkened windows. He snapped a shot of the license plate.

The service for the town's mayor was short. Clarence West read a prayer, as did the minister from a local Protestant church. Barclay watched the faces of the mourners. He noted that no one in attendance was crying. Instead, they were stone-faced and looked as though they'd rather be elsewhere.

Attorney West concluded the service and attendees began to depart.

Barclay watched everyone through the telephoto lens as they returned to their vehicles without speaking to each other. He wondered: was the killer in among the mourners?

After waiting for them to leave, Barclay took a few more pictures of the Jenkins's family plot as cemetery workers were in the process of lowering the hated and slain mayor to his final rest.

The detective's next stop was at the municipal building to see his new friend, Fred Saunders. He walked into the building and asked the receptionist where he could find Saunders.

"Beats me," she said. "Fred called in sick today. You might want to try his apartment. It's behind the barbershop on Main Street."

Finding the barbershop was easy. Barclay got out of his car and walked through the narrow passage between the shop and an empty building.

Before he got to the door, however, he noticed Fred Saunders coming toward him from the other direction, sweating and obviously winded.

"Is everything okay?" asked Barclay.

"What do *you* want?" snapped Saunders.

"I just wanted to tell you that the all-stars will not be practicing at the Complex today. They'll be in Jefferson Township at four thirty. I thought you'd like to know."

Saunders muttered a halfhearted thanks. "Now get out of here." He opened an unlocked door and disappeared into the building. Strange man. Barclay shook his head and walked away.

As he emerged from between the buildings, he saw a policeman next to his Jaguar writing a ticket.

"Sorry, Officer, I didn't see the fire hydrant."

"Have to give you a ticket," the cop said. "Had a complaint." He tore off the ticket and handed it to Barclay; it was for $50.

Now he saw the nameplate, Officer Joseph Sampson. Barclay knew better than to start a conversation with the prosecution's key witness. "Where can I pay this?" he asked.

"At the municipal building, or you can just mail it in," said Sampson. "It has to be paid within ten days or it will cost you more. Have a nice day, sir."

Barclay stopped at the municipal building and paid the fine, then headed to Scranton.

* * *

There, the detective filed the necessary paperwork with the court clerk's office to obtain subpoenas for the dead mayor's phone records; then he headed over to the nearby state office building.

In the Office of Vital Statistics, he was greeted at the counter by a pleasant older lady. "May I help you?"

"Ma'am, I need a copy of a birth record."

She searched around under the counter and came up with a sheet of a paper. "I'll need you to fill out this form, sir."

Of course, the information he wrote on the form was pure fiction. He was trying to obtain the birth record of one Vincent Bonito. He completed the form with lies and handed it back to the clerk.

"It usually takes a week to get the birth records," she told him.

"A week? I need it quicker than that."

LEO A. MURRAY

The clerk told him that procedures for obtaining the information were more stringent since 9/11.

Barclay took a gamble. He took out two $100 bills and held them in his hand. "I'm not a terrorist, and I need this information," he said as he waved the money under her nose.

Barclay could read it in her eyes. She was already thinking about how she could spend such a windfall.

"Wait here," she said.

She returned in a few minutes and provided the detective with Vincent Benito's birth record. He handed her the $200 and started walking away.

"Sir, there is a twenty dollar charge for the certificate," she informed.

"Oh, of course," he said and passed her a twenty.

"Do you want a receipt?" she asked.

"Thanks, not necessary."

Outside, Barclay was delighted. The certificate confirmed the Internet's findings.

The detective then placed a call to Charlie Mars. It was lunchtime.

Mars answered the phone quickly. "Got something for me?"

Barclay asked Mars if he was free for lunch.

"I was just getting ready to grab a bite," he said.

"Where?"

Mars said he frequented a place on Market Street called Simon's. "The food is good and the service is great."

"I'll find it," said Barclay. The detective made a quick stop at Kinko's to make copies of the birth certificate.

Mars and Barclay arrived at Simon's at the same time. Simon's appeared to have been many things before becoming an eatery. Its simple décor made it appear as if it catered mainly to a blue-collar crowd. Barclay noted that the place was extraordinarily clean. Simon's apparently was a friendly place, for most of the people at the counter knew Charlie Mars and greeted him by name. The duo was fortunate to get a booth.

"This is a nice laid-back place," said Barclay.

Mars said he'd been patronizing Simon's for nearly twenty years.

Barclay handed a copy of the fraudulently obtained birth certificate to Mars.

"What's this?" asked Mars.

Barclay then handed the reporter a computer flash drive. He explained to Mars that the certificate and the information on the flash drive was proof that the all-star team from Drewmore was going to field an ineligible player when the district tournament got underway Saturday night.

"How's this related to the Jenkins murder?"

"It's not related directly to the murder, Charlie. Call it a bonus for helping me out."

He then told Mars that the coaches from the Archville team would be challenging the legitimacy of Bonito's ability to play before the first pitch Saturday night. "The information on the flash drive was obtained by my associate in LA. After she downloaded it, she couldn't find it again. Somebody's covering their tracks."

Mars nodded. "That's interesting."

Barclay then suggested to Mars that he sit on the information until Saturday night, and he would have a big story Sunday morning. "You'll want to be at the game anyway, Charlie. Tommy Snook will be on the mound."

Beverly, the waitress, came to take their order and flirt a bit with Charlie. When she left, the reporter explained that she was a notorious flirt.

Soon, they were chowing down on Simon's fine Texas hamburgers. "Not bad," Barclay pronounced.

"I really like the food here," said Mars.

As they parted company, Barclay asked Mars if there was a drugstore nearby with photo processing.

"Down on Green Ridge Street, about four blocks that way," Mars said, pointing.

Barclay thanked Mars and headed to the drugstore. He quickly printed his photos in eight-by-ten format, not looking at the prints until he was in his car. There, he shuffled through the photos until he found the one of the Benz. The plate number was very clear. He took out his cell phone and called his associate.

"Hey there, sweet lips," he said when she answered. "Take down this license plate number. I need a registration on it ASAP."

She took the number, repeated it back, and then gave him several messages, none of which he deemed important at the moment. "I'll get on this right away."

"Thanks, doll. Talk to you later."

Back at the Holiday Inn, Barclay called Sam Cortino and filled him in on the birth certificate and what he had done with it. Cortino was pleased to hear that Charlie Mars had the information. "He's a good reporter," said Cortino. "Will you be at practice?"

"Wouldn't miss it." He told Cortino that he had informed Saunders about the practice change.

"No problem. The boys like Fred."

As Barclay prepared to shower and get ready to go to practice, he thought over the day's events. First there was the funeral where no mourners shed a tear. Then there was the Benz. Could the murderer have been in there?

The biggest question of the day: Where was Fred Saunders coming from that morning? Why was he sweating so much? It was almost like he'd been chased by the devil himself.

*　　*　　*

With very little trouble, Barclay found the field in Jefferson Township. The team was going through some throwing and running drills. He noticed Saunders near the right field fence. The site change had worked, for there were only two dozen or so people watching the practice.

Barclay made his way over to the crossing guard. "Is everything all right, Fred? You looked a little shaky this morning."

"It's my business," Saunders grunted out. "Let it alone, okay?"

"Anything you say," Barclay replied.

The seasoned detective couldn't help detecting: Saunders was hiding something. But what? "I see Tommy's starting against Drewmore," Barclay said.

"I know," replied Saunders. "I can't wait to see him pitch. Saw his father pitch three times in Yankee Stadium when he was with the Indians and won a Cy Young."

"Are you a Yankee fan?"

"No," he replied. "I just like the game."

They watched as Tommy Snook took the mound. Vince Anders was setting up behind the plate, putting extra padding in his catcher's mitt. "Finally," Barclay said, "I get to see the marvelous Three Fingers at work."

"He's something to see, all right," Saunders pointed out.

Tommy Snook went into a wind up and tossed a changeup right through the strike zone. The kid hurled a few more off-speed pitches as he got loose. Three Fingers then went into an unbelievable stride, throwing pitch after pitch right down the middle of the plate, much to the pleasure of the few fans in attendance.

"Okay, Tommy, that's enough," shouted Coach McCracken. "Let's get a live batter up there."

Paul Burns was the smallest of the fourteen players on the Archville team. He was a good shortstop and had uncanny speed on the bases. During the season, he batted .275, and he drew a remarkable twenty-seven walks. His small stature allowed him to crouch down at the plate and make it very difficult for umpires to get a fix on a strike zone when he was batting.

Tommy Snook struck Burns out with three pitches. "I didn't even see the last one," Burns yelled when he left the batter's box.

And so it went, batter after batter whiffed with Tommy Snook on the mound.

"That's extraordinary," said Barclay.

"It's going to be good for the town," mumbled Saunders.

An hour later, Coach McCracken called the players into the dugout for the daily team meeting. "You guys are doing better than we expected," he said. "To show our appreciation, Coach Cortino and I have decided to give you tomorrow off."

The news was greeted with noisy approval from the players.

"Be here Wednesday afternoon at four. Any questions?" asked McCracken.

Paul Burns raised his hand. "Is Tommy going to start against Drewmore?"

"You bet."

Again, cheers and shouts in the dugout. Finally, the boys gathered for their team-spirit huddle. "Go TEAM!" they all hollered as one.

Following the practice, Barclay met with the coaches. "Everything is set for Saturday night," he said and provided the coaches with a copy of the Bonito kid's birth certificate. He reminded them to wait until the Drewmore team was introduced. "If the kid is in the lineup, you know what to do—call time and present the head umpire with the evidence."

"That'll be fun," Cortino cracked.

Barclay informed them he was taking a few days off and would be heading to Upstate New York. "But I'll see you Saturday for the game. You have my cell. Call if anything comes up."

As the detective shuffled away, Cortino and McCracken agreed that Barclay was a decent guy. "He certainly gave us some heavy-caliber ammunition against Drewmore," remarked McCracken, waving the birth certificate.

"He's been talking with Fred Saunders, you know," said Cortino. "You think Fred killed the mayor?"

McCracken's bushy eyebrows went up. "Stranger things have happened. I know goddam good and well it wasn't Jack, but . . ." McCracken stared off into space. "Who knows? Maybe it *was* Saunders," he said. "If it was, they should give him a medal."

CHAPTER TEN

BARCLAY WAS MAKING a quick stop back at the Holiday Inn when his phone rang. "What do you have for me, doll?" he inquired.

"The registration on that Mercedes came back," said Monica, giggling. "And stop calling me *doll*. Almost grounds for a lawsuit."

"Take a number, babe," he replied.

The Mercedes was a 2007 model registered to a company called Number 1 Mine at PO Box 46, Archville. "I checked the company with the Pennsylvania Department of State," Monica continued. "It was incorporated in 1937 and its current officers are—"

"Let me guess," Barclay cut in. "Old lady Jenkins and our deceased mayor."

"You're so clever," she said. "But I bet you dinner you can't guess who the treasurer is."

"Who?" he demanded.

"None other than one Clarence A. West, Esquire."

"The family attorney?"

"I don't know about that," she said. "But according to the records, he has been the treasurer of Number 1 Mine since 1970."

"That was the year the old man shot himself," murmured Barclay.

"Say what?"

"Just thinking out loud. Great job. Dinner's on me, honey."

"There you go with the remarks again. Wait till you get the bill for that dinner, *honey*." She giggled ghoulishly and hung up.

Barclay sat on the bed and looked at the wallpaper. He still had no clue how West, Esquire, fit into the overall picture, but he was willing to bet that the Benz at the funeral had Elizabeth Jenkins as a passenger.

The detective gathered his belongings in a suitcase, went downstairs, and checked out, putting the bill on the plastic. He asked the clerk to reserve a room for Saturday for an indefinite period.

"You got it. That's the last room I have available," the clerk said. "We are now booked solid."

Barclay inquired as to why the hotel was booked solid.

"Big game Saturday night—Drewmore and Archville. Most of the rooms have been booked by media companies. ABC, NBC, CBS, even ESPN. I think the Snook thing has a lot to do with it"

"Imagine that," Barclay said.

The detective drove out of the parking lot, making a beeline to nearby Interstate Route 81 North. He had become adept at looking into his rearview mirror at all times, especially when he was on a case.

At first he thought he was just being paranoid when he spotted a black Chevy Tahoe on his tail. He hit the gas on the Jag and moved into the passing lane as he came upon the exit for Waverly. No sooner had he dismissed the possibility of being followed when the black SUV appeared once again.

To make certain he was being tailed, Barclay exited at the East Benton ramp and looked for a gas station. He gave the appearance that he was just making a routine gas stop. As the attendant filled the Jag, Barclay went into the men's room. Sure enough, when he came out, the Tahoe with two men was just across the street. The driver was pretending to read a map.

He settled up with the kid who pumped his gas and gave him a $3 tip. Then Barclay got back into the Jag and removed his 9-mm Glock from the locked glove box. He quickly devised a plan. On his GPS device, he searched for a truck stop. He located one in Binghamton, New York, not far from the Pennsylvania border.

The SUV followed Barclay back onto the highway, staying back about two hundred to three hundred yards. In New York, Barclay took the exit for Route 11 North. Truck Stops of America was on the right. He pulled into the parking lot and went inside. Just inside the door, he peeked outside and watched the SUV come to a stop. The passenger got out and walked toward the entrance.

Barclay went to the men's room, for he thought that would be the first place the tail would look for him. He was right.

A middle-aged man with a thin build walked briskly through the door. Barclay grabbed him by the collar. "Who are you and why are you following me?" demanded Barclay.

"Wait a minute," the man said. "It's not what you think. We have an offer for you."

Barclay hesitated for a moment, still clutching his shirt. "What do you mean you have an *offer* for me?"

The man then invited the detective to come outside to the SUV and hear him out.

"Okay," said Barclay, releasing his grip on the man. "But remember, I'm armed and I won't hesitate if you try anything funny." The man looked uncomfortable.

The SUV's driver saw the two men exit the truck stop and immediately got out of the vehicle. Barclay was clutching his Glock in his right pants pocket.

The two men, as it turned out, were licensed private investigators. "We were hired to bring you this briefcase. Our client told us there is a note inside the briefcase for you."

The detective eased up on the Glock, took the briefcase, and placed it on the SUV's hood. "Open it," Barclay said to the man he'd confronted in the men's room.

The man slowly opened the briefcase. The eyes of all three men nearly popped out, for the case contained neat bundles of $100 bills. There was an envelope on top of the money with the name of Jake Barclay on it.

Barclay picked up the envelope, opened it, and began reading:

Dear Mr. Barclay:

This briefcase contains $250,000. You may call it a retainer for your services. I apologize for the manner in which I have gone about to hire you. My client in this matter wishes to remain anonymous. All you must do to earn this money and another $250,000 is to stay out of Archville and our county until after the trial of Jack Snook. I am certain you will have questions. However, my client insists that there be no further communication regarding this matter. I have given my client my word that this will never be discussed again. However, if you reject the retainer, the two men I have hired to bring this offer to you will return the briefcase to me.

Sincerely,
Clarence West, Esq.

Barclay pondered the situation for a couple of moments. "Sorry, I'm afraid you two boys will have to tell Attorney West, *Esquire*, I'm not for sale."

"Honest, sir, we do not know anything other than we were assigned to bring you this briefcase and to return it if you rejected the offer inside," said one of the men.

Barclay then asked the men if they were *really* licensed private detectives.

"We are," said one. "My name's Matt Toolan, and he's Jerry Oswald. We have an agency in Scranton."

Barclay then told the men they should stick to working divorces, workers' compensation, and liability cases. "Best you stay away from the hard stuff."

The detective closed the case and picked it up. "Tell Attorney West I will be bringing the case to him personally when I return to Archville."

"But we're supposed to take it back," said Oswald.

"Like I said, you two are amateurs." Barclay then took a Swiss Army knife from his pocket and slit the right rear tire on the SUV. "That's just in case you decide to follow," said Barclay.

The detective got into his Jag and sped out of the parking lot, leaving the private dicks fairly agog. He watched in his mirror as Oswald took out his cell phone, presumably to call West and relate the events that had just transpired. "I'm on to something," he mumbled. "But what?"

Barclay knew it would be useless to continue his journey to the cabin, especially in light of the most recent, unusual development. He steered the Jag off the next exit ramp and got on Route 81 South. He was about an hour from Archville at most.

On his cell phone he dialed up John Lovello. The attorney answered after three rings, and Barclay rattled off the unusual offer of a half million dollars to stay clear of Archville.

However, Lovello said that he had a similar offer apparently passed along to him from counsel hired by Clarence West in Los Angeles. "What the hell have we gotten ourselves into?" asked Lovello.

"I do not know, my man," said Barclay, "but I'm on my way back to Archville to get some answers. I'm going to confront West when I return the briefcase."

"Be gentle. And make sure he writes you a receipt for the return of the money. I'll be near my phone all evening."

Jake Barclay terminated the call and quickly dialed his office in LA.

"What's up, hot stuff," came the voice on the other end of the phone.

"Be careful, honey, sexual harassment is a two-way street," he shot back.

Monica told him she had received a frantic call from Clarence West. "It sounded urgent."

He took the phone number, hung up with Monica, and called West.

The attorney answered on the first ring. "Clarence West."

"This is Jake Barclay. I have something that belongs to you. Where can we meet to talk?"

"There will be no talking," said West. "My note to you was specific. This matter will never be spoken of again."

"Maybe we should speak of this matter with the DA or, better still, with the FBI. You sent two dumb bunnies on roller skates with a bag of greenleaf. They followed me across state lines with a bribe. I'm sure the resident agent in charge of the FBI's field office in Scranton would be most interested."

The attorney was silent for a moment. "All right, my office, tonight at nine."

"It's a date," said Barclay.

He gripped the wheel and let the Jag drift into the fast lane.

*   *   *

That night, Barclay arrived at West's office at precisely 9:00 p.m. It was a storefront office along Main Street surrounded by empty buildings, most of which were at least a century or more old. They were decaying and crumbling.

West was seated in a high-back leather office chair. Most of the other furniture was of the antique variety, even the bookcases holding West's impressive collection of law books. He had the half-anemic expression of the courtroom about him and was puffing on a cigar too big for his face.

"Cuban?" asked the detective.

"Why yes, yes it is," said West. "You must have a discriminating palate, Mr. Barclay."

"I know a good cigar when I whiff one."

"Leave the briefcase on the desk and be gone, Mr. Barclay" said West. He pointed to a piece of paper on the desk. "There is a receipt for the return of the money. I figured you would want one, given the circumstance."

"Not so fast," said Barclay. "You owe me an explanation, Attorney West."

"I owe you nothing, Mr. Barclay. You were offered a retainer by my client and you declined. End of story, Mr. Barclay. Nothing more needs to be said."

"Did you think I would just walk out of here without answers?" asked the detective.

"Why yes, yes I did," said West, puffing on his Cohiba.

"You're dreaming, counselor. I talked to Lovello in LA. He was offered a 'retainer' too."

"That is correct, Mr. Barclay. My client gave the great John Lovello an offer very similar to the one you received. You two either have superior ethics or are holding out for more money, likely the former, in my estimation." West blew the sweet smell of the Cuban cigar in Barclay's direction. "I will not be revealing my client to you or to Mr. Lovello," he said. "So it is best that you be gone."

Barclay looked around the office for a watercooler. There was none. The crafty detective began choking and coughing.

"Are you all right, Mr. Barclay?" asked West.

Barclay continued pretending to cough and motioned to the old attorney that he needed a glass of water.

"I'll get one from the kitchen in the back," West said.

The very second West was out of sight, Barclay picked up the telephone on the desk. If he was right, West had recently called his elusive client, and the number would be in the phone's call list. He committed the last number to memory and hung up the phone moments before West returned with paper cup of water.

He continued his charade until he gulped down the water. "Thank you," Barclay said, coming out of the coughing attack. He stepped to the desk and picked up the receipt noted earlier. As he read it, West assured him it was all in order. "Just checking," Barclay said. "By the way, are you a betting man?"

"Of course not."

"Well, I am," said Barclay. "And I bet by noon tomorrow I'll know who your client is."

The attorney shook his head. "You LA guys are really full of yourselves, aren't you? Even my private secretary does not know who my client is. There is no paper file containing that information, and there is no computer file. You would lose the bet, Mr. Barclay."

"Then it's a bet?"

"What do you have in mind?"

"Well, you obviously have access to Cuban cigars. What do you say to a wager of a box of Cohibas?"

"Very well, a box of Cohibas it is. Noon tomorrow."

"I love a good cigar," Barclay said on his way out.

Back in the car, Barclay chuckled as he called his secretary.

"You again," Monica said. "I was just leaving the office. This better be important."

"Listen, let's not forget who the boss is here. I could put you over my knee, you know."

"Let's see now, would that be sexual harassment or a perk?"

"A little of each, I guess," he said. "Anyway, I need a phone number checked ASAP. This is very important, and I need it by 11:30 tomorrow morning, East Coast time."

"That's overtime," Monica complained.

"Life's hard."

He called Lovello and told him about his knitting session with Clarence West.

"Nice move with the phone fake there," said Lovello.

"I hope he only made one call," said Barclay. "If you find a box of Cohibas on my expense account, don't bitch."

"I won't," said Lovello. "I'll be back there for the big game Saturday night. You have any idea who West's client is?"

Barclay admitted that anything he said would be pure speculation. "We are knee deep into something, John. We may as well let it play out. After all, a million bucks is a hefty bribe. The only one with money like that would be old lady Jenkins. That mystery Benz at the cemetery turns out to be hers."

"Jesus," said Lovello. "Keep me posted."

CHAPTER ELEVEN

BARCLAY WAS AWAKENED at 9:30. The room phone and his cell phone were ringing at the same time. The caller ID on the cell phone told him it was Sam Cortino. He sent Cortino's call through to voice mail and picked up the room phone.

It was Tim Richards, Archville's council president, and he was rattled. "I need to see you as soon as possible. Two FBI agents just left my house."

"I can be there in a half hour," said Barclay.

"No, not here," he said. "Meet me at the municipal building, the mayor's office."

"Fine, see you there." He hung up and thought, *Fine indeed. This was a murder investigation and what better place for a powwow than the very scene of the murder. Add in the other fellow who died there, and you've got yourself a regular small-town killing field in that office.*

Barclay showered and dressed quickly but skipped shaving, a chore he'd hated since college. The *FBI*? Huh? As the kids in LA say, what's *really* going on?

Barclay arrived at the municipal building only to find FBI agents sifting through files. "Excuse me," said an agent whose badge was attached to his belt. "This is a crime scene. What is your business here?"

Barclay reached for his wallet and produced identification for the agent. "I have a meeting with Tim Richards."

The agent nodded toward the mayor's office. "He's in there."

Barclay found Richards on his desk phone, the cord stretching as he paced back and forth. He was breathing heavy and had sweat on his brow. "That's right," Richards was telling his party, "we've been had. Royally fucked is a better way to put it."

Barclay stood there silently. So far, he liked what he was hearing. He crossed his fingers. Perhaps a new suspect was about to emerge in the slaying of our dearly departed mayor.

"Not now," Richards finally said and put the phone down. He was shaking like a bad actor in a low-budget slasher movie.

Barclay said nothing but simply stood by, watching the council president melt. He'd be easier to deal with in that state.

Richards gasped and hugged himself. He looked at the detective somberly. "It was all a scam."

Barclay slipped into a chair in front of the desk. "Uh-huh."

"There's no company going to liquefy coal to produce diesel fuel," said Richards. "It was all a scam."

Barclay shrugged. "So, you almost got conned. Happens every day. What's the big deal?"

"You don't have the complete picture," said Richards. "What I left out on Sunday is the fact that the council *majority* committed $500,000 of our federal Community Development Block Grant money to the project—without the benefit of a public hearing or an *official* vote by the council. We were *conned* by professionals!"

"Are you telling me that the council gave this Texas company a half million dollars upfront for an 'experimental' project?"

"That's exactly what I'm telling you," said Richards. "The FBI told me today that the men behind the scam also bilked other municipalities here in Pennsylvania and in West Virginia and Kentucky too. The agent said there may be as much as $25 to $50 million dollars involved."

Richards was almost spitting as he told Barclay how the FBI got tipped to the scam by a whistle-blower secretary in West Virginia who discovered that proper procedures for spending federal money had not been followed.

"It hit the papers in West Virginia, and the investigation took off from there," he said. "The agent says they executed a search warrant in Houston, with arrest warrants coming down."

Barclay perked up. "Arrest warrants for whom?"

"He wouldn't say." Richards looked like he was on the verge of a breakdown as he sat down behind his desk. "Now I have to tell the good people of Archville that we've lost the money that was originally earmarked for a badly needed downtown revitalization program."

All the while Richards ranted, Barclay was deep in thought, trying to look at this in a way that would point to other suspects in the murder of Al Jenkins. "Listen, I've got to go," said Barclay. "But I'll keep an eye on the situation and let you know. Keep cool."

"We only had the town's best interests in mind," protested Richards, still sweating. "We didn't steal any money, but that's how it's going to look when this hits the papers."

Outside the municipal building, Barclay called Charlie Mars's cell phone. The reporter answered, and Barclay filled him in on what was transpiring at the Archville Municipal Building.

"Thanks, Jake. I'll get right on it."

It was now 11:15. Barclay had a bet to win.

Monica answered the phone on the first ring and proudly announced to her boss that the phone number belonged to Elizabeth Jenkins. "It was hard to get," she explained, "because it's been unlisted for over two decades."

Barclay remained silent.

"Jake, you still there?"

"I was kind of expecting that name. This could be a big break in the case. Stay by the phone. I'll have a couple of things for you later."

At precisely 11:30, Barclay quietly stepped into the West Law Office on Main Street. The secretary was seated at a desk to the right. She appeared to be in her late fifties and looked very professional. "You must be Mr. Barclay," she said. "Go right in. Mr. West is expecting you."

West was standing at one of the antique bookcases holding a law book, his glasses perched on the tip of his nose.

Barclay noticed faint traces of mud on the attorney's shoes. "At the cemetery today?" asked the detective.

"So, Mr. Barclay. You know my routine?"

The detective acknowledged that he did indeed know of the daily cemetery visits.

"But how are you with clients?" challenged West.

Barclay didn't waste time with preliminaries. "Why was Elizabeth Jenkins willing to spend a million dollars to keep me and John Lovello out of Archville?"

The old attorney was unsteady as he put the book away and made his way to his desk. "But how did you find out? I certainly hope that you and Lovello would not stoop so low as to bug my office. That would be breaking the law." He fingered the buttons on his vest as if they were some kind of a control that would transport him away from a very awkward situation.

Barclay assured him there were no bugs. "Now tell me why old lady Jenkins wants me and John out of Archville."

"First things first, Mr. Barclay. I owe you a box of cigars. Let's take a ride."

"Where to?"

"Why to get your Cohibas of course." The attorney pointed toward the rear of the building. "My car is in the garage out back. I'll be right along."

As Barclay left, West went into the outer office and leaned over his secretary's desk. In a faint whisper he told her to call Elizabeth Jenkins and tell her he needed to see her right away. "And find a company that can come in today to sweep for bugs." The secretary looked confused. "The listening kind of bugs, not insects."

"Oh," she said.

The entrance to the garage was just outside the back of the law office. The two entered and West put on a light. It was a two-car garage. On his left, there was a covered car, and on the right was West's older Ford Bronco.

Barclay asked the attorney what was concealed under the drop cloth.

"It's a 1967 Corvette Stingray," he said. "It was my son's car. I could never bring myself to part with it. Clarence Junior loved that car. Paid for it himself with money he earned doing odd jobs and working for me. Here, take a look." He tore back the cover to reveal a bright blue metallic vintage 'Vette.

"I'm envious," said Barclay. West told him he was not the first to envy the car and that he would certainly not be the last. Then he clicked the automatic garage door opener as they got in the Bronco.

"Mind telling me where we're going?" said Barclay.

The attorney slowly backed the Bronco out into the alley behind the law office. "The only place I can get the Cohibas is in Scranton, a place called the Smoke Filled Room. It will give us time to talk, Mr. Barclay."

Barclay grinned. "Guys who pay their bets in Cubans can call me Jake."

"As you wish, Jake."

The attorney asked if he and John Lovello had managed to zero in on any suspects other than Snook.

"Suspects are many," Barclay told him. "But we haven't 'zeroed' in on anyone in particular. By the way, I guess you know about the FBI and the coal scam thing."

"Oh yes, I know about it," said West. "The council's solicitor called me as soon as the FBI contacted him yesterday. Too bad really with the town getting ready to shine in the little league tournament. I hope the negative publicity doesn't hurt the kids."

"I hope not, but you know how the media can stir up things." Barclay looked at West. "You said we'd talk. Let's talk. What interest does Elizabeth Jenkins have in the trial of Jack Snook and why did she try to bribe me and John?"

Crossing the Mulberry Street Bridge, West told Barclay that Mrs. Jenkins had no interest whatsoever in the outcome of any trial—not of Jack

Snook or any other person who may end up charged with her grandson's murder. He explained that Al Jenkins and his grandmother had been severely estranged ever since his return to Archville and that the woman regretted her decision to raise the son-of-a-bitch. "The old lady lost track long ago of how much he'd cost her over the years."

The Bronco came to a stop on a side street not far from City Hall.

"Come on, Jake. I'll treat you to a cigar."

The pair entered the Smoke Filled Room and was greeted by a clerk wearing a bowtie and suspenders.

"Two of your finest cigars from the island," said West to the clerk. Barclay later learned that that was the code to order a Cuban cigar because possession of Cuban cigars in the United States was a crime.

Nevertheless, the clerk clipped two Cohibas and handed them to West. "I will need a box to go too," said West.

He handed the clerk a credit card and signed the slip.

Barclay followed the attorney to a back room decorated with pictures and sports memorabilia, most of which consisted of Pittsburgh Pirates and Steelers items. The two men sat in the big leather easy chairs and fired up their cigars. They were the only customers there.

"Now, are you going to tell me about Mrs. Jenkins's bribes?" asked Barclay.

"No, I will never tell you the reason for the bribes. She has become accustomed to buying anything she wants, Jake. Everything, so they say, has its price, and she believes that you and Mr. Lovello do as well."

The attorney said he had cautioned his client that Barclay and Lovello would likely never compromise themselves, but she wouldn't listen.

"Jake, small towns keep large secrets, and Archville is no different. Long ago, things happened in Archville that should never have happened. They are dark secrets and should stay where they've been all these years—in the past." West told the detective that he was on track to discovering one of those secrets and that he should let his conscience be his guide when he uncovers a truth or two. "That's all I have to say for now, Jake. No more questions."

Barclay picked up the remote for the large screen television in the back room. Ironically, it was at the precise time that the local NBC affiliate was headlining the unfolding story at the Archville Municipal Building. "Federal agents raid the Archville Municipal Building. We'll have team coverage tonight at six," said the woman on the screen.

"I think we best be getting back to my office," said West.

Neither man spoke more than a word or two on the return trip.

West pulled the Bronco into a spot behind Barclay's Jag on Main Street. "Before we part, Jake, please tell me how you found out that Elizabeth Jenkins was my client."

Barclay thought for a minute. "Well, no big mystery. When you went to get me the water last night in your office, I looked at the call log on your desk phone, remembered the number, and the rest was easy in our online world."

"Bravo, Jake, bravo," he repeated in a soft voice. He did not appear to be rattled at all. "You knew that I most likely called my client to inform her of the misfired bribe. Bravo. I guess you LA guys are full of yourselves for a reason. Just remember what I told you about secrets, Jake, and enjoy the cigars."

Barclay stepped from the Bronco and West drove off, heading up Main Street at good speed. Obviously, the old attorney had to report to his client. *Always the client.*

CHAPTER TWELVE

B ACK IN THE Jag, Barclay called Monica.
"Hi, hot stuff," she answered. "The feds in Texas are looking
for a man named Edward Cook and one of his cohorts by the name of
Eugene Morrison."

"Where'd you hear this?"

"I've been following what's been going on in Archville on the web, and
I've been doing some snooping of my own."

Monica had undergone training for the LAPD and was working in the
department's IT division when he hired her away. "One of these days," he
told her, "you'll be telling me you're striking out on your own."

She laughed. "But then I wouldn't have you to pester. Anyway, Cook
and Morrison ran a company called Changeable Energy, Inc., founded in
Texas a year ago. Other than that, there's very little about the company on
the net. The indictment handed up last week by a federal grand jury in
Houston lists twenty-four separate counts against the pair in a scheme to
defraud a dozen or so municipalities of millions of dollars. By the time the
Feds arrived with warrants at the storefront office they had in a Houston
suburb, Cook and Morrison were gone. However, they left behind a pair
of badly damaged computer hard drives, which were confiscated by the
feds. The digital dogs at Quantico sniffed out the information that led to
Archville and numerous other cities."

Barclay said, "Jesus, real Bernie Madoff wannabes, huh?"

"Wait, it gets better." Monica said she had googled both names and
learned that the pair had MBAs from Harvard. "And breaking news! They
were in the same class as a certain dead mayor named Al Jenkins. And this
just in—the indictment was handed up the *same day* Jenkins was killed."

"Wow!" said Barclay. "Not one but two suspects."

"Not so fast there, lover boy," Monica said. "I haven't been able to tie
the trio together recently, but I am going to keep trying."

Barclay told her to keep digging. "Any pictures available?" he asked.

"Yes," she said. "The *Houston Chronicle* ran their driver's license pictures
when it published the story on the indictments."

Barclay told her to e-mail the link ASAP.

"Great job, dolly," he told her. "And I don't mean that in a sexual harassment kind of way."

His next call was to Sam Cortino. He had neglected to call the coach back from earlier. He hadn't even listened to the voice mail he'd left. When he connected with Cortino, he asked if he had a computer with a printer, and when Cortino answered in the affirmative, he headed straight over to his home.

The detective arrived in about five minutes. He took little notice of his surroundings, beyond the fact that he was standing in what appeared to be a well-kept rustic-style suburban home. "Where's the computer?" he asked.

Cortino told him it was in the basement and led the way.

"What do you think about the broadcast?" asked the coach on the way to the basement.

"Huh?"

"You know," said Cortino, "my voice mail from this morning."

Barclay apologized. "I haven't listened to it yet. I've been busy with something else." The distraction in his voice made it clear that he was in no mood to talk about anything until he had accessed the e-mail file he was seeking. Barclay jumped on the computer and tried to log onto his MSN account. "Is this computer always this slow?" he asked.

"Always," replied Cortino. "It's an antique, must be eight or ten years old."

Nevertheless, his e-mail popped up, and Barclay opened the new message from Monica. The pictures of Cook and Morrison were included. "Print that for me, will you, Sam?"

The printer was an antique too. The pictures printed, but they were of poor quality. "They'll have to do," Barclay said. He folded the paper containing the pictures and turned to Cortino. "So what is this about a broadcast?"

Cortino told him that the local ABC affiliate was going to broadcast the game Saturday between Archville and Drewmore.

"Great," said Barclay. "But it may be the shortest sportscast in the history of television."

They both laughed. "That's the same exact thing that McCracken said when I told him."

They laughed again. "Great minds think alike," said Barclay. He told Cortino that he was very busy with the Snook case, bid him good-bye, and thanked him for the use of the computer.

As he was walking out, Cortino informed him, "Practice will be on Wednesday in Jefferson Township at 4:30."

Barclay gave him a thumbs-up. "I'll be there." Then he climbed into the Jag and headed directly for Tim Richards's house.

A news crew was out front with the same pushy blonde reporter from the Complex.

She walked right up to him, flaunted a pair of 38Ds in his direction, and asked what the "famous Jake Barclay" was doing at the home of Tim Richards. The detective ignored her and kept moving. "Get that camera rolling," she snapped at her cameraman photographer.

Barclay was let into the house by a frantic council president. He ran fingers through his thinning hair and looked out on the gaggle of newsies. "It's been like this for the last two hours. Of course, the borough solicitor warned me not to make *any* statements."

"Good advice," said Barclay. Once they were safely hidden in the kitchen, he pulled out the printed e-mail copy. "These guys look familiar?" The poor quality of the printer coupled with the folds in the paper made it difficult to make out the smallish DMV photos.

"Got a computer?" Barclay asked.

"A laptop," said Richards.

"Get it."

The detective logged into his account and pulled up the e-mail from Monica.

"My god," said Richards. "That's them. Those are the two guys from Changeable Energy, Inc."

Barclay was pleased. For whatever it might be worth, he could establish a recent link between the dead mayor and the two con artists way after Harvard. It wasn't a lot, but it was an opening. "Gotta hop, Tim. Keep away from the cameras." Barclay left Richards to his fretting and dismal situation. Outside, he ignored the shouts of the news crews and hopped back into the Jag. As he rolled away, he got Lovello on the mobile.

"Talk to me, Jake."

Barclay laid out what he'd learned about the phony fuel company and how the two con men were linked to Jenkins.

"Do we know where Cook and Morrison are now?" asked Lovello.

"I just got the names, John. I'm following up on a few leads as to their whereabouts. Remember, this is FBI territory now."

"Does that bother you?"

"No," Jake replied, "not really. I like to mix it up, you know that."

Lovello laughed. "So do I. But you have to find those scam artists. It could be our only chance to clear an innocent man."

"I'm on the case," Barclay said. "However, I need Monica out here for some fieldwork."

"All right, if you need her, make it happen."

Barclay called Monica, and she was pleased to hear she had a reason to get out of LA for a while. "Get a flight into Philly and grab a rental. You won't have any trouble finding Drewmore. Call me when you get in."

Next, he called Charlie Mars.

"Hey, Jake. I'm at the Archville Municipal Building. We're all waiting for an assistant US attorney to make a statement. I'm surprised you're not here."

"Standby," Barclay said.

*   *   *

Barclay's Jaguar pulled up a couple of blocks from the municipal building. The whole area was littered with news trucks and hungry reporters waiting to be thrown a bone. He saw Mars and waved him over. They talked a minute, and Barclay brought the reporter up to speed on everything, including the revelation that the murdered mayor was in the same MBA program at Harvard as the two suspects in the coal to fuel swindle.

"Son of a bitch!" Mars cracked. "Hang tough a second." He ran to his car, retrieved his laptop, returned, and got into the Jag. He logged onto his e-mail and, as Barclay watched, knocked out a three-hundred word piece for his paper's website. He typed "Exclusive-Exclusive-Exclusive" on the subject line and launched the message to his editor in Scranton. "There you go, on-the-spot coverage. Those other chumps over there can read all about it in fifteen minutes."

The Jag was already in motion. "Hell with the press conference. Let's grab a bite," Barclay said. "All those reporters will get out of the US attorney is a big "No comment." Of course, your article makes only a weak connection, wouldn't you say?"

"Sure it's a weak connection," Mars agreed. "The news business is built on weak connections. Besides, *any* link between the murder of Al Jenkins and *any* kinda multimillion dollar rip-off is news."

They stopped over at Dunnigan's for a sandwich. There were a handful of older patrons at the bar. Some of them could be heard talking about the $500,000 the municipality had lost in the fraud.

Mars and Barclay took a table off to the right. "Charlie," Barclay said, "can we go off the record?"

"Does it rain on rhubarb?"

"Look," the detective, "we've been straight with each other. I know you can be trusted. What I'm about to tell you is not for the paper. Are you okay with that?"

Mars paused, thought about it a moment, then nodded.

"Ever seen half a million in cash?" Barclay inquired, and Mars perked up. He told him about the two klutzy private eyes who had delivered the briefcase of money while the same bribe to back off was also delivered to Lovello. Barclay went into detail about his subsequent meetings with Clarence West as well as how he'd uncovered the source of the bribe, much to West's chagrin and a box of Cubans.

"Cute business with the phone log there," Mars complimented. "But why would old lady Jenkins want to bribe you and Lovello to stay off the case?"

"Right now, I have no real idea. But West told me the town held *secrets* from long ago. He said he was close to 'uncovering' something. Naturally, he didn't say what."

After they downed some roast beef on rye, the two left, and Barclay drove Mars back to his car and the media circus at the municipal building. They were in time to catch a geeky-looking assistant US attorney at the mike. "This should be good," said Barclay as they got out of the car and listened.

"My office has just received word that Mr. Cook and Mr. Morrison have been picked up by Interpol in London. According to their passports, they've been there the last twelve days."

As the speaker droned on, saying nothing, Barclay and Mars exchanged a look.

"If they've been in London the last twelve days . . . ," Barclay began thoughtfully, "it'll be tricky connecting them with Jenkins's murder a week ago. Obviously, they could've brought in hired muscle."

"Doesn't take a lot of muscle when you're wielding a baseball bat," Mars pointed out.

Barclay stepped aside, rang up Lovello, and explained what he'd just learned.

"Not good," said the attorney. "We're more or less back to square 1: no viable suspects."

"Tell me about it," Barclay said and disconnected.

Mars was shaking his head. "Complicated, ain't it?"

"See you later, Charlie."

Barclay dashed to his Jag and sped up the street to Tim Richards's house. The news people had apparently gotten tired of waiting around, and the neighborhood was quiet. The detective hustled to the door and looked in the window. Richards, his wife, and two kids were at the dinner table. Barclay knocked anyway.

Richards was wiping his mouth with a napkin when he opened the door.

"Sorry to disturb you, Tim, but I have to ask you a question."

"Sure, go ahead," said Richards.

"When I was here on Sunday, you told me that the lawyer for the Texas company insisted upon confidentiality with regard to the project we now know was a scam. Do you know who he was?"

"Why yes," said Richards. "I have his card in my briefcase."

Barclay got the card, thanked Richards, and went back to his car. The business card read, Irving R. Fellerman, Attorney and Counselor at Law. It had a Houston address and two phone numbers, one for voice and one for fax.

"Probably fake," said Barclay as he punched in the voice number on his cell phone.

Surprisingly, the phone was answered by a cheery female. "Fellerman Law Office. How may I help you?"

"My name is Jake Barclay. I'm a private detective from Los Angeles. May I speak to Mr. Fellerman?"

"I'm sorry, Mr. Barclay, but Mr. Fellerman stepped out. I'll be glad to have him return the call however."

Barclay gave the receptionist the number and hung up. He went back to Richards's and asked to use the laptop, which was quickly produced. Barclay logged on and did a search for "lawyer Fellerman Houston."

On the attorney's elaborate site, he found pictures of Fellerman and six associates. It also listed the firm's specialties with a complete biography for every lawyer, paralegal, and secretary.

Barclay showed the picture of Fellerman to Richards. "Is this the attorney from Texas?"

Richards looked at the picture on the screen and sagged. "That's him. That's the bastard who made us sign that confidentiality agreement. At the time, it seemed logical. Morrison said they were just protecting everyone's investment. Didn't want word leaking out prematurely. *Hah!*"

"You weren't the only ones," said Barclay. "Those guys duped more than a dozen communities."

Barclay's cell phone rang. He looked at the caller ID with a Houston area code. "Speak of the devil," he said and clicked a button. "Barclay."

"This is Irving Fellerman returning your call, Mr. Barclay. What can I do for you?"

"Thanks for getting back to me, counselor. Quick question: do you represent a company called Changeable Energy?"

"I did," replied Fellerman.

"They're no longer clients?"

"The company principals, Ed Cook and Gene Morrison, were indicted recently by a federal grand jury here in Houston on various fraud charges. According to the FBI, millions of dollars were stolen." Fellerman said he no longer represented the pair and hadn't heard from them in nearly a month. "I met with the FBI twice. Told them what I knew."

"So you were the attorney of record?"

"I set up their corporation. It was in full compliance with Texas and US law."

"I see," replied Barclay.

"Understand now, I'm not in *any* way associated with Changeable Energy. I was the lawyer for the corporation and that's all. They put up a retainer, and my expenses were paid in a timely manner."

"It all seemed legit on the surface, huh?"

"No, no, it didn't," Fellerman continued. "Like I told the FBI, I didn't for one minute believe that Morrison and Cook had the wherewithal to pull off a technological feat like turning coal into diesel fuel. However, here in Houston, energy companies with great ideas are a dime a dozen. It was not my place to question their ideas or their abilities. I merely represented them."

"I guess you've heard the latest," said Barclay. "Cook and Morrison were arrested today in London."

"No, sir. I hadn't heard that."

Barclay played a hunch. "Ever meet Archville's mayor, Al Jenkins?"

Fellerman said he had never met Jenkins. "But my clients mentioned him a few times. Apparently they were college pals."

"Did they ever mention Jenkins in any capacity beyond their years at Harvard?"

"Actually, yes," Fellerman said, a trickle of excitement entering his voice. "According to Cook and Morrison, they were at one time partners in a political consulting firm. Jenkins had been a client of theirs when he ran for Congress back a few years."

Barclay thanked Fellerman for the information. "You've been most helpful."

"Please," said Fellerman graciously, "call me if you have any more questions."

"I appreciate that, sir. Have a good day." He hung up and looked at Richards. "This deal's getting curiouser and curiouser."

Richards rubbed his face nervously. "And I'm about ready to lose it."

Barclay offered a few words of comfort and drove away.

It was nearing seven o'clock, and he needed to catch the local news. He parked outside of a pocket pub on Pine Street. The place was almost empty. He asked the woman behind the bar if it would be possible to watch the news. "You got it," she said and picked up the remote. "What channel?"

"Try the local ABC station."

It was the top story, the accused and the audacious crimes spelled out in the indictment. Pictures of the two suspects were plastered on the screen, and a voice-over explained that Cook and Morrison had been apprehended in London. The image cut to the blonde reporter Barclay had snubbed earlier in the day. "We attempted to get comments from members of Archville's council. But they've referred all questions to the municipal solicitor, whom we were unable to reach. Coming up, a look at what the loss of $500,000 will mean to Archville's downtown revitalization project."

Barclay had seen enough and got up to leave. He hadn't ordered anything, so he dropped a couple of singles on the bar and thanked the lady for her courtesy. "By the way, know of an arts and crafts store nearby?"

"Nearest'd be at the Crossings over in Dickson City." She grinned. "Like to crochet?"

"Needlepoint," said Barclay and was halfway to the door before she caught on and started laughing.

The detective picked up some poster board and markers at the Crossings and returned to the Holiday Inn, where he showered and shaved. He wanted badly to fire up one of the Cohibas he had won in his bet with West, but smoking in the hotel was banned by law.

He tore open the package of art supplies. Taking a black marker, Barclay began working up a timeline of the events that had occurred since he'd arrived in Archville. He often did this as a way of backtracking his steps. He had to find out what he was missing and, more importantly, what alleged secrets he was getting close to.

CHAPTER THIRTEEN

THE CELL PHONE awakened Barclay from a deep slumber. He squinted at the clock on the nightstand: 11:00 a.m. He wiped the sleep from his eyes and grabbed the phone.

"I'm in Philly," Monica reported. "I should be there in about two hours."

"How was the flight?"

"Bad food. Bad service. Bad attitudes. Any questions?"

"Sounds lovely. Okay, find the northeast extension of the turnpike."

"Got my GPS thingy," she replied.

"Set it for Moosic Street in Scranton. Find a scenic place they call the Lookout. Ring me when you're there. Low key now. I do not want us to be seen together."

"I don't blame you. People'll wonder why a good-looking chick like me is hanging out with a questionable character like you. Ha ha ha! See you at this Lookout place."

She was good. Monica had only been in the field with him on a few occasions since she had come on board two years earlier. Her primary function was handling the day-to-day office chores and the computer work. She was right about the good-looking chick thing. Five-ten, gorgeous red hair, striking features. Quick with the mouth but also the brain.

Barclay had slept later than he liked and now hopped to it, showering, dressing, pulling himself together. He read over the timeline he had prepared, but it looked the same in daylight as it had in moonlight. Nothing clicked.

Within two hours, Monica called; she was ten minutes from the Lookout.

On the drive, Barclay kept an eye on his rearview mirror. He took a couple of deceptive lefts and rights, then cut through an alley. No tail. So far.

In the parking lot at the Lookout, Monica got into the Jag. "Hey, bright eyes," she greeted him.

"You look as adorable as ever," the detective said.

"Thanks, you look kinda wrecked."

"Too much sleep," he replied.

Barclay proceeded to lay out Monica's assignment in detail. Her main function was to conduct sporadic surveillance on the Jenkins's Mansion, Clarence West, and last but not least, Fred Saunders.

"Why Saunders?" she asked.

"My mind keeps going back to the day of Jenkins's funeral." He told her that Saunders had called in sick and that the crossing guard was in somewhat of a state of panic when the detective visited his apartment that morning. "It's just a hunch," he admitted.

He gave her the addresses she would need and one of his credit cards for expenses. "Stay in touch," he said. "And don't get carried away with the credit card."

"Okay," Monica said, "but there's something vaguely sexist about that remark?"

They both laughed like kids as she got out of the car.

Monica was itching to get started. She drove her rented Ford Focus to the Clarion Hotel she had noticed near the River Street Exit and took a small, cozy room. After hooking up her laptop and checking the Internet connection, she was ready. Time to see Archville.

She stopped in the lobby and purchased the local paper, which featured Charlie Mars's lead story on page 1. It would be reading material for her first surveillance.

Two businessmen were entering the Clarion as Monica was leaving. She could feel their eyes peeling off her tight designer jeans and loose-fitting blouse. "You wish," she murmured.

Meanwhile, Jake was back in his room. With a series of boxes and arrows drawn on his timeline, he methodically retraced his steps. Nothing jumped out as helpful. It then dawned on him he had not fully reviewed the pictures taken at the cemetery. Laying them out in the order they were taken, he marveled at the quality of the digital imagery, quite superior to the old days of 35-mm film. But once again, nothing suggested a direction, a lead.

Barclay left the hotel and headed for Jefferson Township.

Since he would be taking a different route to the baseball field than usual, he set the GPS for the trip. On the way, he called Lovello to report there were no new developments. "I've got Monica conducting surveillance on three individuals.

"Whatever it takes," said Lovello. "We need a suspect or two, and we need them badly."

"I hear that," responded the detective.

As Barclay's Jag rolled into the field's parking area, he spotted Gloria Snook and Sally Powderly. Tommy was playing catch with one of the other boys.

He strolled over to Gloria and Sally. "Hello. How's Jack holding up?" he inquired.

"As well as can be expected," said Gloria. "Of course, he's upset he'll miss the game on Saturday."

Barclay told her it was going to be televised.

"I don't think TV is one of the amenities provided in the county jail," Gloria snarled.

"Oh, a lot of lockups allow television."

Gloria just shook her head and walked away. Sally Powderly, however, lagged behind. "Do you have any suspect besides Jack?" she asked.

"We're looking at a few," he responded.

"Who are they?"

"Confidential for now."

Powderly walked away without saying another word.

All the ballplayers were now on the field. Coach McCracken started with some running and throwing drills. Later, he hit some grounders to the boys who would be in the starting lineup on Saturday night.

Barclay looked out toward the right field fence. No sign of the crossing guard. Barclay found this interesting as he knew Saunders was aware of the practice time and apparently seldom missed one.

Coach McCracken called his team into the dugout for their daily briefing. He thanked the boys for the effort they put forward in preparing for one of the biggest games of their young lives. "I can't tell you how much Coach Cortino and I appreciate the contributions each and every one of you make. You're a great team, and it's a pleasure to be your coach."

The boys rang out a quick cheer.

"Today is Wednesday," continued McCracken. "We will practice here tomorrow at the same time. On Friday, we will run through our drills at eleven back at the Complex—"

Another quick cheer, this one for their home field.

"Friday evening, Coach Cortino and I will host a cookout for the team in the picnic area of Jermyn Park."

That brought them all to their feet with a clamor and much shouting.

McCracken cautioned the boys not to get involved in any pickup games or strenuous activity. "I want everybody healthy for Saturday night. Now get out of here."

Later, Barclay helped Coach Cortino gather in the equipment and gear.

"I hear the Bonito kid is still in the lineup," said Cortino.

Barclay smirked. "I guess that means we'll be able to execute our plan." The detective said he'd like them to take a look at some pictures from the Jenkins funeral. They agreed to meet at Marty's in an hour.

*   *   *

Monica set up surveillance on the Jenkins mansion. It was a stately structure, built in the 1940s and upgraded through the years. The house sat atop a hill overlooking Archville. There was only one way in and one way out, thus making it easy to monitor comings and goings.

She didn't have to wait very long for some action. She watched as a late-model Mercedes backed out of the four-car garage. The car rolled to a stop at the bottom of the hill and turned right. The tag on the car was the one she had traced for Jake.

Monica was excited and nervous. Her first real field assignment for the boss. It was an adventure she was more than ready for.

She followed the Benz up Main Street where it turned onto Johnson Drive and into a parking lot near a grocery store. A tall, elderly gentleman in a chauffeur's uniform got out of the car and went into the store.

Monica backed her Ford rental into a parking spot and got out.

Inside, she shadowed the chauffeur as he pushed a cart from aisle to aisle, picking up items here and there. When it appeared he was about finished, Monica picked up a few small items and managed to get in front of the driver at the checkout. She took her bag of items and stopped at the newspaper rack near the door to listen as the chauffeur put the groceries on the Jenkins's account.

"Very good, Mr. Forbes," the clerk replied.

While the chauffeur was signing the charge slip, Monica returned to her car.

Forbes drove to a liquor store a few miles away in a neighboring town. He was in the store a short time and emerged with a bottle in a bag. She watched as the chauffeur got back into the car. Surprisingly, he opened the bottle and took a drink from it. Monica rapidly snapped several pictures with her Canon. *A tipsy chauffeur,* she thought. *Hmm.*

Forbes drove back to the mansion, and Monica followed at a good distance.

She called Jake and filled him in on what she'd gathered so far.

"Forbes, huh? Into the sauce," said Barclay. "So noted. Let me see what more you can find out about him. Keep me posted."

*   *   *

Over at Marty's bar, Barclay, Cortino, and McCracken were huddled together at their regular table. McCracken and Cortino were getting wishes of support from every patron in the place.

"This game has taken on a life of its own," said Cortino.

"We're doing an interview with the sports editor of the local daily tomorrow morning," said McCracken. "We only agreed to do it under the condition there will be no references to Snook or the murder of Al Jenkins."

"He agreed?" asked Barclay.

"He did," said Cortino.

Barclay brought up the chauffeur Forbes. "What's his story?"

"Oh, he's been working for the Jenkins family for years," said McCracken. "He wears a lot of hats. Chauffeur, handyman, gardener. Anything the old lady needs done. He lives in a cottage behind the main house." The coach had done some electrical work at the mansion a few years back and had found Forbes quite standoffish, uttering hardly a word despite McCracken's attempts at conversation.

"There's a woman who works full-time at the Jenkins place," said Cortino. "Don't know what her name is, and she's rarely seen in town. There was a rumor she's the chauffeur's wife."

"Makes sense," noted Barclay.

The detective then took out the photographs from the funeral and handed half to Cortino and half to McCracken. They quickly identified one mourner as old Dr. Fisher, an MD who closed his practice in Archville three years earlier. "Still made house calls up to the day he shut down the office," said McCracken. "He was the last physician we had in town. Now we have to go to Scranton or Carbondale for a doctor."

Other than Attorney West and the retired doctor, the two coaches could not identify anyone else in the photos.

"Sorry, Jake," said Cortino.

"It's no big deal." For a moment, Barclay considered asking them why Elizabeth Jenkins would want to bribe him and Lovello. However, he scrubbed the idea, thinking he might regret it.

McCracken picked up a photo from the pile and tugged his reading glasses from his backpack. He took a closer look at the image.

"Who's that in the woods, on the other side of the graveyard?" He held the photo up toward Barclay and pointed to a shadow in the trees.

Barclay examined the photograph himself. Sure enough, there was the outline of someone or something in the woods. "I never noticed this," he muttered.

All three men looked at the photo, passing it around, trying to decipher the form. "It's definitely a human," said Cortino.

However, they couldn't make out who it was.

Barclay stared at the photograph. "I'll get it blown up. That might help. Good eye, guys."

The three men ordered hot wings and french fries. They sat for a while and talked about Saturday's game. There was pool table in the back, and they impulsively decided to play.

Barclay warned them, "I was the LA County eight-ball champion four years running after I got out of the corps. I even gave serious thought to turning pro."

While the coaches raised their eyebrows at the claim, they soon saw that Barclay was not exaggerating. They played a few games, but Cortino and McCracken were not in Barclay's league.

CHAPTER FOURTEEN

O N THURSDAY MORNING, local papers had follow-up stories on the federal raid in Archville and five other communities. The question they were all asking: how could honest officials fall for such a farfetched scam? Reports were that six local municipalities had been bilked out of some $3 million by the con artists. AP reported that Cook and Morrison were being extradited from the UK to face charges in Houston. It was also said that the pair would face additional charges beyond those in the original indictment.

Jake Barclay was reading the papers in his hotel room. He was still trying to figure out why, as Tim Richards had told him, the mayor was trying to change the site of the so-called experimental plant. Barclay wondered the obvious—how could the good Mr. Mayor have *not known* his college buddies were flimflamming everyone? "Of course you did, you son of a bitch," Barclay muttered.

The room phone rang. It was John Lovello. "What are you doing up at this early hour?" the detective asked.

"Been up all night," said the attorney. "The Internet is full of stuff about the big rip-off." Lovello said the senior FBI agent in charge of the probe in Houston was an acquaintance from long ago. "I talked to him last night." According to the agent, Morrison and Cook gave statements to the bureau agents who were dispatched to London. In separate interviews, the attorney said, they told identical stories.

"The mayor was, in a manner of speaking, in on the con," said Lovello. "However, Jenkins wasn't looking for money. Apparently, he participated in the deal only to make the council's majority look bad when it came out that the town had been bilked."

For Barclay, the news was clear: he was now back to square 1, with even more questions and just as few answers. He realized he would be starting anew in a desperate search for a suspect—any suspect.

Lovello said, "Talk about a couple of numbnuts. Morrison and Cook actually thought they could get away with the scheme. At least, long enough to disappear with the loot and live on Easy Street in Europe for the rest of their lives. They admitted it to the FBI."

"I don't know if numbnuts covers it," said Barclay.

According to the senior agent, Lovello explained, Mayor Jenkins pressed for a site change knowing the council's majority wouldn't cave in to his request, giving the whole con a seemingly arm's-length credibility. "In the final analysis, it was the mayor's plan to let his buddies bilk the town and, after they were safely out of the country, expose the whole gig and show up the majority for squandering federal monies. When the shit hit the fan, Jenkins would be the good guy."

"Cute," interjected Barclay. "Real cute."

Lovello said Cook told the FBI in London that Jenkins even planned on giving Archville half a million from his family fortune to replace the lost federal funds, enabling the downtown revitalization project to continue. "He'd be the town hero. But don't forget, Jenkins's agenda included a run for the state senate. A stepping stone to even higher office. In short, he wasn't in it for money but power. Which is always worth a lot more."

"You know, John, the people I've talked to are right. Jenkins was a prick, and we've got a town full of suspects."

"The whole scam fell apart when that West Virginia whistle-blower tipped off the feds. Morrison and Cook had to move their timetable up a notch or two."

The detective gathered his thoughts. "Perhaps one of the council members found out about the con and decided to end Jenkins's life."

"It's certainly a possibility, Jake." Lovello told Barclay to take a look at the other three members who held the majority with Tim Richards. "We still need a suspect or two."

When they hung up, Barclay thought hard. He recalled a paragraph in the morning's lead story stating that Archville's council had called a special meeting for seven that evening to address the lost federal funds.

He called Richards. "Would it be possible, Tim, to arrange a meeting for me with yourself and the three other majority council members? Say, tonight, after the special meeting."

The council president said he would try but then warned Barclay that the special meeting could get ugly.

"Much appreciated," said Barclay.

He touched base with Monica. She was already on her way to Archville to stake out Clarence West's office for the morning. He brought her up to speed on the conversation he'd had with Lovello.

"Four possible suspects with motive," she said. "Do you want me to watch any of them today?"

"I'm not sure. For now, stick to the original plan. Let's talk in a couple of hours."

Barclay showered and dressed. He called Charlie Mars and invited him for a quick breakfast. Mars recommended Simon's Diner. "See you there at ten," said Mars.

*   *   *

When Barclay walked through the door at Simon's, the reporter was already there in the same booth the two had shared the other day. The waitress, Beverly, was again flirting with Mars. "I have two hot buns for you, Chuckie," she was saying as the detective slid into the booth across from Mars. She winked and hurried off.

"Hot buns, huh?" Barclay cracked.

"She's all show and no go," said Mars. Mars explained that he had been coming to Simon's for more than twenty years, and the flirting had become a rather enjoyable staple in his day-to-day life. "It's not the Olive Garden," he said, "but I do feel like family when I am here."

Once the coffee was poured, Barclay briefed Mars on his conversation with Lovello. Mars perked up on hearing that the dead mayor knew the experimental plant was a scam. "Can I print this?" he inquired.

The detective told Mars that he could indeed print it. "But I assume you will be quoting *reliable* sources in your story and not me or John Lovello."

"But of course," replied the reporter. "And I appreciate your trusting me."

Just then, Barclay's phone rang. It was Tim Richards. He told the detective the other three members of the majority, on advice from their lawyers, would have nothing to say after the meeting.

"Damn lawyers," said Barclay as he ended the call and described to Mars his struggle to gain some new information, some new suspects.

Mars listened closely as Barclay told him about the meeting he had tried to set up with Richards and the other three majority members of the council.

Their breakfast arrived, and after a few minutes of focused eating, Barclay asked Mars if he was close to any of his paper's photographers.

"Sure, what do you have in mind?"

Barclay explained about the mystery figure hidden in the background of a photo he'd taken at the Jenkins burial site.

"Think it's a ghost?" snickered Mars.

"Could be. Just another strange element in a strange case."

Mars said he was a seasoned photographer himself. "Want me to take a look?"

"It's going to take more than a look," said Barclay.

"We can go to my apartment after we eat. I'll take a look on my computer."

"Great, but I can't do it now, Charlie. The camera's back at the hotel."

"Just let me know when," said Mars.

When they finished breakfast, Beverly was flirting with another customer at the counter. "Hey, what's a guy have to do to get a check in this place," yelled Mars.

Beverly slinked over to the table writing up the bill. She whispered into Mars's ear, and he laughed.

*   *   *

Monica had taken up a position on Main Street and was keeping a keen eye on the West Law Office. The buildings in the area were a mix of commercial and residential dwellings, probably built way back when the coal mines thrived. She sat up and rubbed her eyes. The Mercedes from the day before turned into the alley behind the law office.

She got out and wandered up the street. Now she could see the driver, Forbes, helping a passenger out of the back seat. Monica knew it had to be old lady Jenkins herself. At the same time, an elderly gentleman in a suit let himself out on the other side. Forbes escorted the woman and the gentleman to the back of the law office, then returned to the car.

The Jenkins woman had not seemed quite as ill as had been reported, Monica noted.

As Forbes drove away, Monica returned to the Ford to retrieve her Canon and telephoto lens. She strolled along another street and along the perimeter of a dilapidated building. The rear of the property was overgrown with weeds—good cover to hide in until the old lady and the man left West's office.

Monica waited nearly half an hour until the Mercedes returned to the alley. She focused the long lens on the people coming out of the law office. Once she was sure she had good pictures, she ran back to the Ford. She threw the camera on the back seat and prepared to follow the Benz. In a few moments, it appeared at the end of the next block. Forbes turned onto

Main Street. Monica set her GPS system so she would know exactly where she was if the Benz went on a long trip.

At a red light, she reached back and grabbed the Canon off the back seat. She queued up the photos she had taken. She was in such a rush when snapping the photos, she failed to note how many people came out of the law office.

She counted three. She assumed the third was Attorney West.

She stayed back far enough behind the Benz to barely keep it in sight. Her GPS told her she was in Scott Township. The Benz continued out into a farming area; at a crossroads, the car turned right.

Monica approached the road where Forbes had turned. A sign posted there said the property was private and that trespassers were not welcome. Up the road a piece, she could see a small guardhouse and a gate. There were no other signs indicating what was beyond the gate.

A quick recon around the place showed Monica that the entire area was protected with a ten-foot barbed-wire fence. She looked at the GPS and made a notation of the latitude and longitude of the location for future reference. Then Monica drove up the road and found a spot to turn around. She parked on the shoulder of the road and waited an hour for the Benz to emerge from the private road. It turned left and headed back in the direction from which it had come.

Without any detours, the Benz returned to the West Law Office. In the alley, one man—the one she believed to be Attorney West—exited from the front passenger seat. The car sped off. Without hesitating, Monica decided to stay with the Mercedes.

However, the car went straight back to the Jenkins's place.

At that moment, Monica had a strange feeling of fulfillment, for this task was certainly more exciting than the mundane things she did in Jake Barclay's LA office. She relished the thought that, like Jake said earlier, she would strike out on her own someday.

Monica decided to keep an eye on the Jenkins mansion for the time being. She hoped that whoever the other man in the Benz was would be departing soon.

She did not have to wait long. An older Chevrolet sedan came down the hill right at that moment. Monica followed the sedan to Evans Street, where it turned into a driveway. A sign attached to the house read: Evan Fisher, MD.

The garage door opened, and the sedan disappeared as the door rolled closed.

Monica called Jake and rattled off the morning's surveillance activities.

"Excellent work," he complimented. "What's your next move?"

"I'm kinda nosy," Monica said. "I want to know what's beyond that gate out there in the hinterland."

"Me too. Go for it and keep me posted. And be careful!"

Monica put the coordinates into her GPS and started back to the place she was at earlier. She passed the road where the Benz had disappeared. Up the road a little further, she saw two fishermen alongside a creek. She pulled off the road and got out of the Ford. "Excuse me," she said, "but I think I'm lost."

The fishermen appeared to be in their late teens or early twenties. "What're you looking for?" one asked as he looked her up and down.

"I was supposed to pick someone up, and I can't find the private road I was supposed to turn onto." She added that she was on a strict time schedule.

"The only private road I know of around here is the one back there about a half mile," the younger one said. "It leads to the Glenside Sanitarium."

Monica felt a little uncomfortable from the way the two young men were now eyeing her. "Do you mean sanitarium like for crazy people?"

"It used to be just for crazy people," the older one said. "Now it's a drug and alcohol rehab place for rich people and celebrities."

Monica thanked the fishermen and sped away. "The plot thickens," she said aloud.

Back in Scranton, Monica went straight to her room at the Clarion. She searched the web on her laptop for "Glenside Sanitarium" and was amazed at how many page references popped up. After sifting through the bullshit, she finally found what she was looking for: Glenside Sanitarium, RR 70, Box 256, Montdale, PA. The site described its "discreet" services and claimed Glenside was the "modern alternative for curing drug addiction." The facility had been founded in 1971 by Dr. Evan Fisher, MD, and for the last ten years, the facility was under the operational control of Seth Fisher, PhD, grandson of Evan Fisher. Monica read that Glenside offered 180-day programs for the treatment of addiction, while longer stays were necessary for the treatment of mental illnesses.

Just then, Jake rang her cell, and Monica filled him in on what she'd uncovered.

"Looks like we're going to have to get inside that place," the detective said.

"How do you propose we do that?"

"Give me the phone number," he said and told her they would talk later.

*   *   *

Barclay called Lovello and told him the latest. "I have to get inside this Glenside place, John."

"I hear you, but don't get arrested like you did in Florida. You almost lost your PI license, remember?"

"How could I forget when you keep reminding me," Barclay replied, and they shared a laugh. Barclay recalled the incident well. He had been shadowing a suspect in a multimillion dollar stock swindle and walked into an FBI sting with forged papers identifying him as an investigator with the Securities and Exchange Commission. Lovello had to pull some big strings to get him out of that mess.

Barclay checked his watch: it was close to four o'clock—almost time for baseball practice. Before leaving his room, he placed a call to an old friend in LA.

"Well, Jake Barclay," said the voice on the other end. "You must need something, you big handsome lug of a man."

The detective enjoyed it when the opposite sex flirted with him. His graying hair and dark green eyes gave him a distinguished look the ladies seemed to like. He'd married once a long time ago, but being on the road most of the time was a romance killer. He divorced after only two years of what he commonly referred to a "bliss-less" marriage.

"How have you been, Dolly?" Dolly Myers was a retired gossip columnist who at one time knew everyone who was anyone in Hollywood. She used to have a serious thing for Jake in her younger years. Even in her seventies, Dolly looked better than most women much younger.

"I'm upright and sucking wind, honey. How are you?"

He told Dolly he was fine but needed a little of her professional help.

"Shoot," she said.

"Did you ever hear of or write about a place in Pennsylvania called Glenside Sanitarium?"

"Oh, yes," she said. "It's very expensive and very discreet. I mentioned it in several columns over the years when our so-called stars were rehabbing there. Why, what's up?"

"I need a ruse to get inside and take a look around."

"Well, I'll be! The master of ruses needs Dolly's help to pull off a sting. All right, it's simple. Go in posing as a well-to-do person seeking help for an addicted family member. Remember, Glenside is all about money, money, money."

"Pose as a customer," said Barclay. "That's a good idea. I'll try it. Thanks, Dolly. See you when I get back home."

"I hope it's more than a quick visit, you big hunk."

"Count on it," he said.

Barclay left the hotel and dashed off to baseball practice.

At the field, there were broadcast vans from three local television stations in the parking lot. The big game was now only two days away, and anticipation was mounting.

Coaches McCracken and Cortino were being interviewed by a reporter from the NBC affiliate.

When the interview was concluded, Cortino removed his cap, wiped the sweat off his brow, and approached Barclay. "You know," he said, "I'll be glad when this is over."

McCracken soon joined them and told the detective they had decided to give the media access to the team. "I need to get them off our backs at this point. But they were cautioned that questions about Jack Snook are off-limits, and they said they were fine with that."

"It won't stop them from putting comments about Jack in their aired pieces," Barclay said. "The vultures don't care who they step on to get the story."

McCracken picked up a bat and began hitting grounders to the infield and fly balls to the outfield. Tommy Snook was in center field. "Catch three and you can go to the dugout," he shouted to the boys.

Now, Barclay noticed that Fred Saunders was in his usual spot by the fence in right field. He had on the same clothes he'd been wearing on Monday outside of his apartment building. Barclay sauntered out to the crossing guard and attempted to make small talk.

"Leave me alone," snapped Saunders.

"Okay, I'll leave you alone. But that's subject to change, Freddie."

Saunders looked at him with hard eyes.

"We'll talk some other time," said Barclay and walked away. Suddenly, Saunders was looking very good as a murder suspect.

Barclay, Cortino, and McCracken went to Marty's after practice. The detective told them about the cool reception he got from Saunders. The coaches agreed that the crossing guard was a loner and mostly kept to himself. "He works hard and goes home every night to that small efficiency he has behind the barbershop," said McCracken.

"He's lived there since he came back from Vietnam," Cortino added. "He has no family, no friends that we know of."

Four beers later, the trio headed out to the parking lot. Cortino and McCracken shared a hesitant look.

"What?" asked Barclay.

Cortino cleared his throat. "We were wondering how the investigation's going."

Barclay sighed and shook his head. The beer had made him tired and slightly discouraged. "I'm just following leads. If I get a break, you guys'll hear about it."

"Everybody knows Jack is innocent," said McCracken.

Barclay nodded. "I agree, but the problem is, we have to prove it."

"I thought you were innocent until proven guilty," Corino observed.

Barclay yawned. "That's what they tell you in school. But a lot of times you're guilty until proven innocent. I think this might be one of those kind of cases. Have a good night."

CHAPTER FIFTEEN

E ARLY FRIDAY MORNING, Jake Barclay placed a call to Glenside Sanitarium.

"May I help you?"

"I hope so. My name is Carl Abbott. My niece is nineteen and has a drug problem. We've had her in three rehabilitation facilities in the last year and a half. Nothing's worked. We're from California, but I'm here in Pennsylvania on business. I've read about Glenside and figured since I'm here, I would look into your program."

A smooth, yet emotionless, voice responded, "Please hold and I will connect you with our administrator."

Moments later, a woman came on the line, also with an emotionless tone. "This is Donna Patterson. Is this Mr. Abbott? Our receptionist told me about your situation, sir. Would you like to see our facility?"

"If that could be arranged, I would appreciate it."

"We're somewhat off the beaten path," she said. "Do you think you could be here by noon?"

He told her he was staying at the Holiday Inn in Drewmore. "I'm pretty good with directions," he said. "Let me get a piece of paper." Monica had already given him the GPS coordinates, but he pretended to take the directions.

"See you at noon, Mr. Abbott."

Barclay checked in with Monica. She had just gotten the pictures from Thursday processed. "Not much to see. I doubt they're very important."

"You never know," said Barclay. "Meanwhile, let's keep up the surveillance on the Jenkins estate."

"Will do," she said. "What's on your agenda?"

"I have an appointment, or rather a guy named Abbott does, to see Glenside at noon."

"That was quick. Let me guess, you're going in as a nutcase looking for help."

He chuckled. "Close enough. Now listen, I need some of your electronic wizardry." Barclay explained that he wanted one of the office numbers out in LA to have a voice mail message from Carl Abbot. "Use my private line.

Record a message like you are Abbot's secretary and say he's out of the office for the week."

"Not a problem," Monica said. "I'll just reprogram your line out there. Consider it done."

*   *   *

Five minutes before noon, Jake Barclay pulled up to the gate at Glenside. A security guard in a wrinkled blue uniform came out of the booth and greeted him solemnly. He was about a hundred pounds overweight and missing two front teeth. Barclay thought he looked like one of those hillbillies in that film *Deliverance*. "I have an appointment with Donna Patterson."

"Yes, sir. May I see some identification?"

The detective presented one of his prepared aliases, an ID card from Abbott Technologies of Irvine, CA. His picture was on it and a telephone number.

"Do you have a driver's license, sir?"

Barclay was ready for that one. "My trip out here came up unexpectedly, and I left my license in my Ferrari in California."

"Wait here," said the guard, with a hint of suspicion in his tone.

Barclay watched him using the telephone in his guard shack. He kept one eye on the detective the whole time. Shortly, the guard returned the ID card to Barclay and raised the electric gate. "Sir, the office is right inside the main entrance."

He thanked the man and drove on, parking the Jag in one of the visitor's spaces. The sanitarium was a two-story brick structure with a main building and two wings, which had obviously been added after the original construction. There was a small picnic area and what appeared to be a maintenance building in the back. The whole place was, quite literally, in the middle of nowhere.

Donna Patterson greeted the detective at the main entrance. She was wearing a traditional business suit and appeared to be in her early sixties though it was hard to tell with all the makeup plastered on her face, like she'd put the stuff on with a trowel.

"Sorry about the delay at the gate, Mr. Abbott, but we have to be careful who we admit. Privacy issues, you know."

"It's perfectly understandable. You can't be too careful."

As he followed the administrator down the hall into her office, he caught the pungent odor of urine and bleach, the kind of smell that always seems to hang around medical facilities. For Barclay, that smell always reminded him of a latrine in a combat zone.

Patterson showed him to an armchair, and she sat behind a cluttered desk. "As you know, Mr. Abbott, Glenside is a private facility specializing in the treatment of drug and alcohol addiction and mental illness. We have a full-time psychiatrist, a full-time medical doctor, and fifteen therapists. We also have around-the-clock nurses and a dozen psychiatric security aides."

Barclay took it all in, nodding, looking impressed.

"Let me get a little background, Mr. Abbott. Where has your niece previously been treated?"

"My brother was in charge of that," he said. "I really don't know the names of the places she went to, but I do know that the last one was in downtown LA. As far as my wife and I are concerned, downtown LA is not a good place for a rehab facility. My niece got out one night and bought an eight-ball of cocaine a block away."

He could tell Patterson swallowed the story. She was nodding and making soft, sympathetic sounds in the back of her throat. But there were dollar signs in her eyes.

"Well, Mr. Abbott, you won't find that kind of a problem here at Glenside. We are a lockdown facility. All visitors here consent to a search before they enter, and all visitations are monitored by a superior surveillance system. In fact, you've been on camera from the second your car turned off the highway." She went on to explain that the 1,100-acre site was protected by a ten-foot barbed-wire fence and that no patient has ever escaped Glenside.

"That's comforting," said Barclay.

"Well, shall we begin the tour?"

Patterson led the detective from her office to the wing on the left of the building. "Here we have our meeting rooms, where patients get together with counselors for one-on-one sessions."

Barclay feigned interest in the meeting rooms, the decor, and the art hung in the hallway. It seemed odd there was no one around except for the two of them. They walked in solitude throughout the entire wing. "This place is very quiet," he observed. *Like a morgue,* he thought.

"Right now, everyone is having lunch in the basement cafeteria," said the administrator. "Three meals with special menus are prepared each and every day of the week." She explained that nutritional meals are essential when treating addictions. "We try to impress upon our patients that in order to stay healthy, they must eat healthy."

When the walk-through on the drug rehab side was concluded, Ms. Patterson led the detective to the wing on the right. They passed through the connecting door and saw a young woman sitting in a chair as a nurse attended to brushing her hair.

"Nurse Roberts!" Patterson said sternly. "You were warned that we had a visitor today. Why is this patient in the hallway?"

The nurse did not immediately answer the question.

"Return this patient to her ward and then wait for me in my office." Donna Patterson turned to the detective and apologized. "Have you seen enough?"

"Yes, thank you. I was really only interested in the drug rehab side anyway." He gave Patterson his card and asked if she would mail the financial information and any literature she had to the address on the card. "When I return to California next week, I'll go over it with my brother and his wife."

"Very good, Mr. Abbott." Patterson did a little more of her sales pitch as she walked him out to the main door.

Walking back to the car, Barclay wondered about the harsh manner Patterson had used with the nurse and by her anger at what appeared to be a minor offense. The nurse looked to be about thirty years old, and Barclay had made a point of noting her name tag: Evelyn Roberts, LPN. It was very odd, he decided, Patterson getting so worked up over a visitor seeing a patient in the hallway. Why? There was something not quite kosher about all that.

He was stopped at the gate on the way out. The guard handed him a clipboard with a sheet of paper on it. "Just a formality, sir." It was a confidentiality agreement. Under the terms of the legal mumbo jumbo, he was not allowed to discuss his visit to Glenside with anyone other than the person whom he was representing.

Barclay signed the form, handed the clipboard back to the guard, and drove away.

Still bothered by the confrontation in the hallway between Patterson and the nurse, Barclay's instincts told him to stick around awhile to see if anyone left the gated sanitarium. He turned right at the main highway and drove a short distance before making a U-turn, then pulling into a side road out of sight.

Twenty minutes later, a speeding car exited the facility. As the vehicle passed his position, Barclay caught a glimpse of the woman at the wheel—Nurse Roberts.

He followed.

The nurse drove nearly thirteen miles to Mayfield, where she parked and went into a modest house. He jotted down the address, then called Monica.

"How was your grand tour at Glenside?" she asked.

"Enlightening. The head administrator is shifty, and the place is pretty damn weird, like something out of a Hitchcock movie. *Psycho*, for instance."

"Sounds like your kind of place," she quipped. Monica told him about the chauffeur Forbes and his early liquor store run. "Other than that, not much going on at the Jenkins homestead."

He made arrangements to meet Monica at the Lookout in Scranton. "Make it three o'clock, and bring the pictures from the other day."

*   *   *

Barclay found his way to Simon's Restaurant. He was surprised that Beverly was not working. The waitress on duty was a cute blonde with a nameplate: Joanne. She came to his table in her tight uniform, suggesting the New England clam chowder.

"Where's Beverly?"

"I work Fridays," she said. "Hey, aren't you Charlie Mars's friend?"

"I guess you could say that."

"Charlie's a kook, isn't he?" Joanne grinned broadly. "He's always writing about this or that politician." She chuckled. "I'm surprised he's still alive, some of that stuff he's put in the paper."

"It's a tough racket, the newspaper business," he offered, then ordered the soup and a tuna sandwich. He saw the morning paper on the counter and picked it up.

There was a front-page story naming four more municipalities to the list of Cook and Morrison's victims—two in Pennsylvania and one each in Kentucky and West Virginia. Barclay had a feeling the sucker list was not yet complete.

There was an article under Mars's byline: the reporter had bluntly asked each member of Archville's city council leadership to account for their whereabouts at the time Mayor Jenkins was murdered. *The guy's got balls, all right,* thought Jake. And that's a damn good question. The article said all four councilmen claimed to have been on their way back from a conference hosted by the state in Pittsburgh. According to the men, they did not arrive back in Archville until after 4:00 a.m. the night Jenkins was beaten to death. Mars verified their story by reviewing gas station charge slips and the Pittsburgh hotel's checkout records. The upshot was, none of them could have been in Archville at the time of the mayor's death.

Jake Barclay tossed the paper aside, a bit disgusted. Isn't that just dandy? Kicked right back to the starting gate.

Joanne arrived with the food. "Talking to yourself, I see."

"It gets lonely," Barclay told her.

"What does? You mean life?"

He gave her one of his shit-eating grins. "I guess that is what I meant."

That got a laugh out of her, but Barclay wasn't laughing. Losing four potential suspects in one whack wasn't all that funny, and it kind of wrecked his appetite. He downed the soup and nibbled on the sandwich without tasting either, left a $10 bill on the table and ambled out to the car.

He called Lovello, who answered on the first ring. Before Barclay could explain the situation in Archville, the attorney cut in, "I read about it on the net this morning. Four suspects bite the dust." Lovello said he was preparing for the flight east. "I'll be there Saturday. Keep pressing, Jake. We've got a dynamic situation here and can't get discouraged."

"Somebody killed the mayor," stated Barclay. "And we know it wasn't Jack Snook."

"Yes, but that's about the only thing we know."

On his way to meet up with Monica, Barclay rang Charlie Mars. "Saw your piece in the paper. I had my heart set on nailing at least one of those clowns. Thanks a lot."

Mars laughed. "Hey, you know I did you a favor. Saved you time by getting rid of the deadwood. No pun intended."

"Jesus, I've lost more suspects on this case than I have on my last ten."

"Hold onto your hat," replied Mars. "I'm just getting started with my investigation."

"Careful, you've got a tiger by the tail, as they say."

"I know, and tigers can bite. Gotta hop. See you at the picnic tonight."

*   *   *

Monica was already at the Lookout when Barclay arrived. "I heard the news," she said. "We're down four suspects all a sudden."

"And I'm running out of ideas," responded Barclay.

"What about your famous timeline? I assume you did one like you always do."

"Yes, and for the first time, it failed to move the ball an inch."

"Don't worry, boss, we'll get a break," Monica assured.

"We'd better, or they'll cook the Snook." Barclay had her jot down the name and address of the Glenside nurse, Evelyn Roberts. "Do a search and see what comes back."

"You got it, boss. And here, the pictures I took."

Barclay shuffled through them and quickly identified Clarence West and Dr. Evan Fisher. "Right now," he said, "we're assuming that the woman in the car is, in fact, old lady Jenkins." He said he would get a positive ID on her that evening and told Monica to keep plugging. "Let me know right away if you get anything on the nurse."

CHAPTER SIXTEEN

J ERMYN PARK, A sprawling recreational area operated by the county, offered picnic tables, swing sets, sandboxes, and horseshoe pits, which were all getting plenty of use as Jake Barclay parked his Jaguar sedan. Strolling toward the picnic area, he heard a car's horn behind him. It was Charlie Wetzel's Cadillac limousine. The used-car king jumped out and called to Barclay. "Give me a hand, will you, pal?" he said. Wetzel went around to the back of the car where his driver had opened the trunk to reveal several boxes. "Let's take these down to the picnic area."

Barclay glanced at the hulking boxes. "What's inside?"

"Fancy new uniforms for the team."

They hauled the boxes over to where McCracken, Cortino and their wives were sitting.

"Special delivery," said Wetzel.

"What do you have there?" asked McCracken.

"I want the team to look their best for tomorrow's game," said Wetzel. "So I had brand new uniforms made up for the occasion."

McCracken was appreciative but gently explained that teams in the tournament were not allowed to wear uniforms promoting a business or organization.

"Oh, I know that," said Wetzel. "Go ahead and open them up."

Cortino pulled a shirt out of the box that was obviously much too large for any member of the team.

"That's a coach's shirt," said Wetzel. The shirts were blue with red trim on the shoulders and had *Archville* printed in red across the front. The hats were blue with a red *A*.

"Fabulous, Charlie," said McCracken.

Cortino was removing the items from the boxes. "Hey, these are all the right size."

Wetzel explained that the numerical sequence on the shirts went from one to twelve. "Of course, you can hand out the numbers any way you like," Wetzel said. "But remember, Jack Snook wore number 12 in the majors."

Coach McCracken called Tommy Three Fingers to the picnic table. "Thanks to Mr. Wetzel here, we've got new uniforms. What number would you like, Tommy?"

The kid immediately replied, "Number 12, if we have it."

"Number 12 it is," said McCracken.

As the uniforms were distributed, the DJ began playing the song "We Are Family," much to the enjoyment of all in attendance.

Barclay caught sight of Charlie Mars and his photographer. The two stepped aside, and Barclay brought him up to date. "I don't know about you, Charlie, but I think a picture of the boys in their new uniforms might make page 1 in the morning."

Mars agreed and instructed his photographer to get the shot.

"You know, Three Fingers is going to be wearing number 12," Barclay said.

"That's a great angle for the story," the reporter decided.

They watched as Cortino called the team into a huddle and whispered something. On the count of three, the boys all erupted in unison, "THANK YOU, MR. WETZEL!"

There was a tear in Wetzel's eye as he told the boys it was his pleasure to help out in this small way. He almost choked up, telling them they would make Archville proud if they went out on the diamond Saturday night and simply played to their best ability. "When you guys do that, you'll shut 'em down!" That brought another round of shouts and cheers from the young ballplayers.

As the cookout began to break up, Barclay asked McCracken and Cortino to look at one of the photos Monica had taken forty-eight hours earlier. He pointed to the elderly woman being helped from the car by the driver Forbes. "Recognize her?"

The two coaches stared at the picture, looked at each other, then at Barclay. "Nobody's really seen her in ages," McCracken said tentatively, "but I'm pretty sure that's old lady Jenkins. Sam?"

Cortino nodded. "It's her all right. Who else would Forbes be chauffeuring around? Where'd you get the picture?"

"I'd tell you," replied Barclay, "but then I'd have to kill you."

All three roared with laughter.

Cortino said he understood. "It's a need to know thing, right?"

"Something like that" was the response.

Charlie Mars walked over and told them he'd just transmitted his story to the city desk. "And I've got a little something to show you guys."

They all agreed it was time for a beer at Marty's.

*　　*　　*

The four settled at a booth in the back with two pitchers of the local brew. Mars told them he'd had one of his buddies in the sports department obtain a copy of Drewmore's lineup for Saturday's game. He took a piece of paper from his shirt pocket, unfolded it and pointed at the name of Vinnie Bonito. "He's number 8, starting at first base and batting leadoff."

Barclay said, "So they're playing him. Looks like we'll have the fireworks *before* the game."

They all drank to that.

Now, they got down to the Snook murder case. "What about any suspects, Jake?" McCracken wondered.

"All I can say at this point is we have one possible. But it's premature to toss out any names. I've got more digging to do."

"But he looks good, huh?" Cortino quizzed.

"All suspects look good, till they don't," replied Barclay.

"Everybody knows Jack wouldn't harm anyone," said McCracken, "even a butthead like Jenkins."

"One thing's for sure," Mars put in, "somebody harmed the mayor, big-time."

"But who?" asked Barclay. "We have only one *possible* suspect. And it's crucial we don't broadcast that fact."

Cortino, McCracken, and Mars sipped beer and promised they'd keep Barclay's disclosure to themselves.

*　　*　　*

Early Saturday morning, Jake called Monica and told her to be at the Lookout by eleven. He had gone to Simon's for breakfast and read the latest on the big scam. On the front page of the paper, there was a color picture of the Archville all-star team that had been taken the night before at the park. The photo's caption referred readers to the sports section for further coverage.

The headline on the story in the sports section almost made Barclay puke: JAILED EX-MAJOR LEAGUER'S SON TO WEAR NO. 12. While he was downing scrambled eggs, Barclay's cell phone rang. It was Mars.

"I guess you've seen that dumb headline in the paper." The reporter attempted to apologize.

"Hey, I know reporters don't write headlines. It's not your fault."

"Thanks," said Mars. "But I'm sorry nonetheless. Some yokel copy editor in Drewmore slapped that line on there."

"That figures," Barclay told him. "By the way, is that offer to use your computer still open?"

"Of course. Whenever you need it."

"How's this afternoon around one?"

"Lunchtime's perfect." Mars gave the detective his address on the city's southside.

Barclay drove to the Lookout where Monica sat taking in the view of the city and the surroundings.

Monica reported that there was really nothing on the Internet for the nurse Evelyn Roberts, only a short mention of her graduation from a nursing school. "Is she someone I could talk to, girl to girl?"

"That's a good idea. I've got her address in Mayfield. She might be in the mood to spill some beans. I think she may have been suspended or even fired over that patient in the hallway incident I told you about. You're pretty good at getting people to open up." Barclay said to tell Roberts she was a detective working on a case that may relate to Glenside. He passed Monica the photo showing Clarence West, Evan Fisher, and Mrs. Jenkins. "What we need to know is whether she recognizes anyone in that picture."

Monica nodded. "Got it."

For the next half hour, they talked over the case. They reached no new conclusions, and Barclay seemed more annoyed than discouraged. "We're back to where we started," he said. "The name of the game is, we find out who killed Jenkins, or Jack Snook's going down for it."

"Look," Monica said, "we've got a few pieces to this puzzle. All we really need is to fit them together, and this case will get up and fly."

Barclay peeked at his watch. "I have to meet Charlie Mars. Go see what you can wheedle out of our Nurse Roberts."

"That shouldn't be heard. I'm pretty good at wheedling stuff out of people."

"You certainly are," Barclay said.

*   *   *

The reporter lived in an apartment building on Fig Street. Barclay hustled up the rear stairwell to the second floor. As soon Mars opened the door, he handed over the flash memory. Mars wasted no time plugging it into his computer's USB port. The photos downloaded quickly.

He pulled the first shot up on the screen. Barclay shook his head. Mars pulled up photo after photo, while the detective continually shook his head. Finally, the mysterious image appeared.

"Stop there," Barclay said. He pointed to the background. "Zoom in on that."

On the fourth click of the zoom button, they both recognized the figure hidden in among the trees. "Fred Saunders," Mars whispered. "The same guy who found Jenkins."

"The day of the funeral, I stopped by to see Saunders. He was returning to his apartment, shaking and sweating. He looked pretty rattled. I don't know what the hell it means, but there's something fishy about this guy."

Mars agreed. "Damn fishy, I'd say." He clicked a button, and the enlarged color picture churned out of the printer.

Barclay took the photo and thanked Mars. "When I sort some things out, Charlie, you'll hear about it. See you at the Complex tonight."

Barclay drove back to the Holiday Inn. He decided to take a nap until he heard from Monica. But no sooner had he nodded off, and she was on the cell phone.

"You were right, Jake. Evelyn Roberts was fired. We had a productive talk."

"The Lookout in twenty minutes."

Barclay woke himself up with a quick shower and got into some fresh clothes.

He arrived at the Lookout before Monica and gazed out at the distant scenery. It was a spectacular view of a city once the capital of the Coal Region. He was thinking, thinking. All sorts of details ran through his mind. Each time he lined them up in a row, he arrived at the same destination: the picture of Fred Saunders hidden in the woods.

When Monica pulled up in the Ford, she hopped out, talking. "Roberts was fired yesterday for that hallway incident. She told me Glenside is run like a concentration camp as far as employees go. That thing in the hallway was Evelyn's 'third strike,' so to speak. They were all minor infractions though, nothing serious."

Monica explained that once she felt comfortable with the nurse, she had asked her to look at the photograph.

"I showed her the picture, and she recognized the trio as frequent visitors. She didn't know who the people were, but she said they visit a woman who has been at Glenside for a very long time. According to Evelyn, the woman's name is Gail Harding, at least that's what her chart says. She's a patient on the mental side of the sanitarium."

"The mental side," repeated Barclay.

Roberts had said Harding has a difficult time with her mental issues. "One minute she's fine, the next she's ready to tear your head off. In her more lucid moments, she claims her name is—are you ready for this—*Rebecca Jenkins*, and that she's just given birth to a baby boy!"

"The secrets," Barclay snarled, recalling West's phrase. "Had you mentioned the name Jenkins at all?"

Monica shook her head. "You didn't authorize that. You just said see what I could wheedle out of her."

"I don't see any reason to doubt she's telling the truth."

"Oh, I'm sure she is. She also told me Harding is under the *exclusive* care of Dr. Evan Fisher."

"Hmm, Fisher . . . You think she'll tell anyone about your little talk?" asked Barclay.

"I made a point of asking her not to. She agreed. I told her I'd get in trouble if she told anyone I'd been to see her."

Barclay gave her one of his affectionate shoulder squeezes "Good work. Ready for a black-bag job?"

"You make it sound naughty," she cracked. "What's the job, and how black is it?"

"Tonight, during the all-star game, I want you to sneak into Fred Saunders's apartment behind the barbershop on Main Street. He'll be at the Complex, but I'll call you to confirm that."

"That's not a black-bag job, that's breaking and entering," noted Monica. "But no problem, I love committing felonies for you, Jakey."

"You shouldn't have any problems. When I saw him Monday, he went into his apartment without a key. If it's locked, do your B and E thing. And take your camera and get some good pictures of the inside of the place. Snoop around."

"I take it Saunders is an official suspect," said Monica.

"Look at this." Barclay showed her the enlarged photo of Saunders hidden in the woods at the funeral.

Monica shuddered. "Why was he hiding in . . . Don't answer that. I might get more creeped out than I already am."

"Wait for my call tonight before going to that apartment."

On the way back to the Holiday Inn, Barclay got a call from Lovello. The attorney had just arrived at the hotel only to find there were no rooms available.

"Looks like you're bunking with me, my friend," said Barclay. "We'll get a cot put in. Meet me at room 312 in five minutes."

Once they were settled in the room, Barclay brought Lovello up to speed on everything, except the break-in he had assigned Monica. The law was going to be broken, and Barclay figured, there was no need to provide that information to an officer of the court.

"She claims she's *Rebecca Jenkins*?" mused Lovello. "Jesus, Archville has its secrets, doesn't it?"

CHAPTER SEVENTEEN

AT PRECISELY 5:30, Lovello and Barclay departed for Archville. They talked about the elements of the Jenkins murder and the winding road they had taken to get this far.

"When we're done," Barclay said, "this might make a good book."

"How many times have we said that?"

Lovello and Barclay encountered a traffic jam on Main Street in Archville. They parked on a side street and walked over to the Complex.

It was some turnout for a little league game. People were three and four abreast, toting coolers and lawn chairs. "Kind of exciting," said Lovello.

"If the game goes on," observed Barclay. "Let's see what they do with the overage kid."

The team bus from Drewmore was pulling into a reserved parking area. Barclay said, "Let's wait to see if number 8 gets off the bus."

The second player off the bus was indeed Vinnie Bonito. "He's a pretty big kid," said Lovello.

"He's thirteen and too old to play," said Barclay."

They made their way toward the bleachers, but all the seats were taken. There was a crowd standing three deep behind the perimeter fence. Barclay looked for Fred Saunders but did not spot him for a minute. Then, he saw him, atop the home team's bleachers. He decided to wait until the game started before unleashing Monica on the janitor's apartment.

Drewmore took the field to a rather loud cheer from their fans. By an earlier agreement, they would have the diamond for warm-ups from 6:50 to 7:10. Archville would then have their twenty minutes to warm up before the game started.

Barclay shifted his gaze from the stout Bonito kid at first base to Saunders in the bleachers. Old Fred was settled in and wouldn't miss the game for anything. That would give Monica plenty of time.

When the Drewmore team retreated to the visitors' dugout, the Archville boys took the field to thunderous applause. The team and the coaches went straight to the pitcher's mound and performed their ritual huddle, much to the pleasure of the fans. The huddle broke and the team of all-stars took two laps around the field. Then the starters went to their positions and began tossing the ball around.

In the stands, fans began chanting, "Archville! Archville!" The local ABC television news crew had set up on a scaffold near third base and strategically positioned cameramen around the field.

The umpires for the game entered the field near first base, and the Archville team headed back to their dugout to yet another loud ovation. The umpires summoned all coaches to the mound to go over the ground rules. The head umpire was Walt Gursky, a veteran who had been twice selected to umpire in the Little League World Series.

Once the meeting on the mound broke up, the announcer began the player introductions. The name Barclay and the Archville coaches wanted to hear rattled through the air. "At first base, wearing number 8, Vinnie Bonito." The stage was set.

The announcer hurried through the remaining eight players' names and positions.

"And now, ladies and gentlemen, please give a warm welcome to the 2010 edition of your Archville Little League all-stars," proclaimed the announcer. There was pandemonium. But the loudest cheer by far came when the last player was introduced: Tommy "Three Fingers" Snook. He ran out to the mound and was given a brand-new ball by the umpire. Whispers swept through the crowd, "He's wearing his father's number!"

Following the National Anthem, Three Fingers went into a warm-up drill with his favorite target: Vince Anders. The outfielders were tossing a ball around, and the infielders were whipping it around the horn. The Archville chant began anew. The noise was deafening.

The umpires signaled that the game was ready to begin. Umpire Gursky and the two other umpires took their positions. Gursky then cried out the ever-familiar "Play ball!"

Bonito was introduced as the first batter for Drewmore. Coach McCracken waited until Bonito stepped into the batter's box before he walked out of the dugout and called, "Time."

The crowd was quiet. From the back pocket of his uniform pants, McCracken presented Gursky with a copy of the batter's birth certificate. "Bonito's not an eligible player," McCracken stated.

It did not take long for Drewmore's coach to join the conversation. "Where did you get that birth certificate?" demanded Coach Dick Dodge.

"Doesn't matter where I got it," McCracken told Dodge. "Bonito isn't eligible to play in this game because he's overage. The boy's thirteen."

While adults were arguing, Bonito yelled out to Tommy Snook, "Hey, pitcher. My father's here, is yours?" He paused, then shouted, "Oh, that's right. Your dad's in *jail*."

Bonito's remark was heard by a good many people near the fence. "Go back to Drewmore, kid," called a man near the fence.

Meanwhile, Gursky called the other two umpires to a meeting near third base. Gursky showed them the birth certificate, and they conferred. When they had finished, Gursky made his way to the booth where the announcer was sitting and spoke into the mike: "Ladies and gentlemen, Archville is challenging the eligibility of Drewmore's Vinnie Bonito. The Archville coaches maintain they have a birth certificate that shows the player is thirteen years old and is overage at this level. My officiating team and I have determined that we cannot verify this document. Under the circumstances, we are going to allow the game to proceed, but Archville will be playing under protest."

Out of nowhere, Bonito's father came charging onto the field. His face was beet red, and he looked quite crazy. "You son of a bitch!" he shouted as he headed for McCracken. The coach stood his ground and put up his fists, but two policemen jumped in and grabbed the enraged father. As they hurried him away, Vinnie Bonito yelled at Tommy, "You'll need more 'n three fingers to win this game, punk!"

"No more of that, son," growled Gursky. "You've been warned." Once again, he cried, "Play ball!"

However, Three Fingers called time-out. He rushed to the dugout and grabbed a right hand glove. Back on the mound, he asked for three warm-up pitches, and Gursky let him go ahead. McCracken and the others were nonplused. No one had ever seen Tommy throw as a left-hander.

However, before Tommy could wind up and throw, Dick Dodge stormed onto the field yelling and screaming, "We were told we were going against a righty. This isn't fair."

Gursky tensed up and marched toward Dodge. He put his face close to Dodge's. "Shut up," he spewed. "One more word, and you'll be ejected."

Dodge turned on his heels and started back to the dugout, loudly mumbling something, with the word *asshole* clearly audible.

"That's it!" Gurksy yelled and threw his hand toward the stands. "You're out of here!"

Dodge turned and charged the umpire.

But the two cops were quick on their feet, grabbing Dodge and unceremoniously ushering him away.

LEO A. MURRAY

Gursky returned to home plate, shaking his hands. "Let's settle down here! Take your warm-up, pitcher. Let's get this game started."

Barclay and Lovello grinned at each other. "Fireworks before the show as promised," Barclay muttered.

"Nice job, Mr. Detective," said Lovello. "So this kid can throw left-handed too."

Barclay shrugged. "We're about to find out." Then he stepped aside and dialed Monica. "You have a green light," he said.

"Got it" was the only reply.

Now, for the third time, but with plenty of oomph, Gursky proclaimed, "PLAY BALL!"

Tommy Snook went into a slow windup and delivered an off-speed thigh-high pitch that whizzed by Bonito for a strike. The crowd literally roared. Then he fired a fastball for a swinging second strike. That brought the crowd to its feet. Finally, the newly minted left-hander finished Bonito off with a sinker, his father's trademark. The cheers rose up loudly.

*   *   *

At the county lockup, Jack Snook was wiping away tears. Out of natural kindness and more than a little sympathy, Captain Caswell had brought in a TV set so the prisoner could see his son play in the all-star game. The two men sat side by side through the volatile opening arguments as Snook grew pale with worry for his son. But now, watching Tommy dazzle the crowd with his left-handed pitching, Snook was nearly speechless with pride.

*   *   *

Tommy "Three Fingers" retired the next two batters with six pitches. As the Archville team left the field, the crowd was going wild, and it was only the first inning.

In the dugout, McCracken and Cortino pulled their star pitcher aside. "Where'd you get this left-handed stuff?" asked Cortino.

Tommy sheepishly admitted that he had secretly worked out throwing with his left arm when he thought he might never again be able to use his right.

McCraken shook his head. "But why switch arms tonight?"

"I wasn't going to, Coach," said Tommy, spitting in the dirt. "But that Bonito creep pissed me off big-time."

The two coaches cracked up. "Damn, you're good, kid!" exclaimed Cortino, hugging Tommy.

Barclay and Lovello watched the Archville team score three runs in the bottom of the first, aided by a towering homer over the right field fence by catcher Vince Anders. It was almost enough to make them forget they were here because a man had been murdered.

*　　*　　*

Monica had easily gained entry to Fred Saunders's three-room apartment. Jake had been right; the door was unlocked. Snapping on a Maglite, she instantly saw the place was a complete pigsty. Talk about your messy bachelor pad! And this was the guy responsible for keeping the municipal building clean.

She turned the flashlight toward a cluttered kitchen table. Scattered about were newspaper clippings about the Jenkins's murder. Monica looked close and saw there were not only articles about the homicide, there were also accounts of the municipal coal-to-fuel scam. She started snapping pictures with the Canon.

The bedroom was filthy too. The sheets on the bed were soiled and torn. There was dust everywhere. On the nightstand, amid candy wrappers and an empty Fritos bag, there was a small photo in a frame. The picture was of a young man and woman. It was one of those old photo booth pictures. She snapped a few close-ups.

Off to the right was a closet door. Carefully, she nudged it open to find mounds of dirty clothes. Several boxes were stacked up on a shelf. Taking down the most accessible box, she examined the contents. It contained Saunders's military discharge papers and another one of those vending machine photos of the same couple. She put the box on the floor and took several pictures. Beneath the discharge papers was a yellowed newspaper. She carefully picked it up and read the headline: MAYOR'S DEATH RULED SUICIDE. The paper had begun to flake, so Monica just made note of the publication date: October 15, 1970.

*　　*　　*

Back at the Complex, Archville was smashing Drewmore 5-0 in the top half of the third. When Three Fingers took the mound, he was wearing his glove on his left hand, meaning that spectators were now going to get a look at what he could do with his damaged right hand. The crowd was on its feet, chanting, "Tommy, Tommy, Tommy!"

When the Drewmore batter stepped into the box, Tommy went into a big wind up, as though he was going to deliver a blistering fastball. Then he delivered a pitch so slowly, it should have had the cover knocked off the ball. However, the Drewmore hitter, expecting the legendary pitch, was way out in front of it. "Strike 1!" yelled Gursky.

The Drewmore batter stepped out of the box and banged the instep of his cleats with his bat. Then he stepped back in, again expecting a fastball. But Three Fingers knew he owned the hitter. He threw another off-speed pitch right down the pipe. The batter took a cut and missed by a foot. "Strike 2!"

The batter shook out his arms and choked up on the bat, readying for another off-speed pitch. Three Fingers went into his steady, now intimidating, windup and fired a blazing fastball, low and outside. The kid took a power swing and connected with nothing but air.

Gursky punched the air sharply. "You're out!"

The crowd started up the Tommy chant.

Throwing six consecutive strikes, Three Fingers retired the side without them so much as touching the baseball.

For his team's half of the third, Tommy Snook was the leadoff hitter. Coach McCracken stopped Tommy before he left the dugout and told him he was going to pull him for the fourth inning and put in Danny Fitzgerald. In little league, pitchers are allowed only six innings a week. Tommy understood that Coach McCracken was looking toward the next game.

"Anything for the team," said Snook. "I just wish my dad were here to see me."

The coach pulled him close. "Lay down a bunt, Tom. Catch 'em napping."

Tommy smiled.

With Coach Dodge ejected, Drewmore's assistant coach was in charge. He moved the infielders and the outfielders back as Three Fingers stepped to the plate.

The first pitch was in the dirt for a ball. The second pitch was high, ball 2. The third pitch was also a bit high, but Tommy put the wood to it and laid down a near-perfect bunt that trickled along the third base line. The infielders were caught off guard. By the time the third baseman had rushed the ball and picked it up, Tommy was stepping on first base. But the third baseman, off balance, let fly with the ball anyway. The throw sailed over the first baseman's head, and Tommy sprinted to second.

The "Tommy, Tommy" chant rose again.

Coach McCracken then called time. The announcer told the crowd that Danny Fitzgerald was coming in to run for Tommy Snook. The crowd showed its obvious displeasure with the move with a series of "Boos!"

Tommy returned to the dugout, receiving high fives from players and coaches. He sat on the bench and thought about his dad. The Snook family was not very religious, but Tommy reflected for a moment. "Please God," he whispered, "help them find the real killer so my dad can come home."

Pete Harrison stepped to the plate and doubled down the right field line, sending Fitzgerald home from second. The crowd roared.

Before the side was retired, Archville was sitting on a 6-0 lead.

Meanwhile, Barclay was scanning the crowd anxiously. "What's wrong?" asked Lovello.

Barclay shook his head. "I don't see Fred Saunders anywhere." He looked at the attorney as he took out his cell phone. "Just a little hunch I'm working on." Barclay called Monica and said, "Beat it. Now."

"Understood," Monica replied. "I'm done anyway. I got some interesting stuff. Later."

Within a few moments, Barclay spotted Saunders near the refreshment stand. False alarm.

"Everything okay?" inquired Lovello.

"I won't know till later, John."

Lovello looked askance. "Whatever, but I'll keep my fingers crossed."

In the top half of the fourth inning, Danny Fitzgerald walked the first two hitters. And now, Bonito was on deck.

Coach McCracken asked for time. He walked to the mound to settle Fitzgerald down. He told the pitcher to relax, take his time, and pitch his game. McCracken could tell the kid was nervous. He told Fitzgerald the team was on its way to breaking a twenty-year jinx. "When future players look back," the coach said, "they will remember it was this team that broke the jinx."

When play resumed, Fitzgerald faced Bonito with confidence. He threw a pitch that caught the outside corner for a called strike. He leaned forward before going into his next windup, staring hard at the thirteen-year-old batter.

Bonito connected on the next pitch, grounding it back to Fitzgerald. The pitcher scooped it up and whipped it to second for the force out. The second baseman threw to first and caught Bonito by one step for a double play. By that time, the runner from second was rounding third and headed for home. The first baseman fired to Anders at the plate. The catcher joined forces with the third baseman to catch the boy in a rundown. Anders tossed the ball to the third baseman who tossed it back to Anders. The catcher faked his next throw and tagged the runner out.

The crowd loved it.

"A triple play!" an excited television announcer was heard telling his viewers. "Wow, you can't script 'em any better than that!"

Though playing under protest, Archville went on to win the opening game of the tournament with a convincing 7-0 shutout. While the huge crowd gave the athletes a standing ovation, the Drewmore team retreated to their bus, skipping the traditional handshake with the winners.

*   *   *

At the lockup, the elder Snook was on his feet. He shook his head in disbelief. "Can you believe that kid?"

"Believe it," said Captain Caswell. "That's some boy you've got. The team couldn't have done it without him."

Jack Snook hadn't felt this good since he was put in cuffs.

*   *   *

After the game, the field was alive with celebration. Kids, parents, coaches, all shouting and erupting with victory whoops. McCracken and Cortino felt like celebrities as fans huddled around to congratulate them. At one point, McCracken was approached by the TV producer for the game, lanky Ned Templeton. "We'd like to have the entire Archville team and coaching staff on our *Good Morning USA* program," explained the producer. "It's a live broadcast on Sunday morning. What do you say?"

"Thanks. Sounds great, but I'll have to ask the team. I'll get back to you."

"Let me know as soon as you can," said Templeton, handing over a business card.

McCracken saw Barclay and Lovello in the crowd and called them over. "Did you hear that? They want us on teevee."

"Yes," said the lawyer, "but a word of caution. You know the Snook case might well come up. How will you handle that?"

McCracken nodded gravely. "Good point. Maybe the show isn't such a good idea."

"I'd say go ahead," replied Lovello, "but only if you can set some ground rules with the producers. The Jenkins killing should be off-limits."

"Damn, I'd hate to prevent the boys from getting the recognition they deserve."

Barclay stepped close. "Here's an angle. We've just identified at least one suspect, possibly two. If you go on the show and the Snook case does comes up, you have our permission to mention that other suspects are being considered."

"Hey, that's fabulous news!" McCracken was excited. "Maybe we should definitely do the show and let folks know Jack Snook's no killer."

CHAPTER EIGHTEEN

B ARCLAY WAS AT the wheel of his Jaguar, Lovello lounging in
the passenger seat. They were heading for the Lookout to meet
with Monica.

"These other *suspects*," ventured Lovello. "You going to let me in on
who they are?"

Barclay let the car drift into the fast lane. "That was just a ruse to help
Tommy if they go on TV. Anything solid, obviously, I'd have told you."

"Come on, Jake. You've got someone in mind."

"Let's say I've got my eye on someone. He won't be an official suspect
until I have some evidence. Cross your fingers. Monica might have turned
up something." Barclay's cell phone rang. He saw it was Charlie Mars's
number and clicked it on. "Go."

"Hey, big guy, what is this? You got a couple of suspects and didn't
share? We had a deal."

Barclay chuckled. "Relax, Mr. Newsman. That was a bullshit story just
for young Snook's benefit. Take a little pressure off the kid. How'd you find
out?"

"Over at the Complex," responded Mars. "I heard people talking about
it."

"Forget that story. I might have something more substantial a little
later."

"All right, Jake. I won't press you. Keep in touch."

When Barclay finished the call, Lovello said, "You wanted that story
spread around, didn't you?"

The detective gave out a grunt of a laugh. "John, I've said it before, and
I'll say it again, you know how I like to mix it up."

Monica was already at the Lookout when they arrived. She was in a
pair of cutoff jeans, a slim top, and black heels. Lovello greeted her with a
kiss on the cheek. "Why didn't I meet you twenty years ago?"

She gave him a hug. "You say that every time I see you, ya big flirt."

They hung out by the wall while Monica detailed her snooping in
Saunders's apartment. "I know, counselor, breaking and entering. Big
crime."

"Only if you get caught," replied Lovello.

Barclay said, "It's not against the law to keep all those newspaper clippings of the two dead guys, but it's damn suspicious."

"Saunders found both bodies in that office," said Lovello. "I find that god*damn* suspicious."

Monica had obtained prints of the pictures she'd taken in Saunders's dingy quarters. She showed them the vending machine photo of the unidentified couple.

Barclay believed the man in the photo resembled a very young Fred Saunders. The woman was a complete mystery. "According to people I've talked to, Saunders was never married or romantically inclined. But there's a rumor he was jilted by a girl years ago."

"Rumors, speculation, gossip," said Lovello, "that won't get us far. We need a positive ID on the couple in this photo."

"Let's do a little history detective work," suggested Barclay. "There's a lady named Rachel Ormsby. She's Archville's unofficial historian. Go see her, Monica. She might be able to identify the couple."

"First thing in the morning, boss. But now, I need a nice hot bath and a good night's sleep."

Barclay and Lovello stopped at a roadside diner for a bite to eat and some hard thinking, then headed back to the Holiday Inn. Barclay set the alarm in his cell phone for 7:45 so they wouldn't miss the team on TV. They flipped a coin to see who would sleep on the cot. Barclay lost.

*   *   *

In the morning, both men were already awake when the alarm sounded.

Lovello got into the shower while Barclay ordered a pot of coffee from room service. When the attorney's cell phone went off, Barclay picked it up from the dresser. "Mr. Lovello's office."

It was the DA, Morgan Thomas, and his tone was sharp. "Who's this, Barclay? I need to talk to your man Lovello right away."

"Sorry, he's indisposed at the moment."

"Indisposed, huh? Well, have him call me as soon as he's 'redisposed'," Thomas ordered and rang off.

Barclay opened the bathroom door and called over the gushing water, "Morgan Thomas just called and sounds pissed."

Lovello laughed. "No doubt he's heard about the suspects we don't have."

Barclay turned on the television in time to see McCracken and the team in the program's opening. The coach announced, "We are the 2010 Archville, Pennsylvania, Little League All-Star Team, and we're here to wish you . . ."

The team sang out together, "Good morning, USA!"

The scene faded to a female host who said there'd be more coming up later with the all-star team. She then threw it to the anchor desk for the morning's headlines.

Lovello was dressed and pouring a cup of coffee. He had his cell phone open and pushed a speed dial button. "Good morning, Morgan. How's the prosecution business doing?"

"You tell me," said Thomas. "I hear you have a couple of suspects in the Jenkins's murder."

"I know my client is innocent, thus everyone's a suspect."

The DA was not amused. "You've got a reputation for taking things to the edge. But, John, don't try to make a jackass out of me in my own backyard. What about these so-called suspects?"

"What about them?" toyed Lovello.

"Okay, play it your way. But if you step over the line on this one, I'll have you before the Judicial Review Board on a four-fifteen. Am I making myself clear?"

"Quite clear. On the other hand, Morgan, it's been a long time since I worried much about threats from small-town lawyers, or lawyers from any-size town, far as that goes."

"You've been warned," said the district attorney as he hung up.

If there was one thing Lovello took pride in, it was his ability to ruffle feathers. He knew Thomas was afraid he'd be beaten on a case he had already placed in the win column, looking toward that next reelection campaign. "He's getting nervous," said Lovello. "Working the case on a Sunday morning."

"Shouldn't he be in church praying for you to go away?"

When the bottom of the hour came, the Archville team made its national debut. The piece opened with the spectacular triple play from Saturday night, then segued into shots of Tommy Snook throwing first as a left-hander, then with his right.

The reporter did a nice job, and there was no mention of Jack Snook and the murder rap hanging over his head. When Tommy was interviewed, the reporter asked him how he learned to throw so well with both hands, a considerable feat. The kid explained that, after losing two fingers in the accident, he never thought he would be able to use his right hand again. "I just pushed myself," said Tommy.

When the program moved on to other things, Lovello's phone rang. It was Gloria Snook, a call the attorney had been expecting. She wanted to know about the suspects. He told Gloria that they did, in fact, have two suspects they were looking at. "But nothing's definite yet."

"Well, that's certainly comforting." She paused, then added, "Can I ask who they are?"

"Gloria, I can't disclose that information right now." Lovello explained that he and his detective may be wrong about the possible suspects. "But I assure you, we'll let you know as soon as we have something solid."

"Okay," Gloria said in a wavering voice. "I trust you."

Lovello hoped she wasn't misplacing that trust.

Barclay and the attorney went down to the restaurant for breakfast, picking up a newspaper in the lobby. The headline read NEW SUSPECTS IN JENKINS'S MURDER.

They got a table and their waitress, a pleasant grandmotherly type, who poured them coffee and took their orders for scrambled eggs and bacon.

They looked over the article by Charlie Mars. He cited "sources close to the investigation" as saying that two new suspects in the mayor's murder were being looked at.

Lovello tossed the newspaper aside. "Now, we really do need a suspect."

"Couple of 'em."

Waiting for their breakfast to arrive, Lovello called Thomas back. "Look, Morgan, don't believe everything you read in the paper. When I have something I think'll stand up in court, you'll know about it."

Thomas was still a bit perturbed but willing to let it go. "I'm glad to hear that. All I ask is a level playing field."

"I wouldn't have it any other way," assured Lovello. "Listen, I need to see Jack Snook this morning."

Thomas said he'd handle it, and Lovello could get into the jail anytime after eleven. The call ended on a better note than the earlier one.

Barclay finished his coffee and signaled for a refill. "While you're seeing Jack, I'll deal with Monica, then follow up on anything she's uncovered. We've *got* to have an ID on those people in that photograph."

*   *   *

This being Sunday, the friendly Captain Caswell was not on duty when Lovello arrived at the jail. The gate guard didn't know him and had the attorney empty his pockets as he scanned him with the metal-detection wand. Lovello was finally shown into the attorney's meeting room, and Snook arrived a few minutes later.

He'd heard the news too. "Who are these suspects?"

"Jack," said Lovello, "we are indeed looking at two *possible* suspects. I emphasize the word *possible*. For now, let's leave it at that."

The ex-ballplayer nodded and changed the subject. "Hey, I got to see the game, thanks to Caswell."

"Some game, wasn't it."

"It was a fine game," agreed Lovello, "for Archville."

"How do you think they found out about the ineligible player?"

Lovello said he wasn't sure, but the protest was now moot as Archville had trounced the Drewmore team.

"Yeah, they sure did."

"I want you to know, Jack. I've got Jake Barclay helping me on the case. He's one of the best private detectives in the country. We'll get to the bottom of this thing."

Snook shook his head glumly. He was pale, listless.

"Jack, you need to take care of yourself in here. We'll find whoever killed that bastard Jenkins, but I want you to keep your spirits up. Don't go batty on me, okay?"

Snook nodded. "I appreciate what you're doing for me."

"Keep the faith," said Lovello.

* * *

Once again, Barclay arrived at the Lookout ahead of Monica and, once again, marveled at the view as he waited. From the back of his mind, he heard a voice saying, "It's Saunders. Can't be anyone else."

Monica pulled into the Lookout's parking area like the devil was on her tail. She hit the brakes and hopped out, then waltzed slowly over to him. She looked good in tight slacks and a loose blouse. "Okay, it's Fred Saunders and Rebecca Jenkins in the photo."

Barclay felt his heart skip a beat.

Mrs. Ormsby had quickly recognized the couple. Her daughter Melanie had graduated with Rebecca. "She got her daughter's high school yearbook out of the attic. We put the photo I took next to one in the book of Rebecca Jenkins. It's her, all right."

"And it looks like they were a couple," pondered Barclay. "You did well, kid. Take the rest of the day off but pick it up in the morning at the Jenkins estate."

"Where are you headed?"

"It's time I had a more 'official' talk with Mr. Fred Saunders."

CHAPTER NINETEEN

O N THE DRIVE from Scranton to Archville, Barclay wondered just how romantically involved—if at all—Saunders and the Jenkins girl had been. Was he perhaps, just maybe, the father of the deceased mayor whose body he had discovered? Does Saunders know that Rebecca Jenkins may still be alive? The questions kept on coming and kept going nowhere. He couldn't help thinking how this case more than ever reminded him of that Grateful Dead number "Truckin'." That line about "what a long strange trip it's been" seemed an apt description for his own meandering over the last few days.

As he parked the Jag on Main Street, the detective tried to formulate his approach to the secret man Fred Saunders. As usual, he decided to forget preplanning and simply wing it.

Barclay headed along the narrow lane between the barbershop and the crumbling building next door. He spotted Saunders just coming from his apartment. When the janitor saw him, he made a face. "What the hell do you want!" demanded Saunders.

"Well, Fred, I wish I was here to talk about last night's game. However, we need to talk about something more important."

"Like what?"

Barclay watched Saunders closely and said, "Like Rebecca Jenkins."

Saunders's face seemed to short-circuit and then dissolve in on itself, the same washed-up look he'd had after the funeral. It was like a death mask that didn't come off the mold right. "Rebecca," he muttered.

"Look, is there a quiet place we could go for a beer?" asked Barclay. "I mean you no harm, Fred. I'm just doing a job."

The crossing guard was dazed and confused; his natural combativeness had gone limp. Reluctantly, Saunders said they could walk over to the American Legion hall where he was a member. As they set off along the street, Saunders asked how he had heard about him and Rebecca. "That's been kept secret a lotta years."

"Remember, I'm a detective," said Barclay. "I have ways of finding things out."

"Like going through a man's living quarters?" Saunders told Barclay not to bother lying. "I know you were at the game last night, but someone was in my apartment."

Barclay looked surprised. "I don't know who it could have been."

Saunders explained how he always placed a toothpick on top of the door before closing it. "If the toothpick has fallen, somebody's opened the door." He claimed to have started the practice after some kids broke in a few years back.

"Was anything taken last night?" asked Barclay.

"No, but my stuff's been rifled through."

"Did you file a police report?"

Saunders shook his head. "What's the point? Nothing was taken. As you know, I live a meager existence. I don't have much, I don't need much, and I don't want much."

The Legion hall was quiet, with just a few patrons at the bar, the dining area dark. The building had once housed a preschool. However, the woodworking on the walls and the long mahogany bar made for a comfortable lounge. Along one wall, there were photos of local vets who had served as post commanders. There was a photo of Clarence West. According to the description underneath, West had been honored as Veteran of the Year several times. Shortly after his son was killed in Desert Storm, the post was dedicated to the memory of the fallen soldier.

The lady bartender greeted Saunders and handed Barclay the visitor's book. He signed it and then Saunders countersigned, verifying that the detective was his guest. He introduced him to the bartender. Her name was Mildred, a sixty-ish woman who looked more like a Sunday school teacher than a taproom server. "What'll it be, gentleman?"

Barclay flashed a smile. "How 'bout a Yuengling Lager?"

"Our best seller," she said. She glanced at Fred. "Usual?"

She brought over two drafts, a shot glass, and a bottle of Old Granddad. She poured the shot for Fred and waited. Saunders downed the shot quickly, and Mildred poured him another, which he let sit on the bar as a backup.

"A shot for you too, Mr. Barclay?"

He passed on the bourbon, and when she moved away, he got down to business. "Tell me about Rebecca."

Fred Saunders put down the backup shot and started talking like he was all oiled up and ready to go. "I first met Rebecca in 1970. I had just started working at the municipal building. Before the building was remodeled, it was easy to hear everything that went on in any of the offices. It was late on a Friday afternoon, and Rebecca had stopped in to see her father, the mayor. At the time, she was nineteen. I was finishing up cleaning the treasurer's office right next to the mayor's. I heard her ask him to help her get a car. Everyone in town knew the Jenkins family was very rich. But the old man refused to help Rebecca. I remember him telling her she was 'not her brothers' and did not deserve his help. Rebecca started to cry when she reminded her father that Archie and Reginald were gone, and she was his flesh and blood too." Saunders wiped away a single tear. Apparently, he'd already shed many tears over Rebecca and didn't have a whole of them left.

Barclay tried to quiet his mind, which was racing ahead toward a multitude of possible scenarios. Saunders ordered a third shot and downed it. The whiskey settled him a bit. Barclay told him to take his time.

"I heard a crack," Saunders continued, "like a slap or something, and the next thing I knew, the old man packed up his briefcase and left her sitting there sobbing. When I was sure the mayor had left the building, I went into his office. That was the first time I ever saw Rebecca Jenkins. The old man's handprint was still on her face. I felt sorry for her and offered her my hanky. I told her I'd heard everything. Believe it or not, she apologized for her father. She told me he hadn't been the same since her brothers got killed on the mountain." Saunders looked over at Mildred and lifted his empty shot glass. She poured him a fourth shot of Old Granddad. "Thanks, Mill."

"I know this is rough on you, Fred," Barclay said. The more he heard, the more certain he became that he was losing his only potential suspect. "We can stop if you like."

Saunders lifted the shot glass slowly and swallowed quickly. "I've kept this inside for a long time. Not a day passes I don't think of her."

"I can see that," said Barclay.

Saunders took a deep breath. "We started talking that afternoon. She was beautiful. She started to cry again when she recounted how her father would often smack her for no reason at all. She told me it got worse after her brothers were killed. I didn't think that kind of stuff happened in rich families. Anyway, I comforted her with a little hug and told her I was in the building every day if she wanted to talk. You know, just a sympathy thing."

"Sure."

"After that, Rebecca took to stopping in to see me. She always made certain her father wasn't around. One thing led to another, and we started secretly dating. That was in the summer of 1970. We were always very careful where we went because she didn't want her father—or her mother—to know she was seeing the janitor from the municipal building. She knew there would be trouble if they found out."

He paused in his story, and Barclay ordered another round of drinks though Saunders declined more bourbon. "I gotta get up early."

"So, you were dating, but no one knew about it," reminded Barclay.

"For a long while. And then, one morning in October of '70, I come into work and find the old man dead in his office, a pistol on the floor next to him. I called the police right away. Eventually, his death was ruled a suicide. Everybody in town said he killed himself to be with his boys."

"After that, did you keep seeing Rebecca?"

Saunders nodded. "Yeah, for quite a while. I asked her to marry me—must have been a hundred times. She wanted to, but her mother just wouldn't accept the fact that she was settling for a lowly janitor. It was inconvenient for the old woman, us being in love. Neither of us had any interest in other people."

Saunders grew silent and sipped his beer, lost in memory.

"And then what happened?" prompted Barclay.

Saunders said he and Rebecca had a liaison one night in the municipal building. "One thing led to another, and we made love for the first time. She got pregnant but didn't tell me until two months later. I wanted to marry her. I even suggested we run away together. She wouldn't go for that. But eventually, Rebecca said we could get married after the baby was born. She would never say why she wanted to wait."

Barclay downed more beer and sat quietly.

After a few moments, Saunders went on with his story of lost love. "Her mother put the pressure on. She demanded to know who the father was. Rebecca said she wouldn't reveal that until after the birth. She refused to have an abortion. Hell, during the last three months of the pregnancy, I only saw her once."

"When was this, Fred?"

"She had the baby in November of '74."

Barclay knew more was coming, and he stayed silent.

Saunders wobbled on the stool and looked at the detective with heartsick eyes. "When they told me the child was okay, but Rebecca didn't make it, I kinda died myself. I've been about dead ever since."

"And the baby, Fred . . . ?"

Saunders rubbed his face with both hands. "You've figured it out, and now you want me to say it."

"I'd like to hear it from you," murmured Barclay.

Now, the aging janitor put both hands flat on the bar. "All right, I'll say it. To hell with it. Don't matter no more." He glanced at Barclay with worn out features. "Mayor Albert Jenkins was my son. There, now I've said it."

Though he had half expected this, Barclay was still a bit shocked. The secrets of Archville. Now he knew he had to rule Saunders out as a suspect in the mayor's death. At least, the most recent mayor's death. The other one was a closed case, not a cold case. "Thanks for telling me, Fred."

"You can probably figure out why I kept quiet about the boy," said Saunders. "With me as his dad, what would he have? Bullshit, that's what. But with the Jenkins name, he'd be guaranteed a decent life."

"I understand," remarked Barclay.

"Yeah, he had the Jenkins name. And he grew up to be a cutthroat son of a bitch like the rest of 'em."

Barclay touched Saunders gently on the shoulder. "Albert never knew?"

"No. Oh, plenty a times I wanted to set the little prick down and tell him." He shook his head. "I just never got up the nerve. I promised myself I'd do it before I kicked off. Just didn't work out that way."

For a few moments, the detective sat in respectful silence, letting the dirty laundry hang in the air. He finally said, "That's why you hid in the woods at the funeral. You didn't want anyone to make the connection."

"You know about that, huh?" replied Saunders. "Yeah, I had to go. See him put in the ground. Weird thing. There was a car parked a ways back from the burial site and the rear window was halfway down. I saw a woman in the backseat, and my god, it looked like Rebecca." He used a napkin to mop his sweating brow. "Weird."

Barclay nodded sympathetically. "So that's why you were so rattled when I saw you that day."

"Yeah, it was like I'd seen a ghost."

They sat quietly a couple of minutes and then Barclay tugged Saunders's arm. "Let's get some air, Fred."

Without comment, Saunders got off the stool, and they went out into the sunshine.

As they walked back toward Saunders's place, there wasn't much to say; only there was a lot to say. "Fred, I've got something to tell you."

"I don't know if I want to hear it."

"I think you might."

Saunders stopped dead still. "Can't drink the way I used to," he said distractedly. He was clearly scared, with an end-of-the-world look.

Barclay took a deep breath. "I have reason to believe Rebecca Jenkins did *not* die in childbirth. I believe she's still alive."

Saunders staggered and gasped. "Oh Jesus," he moaned and began to cry. "Oh *Jesus!*"

*　　*　　*

Before leaving Archville, Barclay made a stop at the Protestant cemetery. He walked around the Jenkins's family plot, searching for a tombstone with Rebecca's name on it. Sure enough, there was none. It's a wonder the Jenkins family didn't fake a burial. Maybe that was going too far, even for them.

As he drove out of town, Barclay phoned Monica. "I know you're off duty, but I need just a little help."

"Not a problem. There's nothing to do around here anyway. What's up?"

"I just found out Mayor Jenkins was Fred Saunders's son," said Barclay.

"Are you kiddin' me!"

"No, straight business. He admitted it. Now look, get back in touch with our nurse Roberts, ex-nurse. We need to confirm something. Ask her if the woman named Harding was taken out of the facility the day of the funeral, the twentieth of June."

"I've got her number. Give me five minutes," replied Monica and rang off.

In less time, Monica was back to confirm that the Harding patient was indeed driven away from Glenside the morning of the funeral. "Roberts helped her dress and get ready. She also said the woman was very upset and crying."

"Thank you. Go back to doing nothing, and I'll call you later."

At his hotel, Barclay found Lovello examining the timeline on the poster board. "Jake, we're still missing most of everything we need."

Barclay plopped down in a chair. "Here's something that's not missing anymore. Fred Saunders just told me he was Albert Jenkins's father."

Lovello flinched. "His *father?*"

Over the next twenty minutes, Barclay went over all he had discovered. The whole Fred-Rebecca mess and her not being dead, just imprisoned. "It's not unheard of for a rich family to hide their secrets in the loony bin, as my uncle used to call it."

"But why say she died?" asked Lovello.

"Don't you detect the stench of big money?" asked Barclay. There was indeed a great deal of money involved. The old woman was worth at least $40 million. "And John, maybe a lot more. Whatever this is all about, we've got at least three people in on it—this Dr. Fisher, the lawyer West, and old lady Jenkins. They were all in the car when Monica tailed them to Glenside." He grinned. "All three of 'em, just like Wynken, Blynken, and Nod."

"More like partners in crime," said Lovello. "And let us not forget the half million in cash money you were offered *and* the half million in cash money I was offered."

"West called it 'a *retainer*'."

"Actually, the technical term is 'a *bribe*'."

Barclay was pacing around the room, anxious to make a move, almost any move was better than no move. He froze in place. "I just got me an idea."

"I don't like the sound of that, Jake. But if it gets us off dead center . . ."

"We need suspects, and I know where to look."

"Now you're talkin'," said Lovello.

Barclay stopped pacing and stood with arms folded. "You know what'd be kind of fun? You know how Monica can perform wonders on the Internet, right?"

"Yeah . . ."

"I'm going to turn the chick loose on West's office computer. Hack around a little."

"I didn't hear that," replied Lovello. "But if I had, I'd have said that's got promise."

"Look, John, I know we don't want to get bogged down with the Jenkinses and the Glenside crowd and all. But I've got a feeling we're closer to finding the killer if we dig up a few links, no matter how far afield we have to go."

Lovello spread his arms like he was the pope addressing believers. "I don't care where they come from, I just want some good, solid suspects."

Barclay snapped his fingers. "Those Cohibas I won from West. Wanna go somewhere we can light up?"

"Maybe wash it down with a beer, huh?"

"Let's hit Marty's in Archville. They keep the smoking lamp lit."

"Good," the attorney said, "sounds like a *man's* saloon."

Barclay picked up the handsome box of precious, though prohibited, Cohibas from the dresser drawer. "In case we run into any of the locals who like a quality smoke for a change."

*   *   *

In Archville, Barclay's Jaguar tooled along the main street. As they passed the building where West had his office, he slowed up. "Hey, look at that. There's a light on in his window."

"On a Sunday night," noted Lovello.

Barclay slowed the car. "I'm a little curious about that."

"That doesn't make you a bad person."

"You know what the kids in LA say, 'What's *really* going on'?" Barclay pulled into a parking spot at the curb. "Time for a little shuck and jive."

Barclay hustled across the street. At the door to West's office, he knocked lightly, tried the knob, opened the door, and got a nice surprise. He loved surprises. West was standing in the outer office with a conservatively dressed older woman and a distinguished gentleman in an expensive suit. They all looked like actors in a daytime soap opera.

"Excuse me, counselor. Saw your light, thought you might care for a cocktail."

"That's very thoughtful of you, Mr. Barclay, but I must decline. Very busy these days."

Barclay eased out, closing the door. "Well, I won't interrupt you. You got a rain check on that cocktail."

"Yes, another time," said West noncommittally.

Back in the Jag with Lovello, Barclay pulled out and continued on to Marty's bar. "That was worth a peek. Like I said before, Wynken, Blynken, and Nod. West was meeting with a guy I bet is Dr. Fisher and an old body who has to be the Jenkins woman. What's the right word, 'matriarch'?"

"A get-together on a Sunday night in a lawyer's office," mused Lovello. "Sounds like a crisis or a celebration."

It was Sunday night, and Marty's was busy. As it turned out, there was an impromptu party underway, a celebration for the little league win, busting a twenty-year jinx.

McCracken and Cortino were at their usual table and waved Barclay and Lovello over to join them. After a round was ordered, McCracken asked how the Snook case was going. "I know you can't talk about it, Jake, but everybody's wondering about those suspects."

"And they'll have to keep wondering for now," said Barclay. He put the cigar box on the table. "Anybody care for a genuine Cuban seegar?"

"Holy shit, haven't seen one of those in years," said Cortino. "Where the hell'd you get them?"

Barclay shook his head, grinning, delivering one of his trademark lines, "I could tell you, but then I'd have to kill you."

That got a big laugh, and everybody loosened up. Barclay drank his beer and looked around and instinct told him the killer could be in this room right now. Of course, instinct has to be backed up with evidence, and right at this moment, all the evidence he had could dance on a dime.

CHAPTER TWENTY

E ARLY MONDAY MORNING, while Lovello was in the shower, Barclay called Monica and laid out his scheme to hack into the computer at Clarence West's office.

"Now that's something I can sink my teeth into," she told him. "What am I looking for?"

"A few things. There's a company called Number One Mine we're interested in. Anything on that. His main client is the Jenkins family, so there'll be a lot of stuff under that heading. I'm specifically looking for any wills or special court filings on their behalf." "Keep going," said Monica, "I'm taking it down."

"And then there's this whole Glenside business and the Harding patient. We know she's really Rebecca Jenkins, so look for that name too."

"That's quite a grab bag, Jake. I'll have to find out what kind of computer equipment West uses."

"All that takes is a little role-playing," assured Barclay. He gave her a couple of ideas for innocently gaining access to West's office. "You can do it, girl."

"What'd you ever do without me?"

Barclay's next call was to Charlie Mars. "I said I'd keep you abreast of things. Are you sitting down?" He briefly detailed the relationship between Fred Saunders, Rebecca Jenkins, and the murdered mayor.

"Son of a *bitch*!" the reporter whispered.

"And here's another little treat for you, Chuck. Rebecca Jenkins is very much alive and was at her son's funeral."

"Son of a *bitch*!"

"Of course, none of this is printable quite yet. But when it breaks, you're going to have one of those stories that comes along once in a blue moon."

"Sometimes, Jake, you can be such a goddamn nice man."

After a quick breakfast with Lovello, who went off to chase whatever lawyers chase when they're not chasing ambulances, Barclay drove over to the courthouse to pick up the phone records he had subpoenaed. There was an envelope with his name on it waiting in the DA's office; a yellow Post-it note stuck on the outside requested he stop in to see Thomas for a few moments. Barclay knew the guy wanted some juice on the "suspects" played up in the papers. Only he didn't feel like enlightening him on that subject. One of those mood things.

He took the envelope and headed over to the coroner's office. Walking through a maze of marble floored hallways, Barclay glanced into the package of telephone records. There were numerous calls to and from the Houston number belonging to the two con men, Cook and Morrison.

At the coroner's office, Barclay told the middle-aged woman behind the main desk that he was looking for a copy of a death certificate for one Rebecca Jenkins, who passed away in 1974. She promptly entered the information into her computer. In a few moments, the death certificate was being printed out. He paid the ten-dollar charge, thanked the clerk, and left.

On his way back to the car, Barclay read the certificate. Cause of death: complications from childbirth. The document was signed: Evan Fisher, MD, Deputy County Coroner.

Interesting, thought Jake, *very interesting.*

*   *   *

At noon, Monica entered the office of Clarence West, Esquire, simply dressed and sedate looking. She talked to the receptionist, a lady with blue-tinted hair and a Dell computer next to her. Monica explained that she was in need of a Protection from Abuse Order. "I think that's what they call it." Her ex-boyfriend, Monica said, had followed her from California, where there was already an order of protection against him.

The receptionist was properly sympathetic. "I'm afraid Mr. West is at lunch. But I know all you have to do is take your California order to the county court. They'll issue you a new one."

"Is there a form to use for that?" asked Monica.

"Yes, and I can give you one." The receptionist stepped over to a filing cabinet and began rummaging through one of the drawers.

With the woman's back turned, Monica was able to take a good look at the computer desktop, and she had what she came for.

"Here we are," said the blue-haired receptionist, handing Monica a single sheet. "Just fill it out and take it with your California order to the courthouse. Best of luck, honey."

"Thanks, ma'am."

The lady gave her West's business card. "If you have any problems, just give us a ring."

"You're very kind. Have a nice day."

On her way out of the building, she passed a conservatively dressed gentleman who had "lawyer" stenciled on his forehead. She pretended not to see him but knew he saw her.

*   *   *

Barclay sat in the hotel coffee shop looking over several pages of phone records but saw nothing of interest, nothing that stood out. The nice waitress brought a newspaper with his late-morning breakfast. The headline screamed: ARCHVILLE'S CITY COUNCIL MAJORITY RESIGNS.

He read the story detailing the resignations of Tim Richards and the other three members of the voting majority after a federal probe into the coal-gas scam. The four had illegally expended $500,000 in federal funds. Barclay knew the men had had good intentions and were simply taken in like so many had been taken in. Clearly, they were not crooks. The most they should be charged with, he decided, is second-degree stupidity.

The story explained that all four men were Democrats; since there were no provisions in the state code for replacing all of them at once, it would be up to the Democrat Party to prepare a list of possible candidates and submit it to the county court.

Barclay returned to his room and a ringing phone.

"The Benz is on the move," reported Monica without preamble. She said the car had left the Jenkins mansion ten minutes ago and was now heading toward Glenside. "I don't know if the driver's alone or not."

"Keep him company," said Barclay. "Call me when it gets interesting."

He went in and splashed cold water in his face and looked in the mirror. It was not the face of a happy detective.

A few moments later, Lovello was on the phone. "Get the phone records?"

"I did and took a quick look. Nothing earthshaking, but I'll have to go over it carefully." He told the attorney about the death certificate he'd obtained for Rebecca Jenkins. "Get this, John, it was signed by none other than Dr. Evan Fisher. At the time, he was deputy county coroner."

Lovello was not surprised. "If you're going to fake someone's death, you need a death certificate. Damn, this case is a doozy."

Right after that call, Charlie Mars rang Jake's cell phone. "I just found out Thomas has had the Snook prosecution reassigned to himself. He has a press conference set for noon. He's going to announce he'll be seeking the death penalty."

Barclay sagged. "What's that all about?"

"I'm looking into it as we speak," said Mars. "Gotta run, but I wanted you to know."

Barclay called Lovello back and told him the news.

"Jesus," said the lawyer, "one minute they're offering a plea, and the next they're going for the death chamber. That son of a bitch Thomas thinks he's got this case knocked. Not while I'm at the defense table."

They agreed to meet at the courthouse to catch the press conference.

*　　*　　*

Monica had followed the Mercedes from the Jenkins place to Glenside, but by the time she turned around and parked, the car was already leaving the sanitarium grounds.

She tailed the car cautiously even though she figured Forbes would likely have already been hitting the bottle and wouldn't be all that alert.

The Benz got on the Interstate, and Monica followed for twenty minutes. Forbes finally took the ramp for Route 309 South. Three miles up the hill, the chauffeur pulled into the parking lot of some kind of medical facility. Monica parked on the shoulder of the road and watched. It was something to watch all right.

The doors on both sides of the car opened to reveal a female nurse and a male guard struggling to pull a woman from the backseat. She was in a straitjacket. The woman was putting up quite a fight, kicking and spitting. They brought her under control with force and took her into the building.

Monica quickly located a place where she could hide when the trio came out. She took her Canon video camera and tripod across the road and stomped up the embankment. She set up the equipment and waited. She used her cell phone to google the address of the building and found it to be a clinic run by Dr. Evan Fisher, psychiatrist.

Half an hour later, the trio emerged from the building. Monica began shooting. The woman in the straitjacket was now limp and subdued. Monica zoomed in to get some very tight footage. She could see that the woman's mouth was slack and her head lolled to the side.

Once Forbes had driven out of sight, Monica hustled back to her Ford. She made a U-turn and zoomed off after the Mercedes. She caught up and followed the car back to Glenside. When the car left there, she tailed it back to the Jenkins estate. Monica called Barclay but got his voice mail. She left a short message describing what she had witnessed, then added, "Video tape at eleven."

*   *   *

At the courthouse, the print and broadcast folks were all assembled in the press room ahead of the district attorney's appearance. Charlie Mars was sitting in front and nodded casually as Barclay and Lovello slipped into the room.

DA Thomas was fashionably late, groomed and suited in an over-roomy gabardine suit. He was an important man, he was, but he was big enough to apologize for his tardiness. Then he tossed a grenade into the crowd: "Barbara Grochowski, my first assistant district attorney, has been suspended as of nine a.m. today. As you know, she was slated to be the prosecutor in the Jenkins murder. Under the circumstances, I am taking over the prosecution. What's more, my office will be seeking the death penalty."

A noisy murmur spread among the reporters.

"What the hell's this guy up to?" Lovello whispered.

Barclay said, "It's hard to make a name for yourself in Nowhereville. You grab what you can."

When Thomas took questions, Mars jumped in. "Why is she off the case?"

"Sorry, that's not something I'm able to discuss at this time," said Thomas dismissively. He glanced at an iPod screen. "Couple of other announcements . . . The trial date has been moved from September third to August fifteen. In addition, the case has been reassigned from Judge Thomas Mooney to Judge Max Harkins." With that, ignoring the shouted questions, Thomas exited, stage right.

"Can he do that?" asked Barclay.

"I'm afraid so," Lovello replied. "But what I'm concerned with is the *why*." The defense attorney said he was inclined to start filing motions that would keep Harkins quite busy. "On the other hand, maybe we should ride this out and see where it takes us. But first, as you would say, let's go mess with the DA's head."

While the news people hastily departed to file their stories, Barclay followed Lovello down the hall and over to the DA's office.

"I need to see him," Lovello crisply informed the secretary.

She smiled politely, too politely. "Isn't that a coincidence. Mr. Thomas said you might stop by. This way, please."

They were shown into Thomas's rather pretentiously elaborate office with all the fishing trophies and the glad-handing Mr. District Attorney photos on three walls. Lovello spoke right up. "Morgan, what the hell is this? You just cut three weeks off my time to prepare the case. That's highly irregular and, frankly, highly underhanded."

"Yeah, I know," readily admitted Thomas, who was taking an interest in his fingernails. "But I can do things like that, John, because *I'm* the DA in these parts."

Lovello looked at Barclay. "He's the DA, Jake. He can do things like that."

"Uh-huh."

Thomas pointed a cocked finger, the drugstore cowboy emerging. "Look, counselor, your client shoulda taken my offer when it was on the table. Which it's now off of."

Lovello eyed the big man behind the big cluttered desk. He was the badass arm-of-the-law and liked to flex those muscles. "Mind if I ask *why* your assistant is off the case?"

Thomas shrugged, all innocence. "She's not got the stomach to pursue capital murder."

"But you do," said Lovello, heading for the door. "See you in court."

"Have a nice day, guys," called Thomas, a note of hilarity in his tone.

Outside in the hallway, Lovello said, "We're in trouble, Jake, and we're running out of time."

"Tell me about it. Just for shits and giggles, let's stop by voter registration and get copies of some campaign contributions—like those for Judge Harkins and our buddy Thomas."

"Following the money."

"Exactly," said Barclay. "Something tells me that bag-o-cash West was handing out finally found a home, both bags."

Lovello shook his head, exasperated. "It just never quits, does it?"

"What doesn't quit?"

"People."

"Oh, they're the worst," assured Barclay.

At the voter registration office, the young gay intern was accommodating. He quickly printed out the requested public information on a single sheet, put it in an envelope, and handed it over. No charge. While Lovello took a quick peek, Barclay got on the cell and called Monica. "Hey, doll, meet us at the Lookout in thirty minutes. We're shifting this gig into overdrive."

"Overdrive, huh?" repeated Monica. "I guess I better drive over there."

"Now you're getting silly."

∗   ∗   ∗

At the Lookout, the three of them huddled unnoticed by the wall like teenagers sneaking a smoke in the schoolyard. This time, they hardly glanced at the thousand-mile view. Lovello said he knew forces were at work to get them out of the county as quickly as possible. "Like maybe with a tar and feather party."

Barclay was worried that Nurse Roberts might have told someone about her little talk with Monica. It could mess up what little they had in the hopper. "Humor us, doll. Ring her and find out if she's kept her mouth shut. Tell me I'm just paranoid."

Monica was already dialing. She spoke for a minute, then clicked off. "You're just paranoid. She gave me her word. Hasn't spoken to anyone about the mystery patient and all that. Besides, I think she's afraid to say anything having to do with Glenside."

Lovello nodded. "Good. Gives us a chance to take a closer look at this Dr. Fisher, not to mention West and old lady Jenkins."

Monica cued up the video she'd shot earlier, displaying it in the camera's side screen. They could see the woman in the straitjacket being almost carried from Fisher's clinic.

"Dogs to donuts," said Barclay, "we're looking at 'the late' Rebecca Jenkins."

"Jesus," muttered Lovello, "how many years have they kept her like that?"

"Nice people," added Monica.

Barclay was looking over the maze of small print on the sheet disclosing campaign contributions. "Here you go, all three of them—Fisher, West, Mrs. Jenkins—were quite generous to Judge Max Harkins in his campaign for the bench three years ago. Generous to the tune of a hundred gees or so."

"That's damn generous," noted Lovello. He stood thinking for a moment, running fingers through hair that was mostly not there. "I know the assistant state attorney-general in Scranton. He was in a Justice

Department seminar I went to on trying terrorist cases. I'm going to set up a meeting with him. I'll need the video and that bogus death certificate."

"Who said you can't bring back the dead?" offered Barclay.

*   *   *

Back at the hotel, Lovello looked up the number and phoned the state attorney's office. "Leonard Carson, please. John Lovello calling." He looked over at Barclay. "This could be a complete waste of time."

Carson was on the line shortly. "I heard you were in town. What for, a Texas Hold 'em showdown?"

Lovello laughed. "I was just lucky that night and you played too many hunches."

"Ain't that the truth? What can I do for you, John?"

Lovello rattled off a few points about the Snook case and the possible connection with a dead woman who apparently wasn't dead. "I need to talk about this, Len. Let me take you to dinner."

"You got it, buddy. You know Russell's. Meet you there at seven?"

"Till then." Lovello hung up and told Barclay they had a dinner date.

Barclay was across the room, standing at the dresser, going through the pages of telephone records he had subpoenaed. He soon noticed an incoming call to Mayor Jenkins's cell phone at 11:50 p.m., on the night of the murder. He wrote the number down on a hotel notepad. "John, what was that time of death on Jenkins?" asked Barclay.

"The coroner put it between midnight and one-thirty."

"That's interesting. In fact, that's real interesting, isn't it?"

"What's that?" asked Lovello.

"We might have an electronic fingerprint." Barclay hit the speed dial on his cell and got Monica. He gave her the phone number on the notepad. "Get on that laptop I bought you and find a name to go with that number. Like right now, *please*." He turned to the lawyer sitting in the best of the easy chairs. "For whatever the hell it's worth, Jenkins took an inbound call just before midnight on his personal cell. That's right around the time he got his skull bashed in. There were some daytime calls, but nothing else late at night."

"The cops have those phone records. If there was anything there, they haven't shared it with us. Not required until discovery, of course."

Monica was back in just ten minutes. "It's no go on getting any kind of a name, but there's definitely something funny going on here. First off, the phone was a throwaway, purchased at a Walt's Mart on Route 12 in Archville."

"Time of purchase?"

"Eleven twenty-two p.m., the night Mayor Jenkins died. It was purchased with a sixty-minute usage card, paid in cash. Activated right away. There was one call ten minutes before midnight. No other calls on that phone since then. That's what I mean by something funny. It's tied in to the murder, isn't it."

"Starting to look like it."

Barclay put down the cell phone and looked at his watch. He remembered the ominous sign in his fifth grade classroom, posted right under the big IBM wall clock: Time Will Pass, Will You?

CHAPTER TWENTY-ONE

A LITTLE BEFORE SEVEN o'clock, Barclay and Lovello were in the bustling bar at Russel's restaurant, waiting on Len Carson's arrival. While they sipped a drink, Barclay bumped Lovello with his elbow, nodding toward an attractive redhead entering from the foyer. "Nice," he murmured.

"And she's very smart," said Lovello, slipping off the barstool and going over to her. He greeted the redhead with a warm handshake and brought her to the bar. "Jake, meet Barbara Grochowski, the county's first-assistant district attorney."

"Not anymore," she said.

"What happened?"

She shook her head. "I refused to go along with changing judges. And I wasn't in favor of moving the Snook trial up either." Then she leaned in and added, "Morgan's an asshole, in case you haven't picked up on that."

Lovello bluntly asked why the DA was moving forward with all guns blazing when the case against Snook was really not that strong. "Not from where I'm standing."

"That's just it," she said. "He wouldn't give me a reason. It was his way or the highway. I chose the highway."

A well-dressed forty-something gentleman who looked like he belonged on a *GQ* cover walked in, strode up to Grochowski, and kissed her on the cheek. "Are we ready to dine?" he asked.

"Excuse me," she said, and they sauntered away arm in arm.

"Thomas wouldn't give her a reason," mused Barclay. "Why would he keep it to himself? Like I don't know."

"Yes, it's pretty obvious he's been given his marching orders. But from who? Or, is that 'whom'?"

Len Carson came through the door looking like what he was, a state's attorney. Thick glasses, graying at the temples, casually dressed in khakis and a blue golf shirt. While they waited for a table, Lovello introduced him to Barclay, and the two lawyers fell to small talk about Carson's wife and two kids.

Barclay's cell rang. He glanced at the caller I.D. "Pardon me, guys, I have to take this." He politely stepped into the foyer to talk, but it was getting crowded with diners waiting on a table. He went on outside into a warm and still bright evening. "Hey there, Jerry."

"Jake, you son of bitch. You don't call me in a coon's age, and outta nowhere, I get a fuckin' message with *nothin'* nice in it and like it's the end of the world if I don't call you right back in a couple a minutes. You're a pushy bastard, Jake. You got a handful of gimme and mouthful of much obliged." The man broke up into snorting laugher. "Anyway, how the hell are you, big guy?"

Barclay was grinning. "I'm doing okay, but no thanks to one Jerry Elias."

"What, that thing up in San Francisco?"

"Yes, that thing up in San Francisco. Here I am, trying to help out my old sergeant buddy with his problems with the ex-girlfriend, and next thing I know, I'm hooked. Takin' the chick out for goddamn eighty-dollar sushi platters, two-hundred dollar ballet tickets. Dropped over a grand on her that week. Then come to find out you knew all along she'd put the make on me and I was going to like it. I thought I was being hired as a private eye, in fact, you were setting me up on a blind date so you could get rid of the lady." Barclay laughed. "I won't deny there were certain side benefits to the assignment."

"Here I hand you, *hand* you," said Elias, "some of the finest trim in California, and this is the thanks I get. Besides, I told you to send me a bill and you never did."

"What was I supposed to do, bill you for, stud services?"

Elias broke up. "That's a good one. All right, enough beating around the bush. I know you'd only call if you needed a favor or wanted me to do something you should prob'ly do yourself. So, what is it this time?"

"Here's the situation, Sarge. I'm up to my eyeballs in a murder case out here in Pennsylvania, and I need a peek at the surveillance video from—"

"Thanks for not saying 'videotape'," said Elias. "That went out with the Civil War. What is it, one of Lovello's cases?"

"Yeah, John's here with me. Now listen, there's a Walt's Mart in a town out here called Archville. I got a receipt, time and date stamp, on a cell phone bought with cash. I have to track down who that customer was. Got a pen?"

Elias could be heard scribbling as the information was fed to him. "Okay, got it. I assume you need to look at this surveillance footage ASAP and I should drop everything—sex drugs and rock 'n' roll—and put all of my energy into it. Is that about right?"

Barclay said, "Well, that *would* make up for that strenuous week you put me through in San Francisco."

"All right, big guy. I'll get back to you after I talk to Ned Jameson. He's eastern security chief at Walt's Mart. We did a tour together, FBI Denver. And that reminds me. Ned owes me a favor. I was one of his references for the job at Walt's Mart."

Back inside, Barclay ordered the same gin and tonic the other two were having. The place was getting crowded, and the general hubbub made for a wall of privacy at the table. "You guys got a game plan cooked up?" asked Barclay.

Carson leaned toward him. "John's been putting me in the picture. What I see, at minimum, is bribery of a public official, abuse of office, and probably witnesses tampering. And frankly, that might be the tip of the iceberg from what I'm hearing. What are you looking for, a wire package?"

"That's right," said Lovello. "One tap on the lawyer West, one on Dr. Fisher, and one on Mrs. Jenkins. With my complaint, you'll have probable cause, Len."

Carson took it in and nodded. "Okay, but I'll need a judge to sign the warrant." He grinned. "Didn't you just tell me the Honorable Justice Thomas Mooney was replaced on the Snook docket? Something tells me Judge Mooney'll be in a warrant signing mood when he hears the bribery case could be linked to the Jenkins homicide. Maybe I'll even put a little pressure on with a visit to Clarence West."

Lovello lifted his glass. "Len, people always said you weren't as dumb as you look."

"That's what my wife tells me," cracked Carson. He looked at Jake. "What's your take on all this?"

Barclay drained off some of his drink. "I'm totally convinced the district attorney and the judge have taken money from old lady Jenkins, with West as the conduit. Fisher's got reasons other than money for wanting the Snook case wrapped up fast. Keeping Rebecca Jenkins in illegal confinement like he is . . . Well, I don't know how it all fits in, but I know it does."

After dinner, Barclay and Lovello returned to the hotel. There was a message to call the DA. He rang the number.

Thomas was all business. "I thought you'd want to hear my witness list as soon as possible, John. I'm only calling five." Thomas rattled off the list: Jeff McCracken, Fred Saunders, the coroner, a forensic pathologist, and Officer Joseph Sampson of the Archville Police Department.

Lovello offered a halfhearted thank you and hung up. He went over the list with Barclay. "What about this cop Sampson?" asked Lovello. "What's his story?"

"All I know is he was the one who talked to Jack Snook the night of the murder."

Lovello was lost in thought a moment, then said, "He'll be the sledgehammer for Thomas, the 'star witness' as they say on those stupid lawyer shows. Jake, go see that Richards guy and some of the others. Let's find out what skeletons Sampson's got rattling around in his closet."

"We've got a town full of skeletons rattling around," observed Barclay. "And some of them are alive."

Lovello hit the sack before he fell out.

Barclay sat down, rubbed his face, and called Charlie Mars. "Another update, Chuck. Keep this strictly to yourself, understand?"

"Does it rain on rhubarb?"

Barclay explained the situation with Len Carson and the request for a wiretap warrant on the three characters they were now focusing on.

"That's a smart high-power move, Jake, the state's attorney. Good show. Don't worry, I'll keep my mouth shut *and* my fingers crossed."

*　　*　　*

Monica was hunkered down in her hotel room on the laptop. She had used a simple program downloaded from a German hacker's website, which had enabled her to gain access to the main hardwired telephone line in West's office. From there, it was not difficult to jump into the computer connection and view the desktop on the secretary's computer. Fortunately, they were running funky old Windows XP Pro, the Edsel of operating systems, Monica always called it. She snooped around for half an hour, looking in files, pulling up documents in Word and various spreadsheets. All very dull, little more than bookkeeping files.

Finally, she came upon a folder labeled RMJ. "Well, well," she mumbled. "We know who that is, don't we."

However, the RMJ file was password protected, unlike the others. Monica set to work with purpose. Over the next twenty minutes, using a goosed-up backdoor path, she was able to easily crack the password, thanks to those helpful German hackers and Microsoft's rinky-dink encoding. It turned out the password was "Stingray." Yes, Jake had said West owned a vintage Corvette.

The file had separate documents pertaining to various matters, from power of attorney assignments to estate briefs. One file memo was headed Confidential and Personal. As she read into the text, she saw it was a summary of events pertaining to the Jenkins estate. It took less than ten minutes to read the entire four-page memo. It was an eye-opener, to put it mildly. Monica launched a new window and logged into her Cloud account. With a couple of clicks, she copied the entire RMJ file into her Jake's Junk folder, the one with the doggie icon on the front. She double-checked to make sure she had left nothing in the Recent Documents list, found it clean, then shredded her own DLL nuggets as she deftly danced out of the hacker program, leaving not a single disturbed memory.

Monica sprang from the tiny hotel desk to the tiny dresser for her cell phone. Barclay was on the line in ten seconds. "Jake, I just robbed Clarence West blind. I got the goods you were looking for and I mean the goods."

"I'm listening."

"There's a whole file of stuff on the Jenkinses that I copied. File was created last summer, probably scanned in. From what I can tell, based on this memo I read, back in 1970, Elizabeth Jenkins was having an affair with Dr. Evan Fisher."

"Really?" said Barclay.

"Yeah, this is like a soap opera. Archibald Jenkins found out about the affair and threatened a messy divorce. The Jenkins family apparently didn't like that idea. So to avoid a public scandal and keep the family together, at least in appearance, Elizabeth was forced to sign a stipulation that granted her just $250,000 upon his death. See where this is going?"

"Rebecca," said Barclay.

"You bet your sweet-ass Rebecca. She was named beneficiary for the umpteen millions the old man had. Payable on her twenty-fifth birthday, if Archibald died before that occurred."

Barclay skipped a beat and said, "So that's why Rebecca Jenkins has been confined for thirty-five years in that Glenside prison, which is what it is. She's the rich lady, not her mother. I wonder how they got West to go along with it."

"Remember what the nurse said about her acting 'crazy.' The poor woman, after all that time locked up, of course, she's gone crazy."

"This guy West is a cute one," stated Barclay. "But we've got a little deal cooked up for him." He told her about the involvement of assistant AG Len Carson, their bid for a prosecutorial misconduct charge, and the petition for wiretap warrants. "Carson's going to 'drop by' West's office tomorrow just to rattle his cage and see what happens. I need you watching that office like a hawk. Video would be nice."

*   *   *

The private eye's alarm sounded at 5:15 a.m. He showered and shaved and was on his way. It was sunny and hot, a nice day for unmasking a killer.

Pulling up across from Fred Saunders's apartment, he could see a light on. Barclay walked around back and lightly tapped on the door. Saunders opened it holding a Styrofoam cup of coffee. He saw the detective eyeing it. "I don't like to wash dishes," he said with a grin.

"Let's grab a quick breakfast."

"All right, Jake. But I have to be at work by six thirty."

"Sure, but we've got time."

As they got into Barclay's Jaguar, Saunders said he'd always wanted something decent to drive. "Closest I ever got was a five-year-old Pontiac Bonneville."

They ended up at a little diner on Route 5. Both ordered breakfast sandwiches and coffee. Once they were settled in a booth, Barclay said, "Fred, I've learned a few more things in the last twenty-four hours. I can definitely confirm that Rebecca is alive. However, I can't say what condition she's in."

Saunders's hand was trembling as he sipped the coffee, his eyes watering. "Where is she?"

"She's being held against her will, Fred, at Glenside."

Saunders's features were slack and hopeless. "My god, all this time. What's it all about?"

"What's it ever all about?" replied Barclay.

Saunders spoke a single dirty word: "*Money.*"

"I don't know the details, yet but we're working on it."

Saunders lowered his eyes, looking backwards. "I almost killed myself a couple a times. You know, so I could be with her. Had that forty-five of mine chambered, cocked, and up against my head. But each time I chickened out, didn't have the guts." He was more or less talking to himself.

Barclay cut in. "You could help us get to the bottom of this nightmare, Fred."

Saunders looked up, a mean, tough man ready to take care of business. "Whatever you need, Jake. Whatever you need."

"Look, somebody killed your son. I know he was a shit and all, but he was a human being. The thing is, you know and everybody else knows, Jack Snook didn't do it. However, we've got a DA working overtime to hang him. He's looking for a ticket to better places."

"That motherfucker," muttered Saunders.

"You've been working for the local big shots a long time now, Freddie. Tell me what you know about this cop Joe Sampson."

Saunders scratched his head. "He's a tough guy to get a read on. But I do know he got screwed in January."

"What do you mean *screwed*?"

He told the detective Sampson was supposed to be named chief of police at the January council meeting. "Supposedly, he had the four votes needed, but he still didn't get the job. It went to a guy who was a friend of Albert's." He'd only heard about it second—or third-hand, but the newspapers played it up. "They said the council was deadlocked in a three-three tie, and the mayor broke the tie with a vote for his own man."

"How could you have a tie with seven men on the council?"

"One of the guys—I don't remember which one—was not at the meeting. That's what caused the tie vote. That gave Mr. Mayor a rare voting opportunity. In other words, he aced Sampson out of the job."

Barclay nodded solemnly. "You think that could be a motive for murder?"

"Well, I thought of that, of course," remarked Saunders. "But it's kinda hard to swallow."

"A lot of this business is hard to swallow."

Barclay dropped him off at the municipal building. "I'll keep you informed about Rebecca, Fred. We'll sort this out."

Saunders looked at him like a bewildered child. "It's the end, isn't it?"

"What do you mean?"

"I don't know. But thanks, Jake. I got a lot to think about, and I ain't all that good at thinking."

It was too early to call Tim Richards, so Barclay drove back to the hotel, keyed up and hyper. He went to his laptop and searched the local paper's morgue online and found the article about the city council's vote for police chief. He quickly verified what Saunders had told him. According to the article, council member Steve Myers was not in attendance. The reporter mentioned it was the first meeting Myers had missed in nine years. Barclay put Steve Myers down as a man he'd be talking to in the immediate future, whether Myers like it or not.

A little after nine, Barclay called Tim Richards but reached his wife. She said Tim was at his full-time job as an auto mechanic and gave Barclay his cell phone number. He quickly got hold of Richards. "Tim, you forgot to mention that tie vote for police chief. Sampson had a good motive to kill Jenkins, didn't he? You're not trying to cover up something, are you?"

There was silence on the line.

"Spill it, Tim, or I won't be such a nice guy, and you won't like it when I'm not a nice guy."

"I didn't want to confuse the issue. That's why I didn't bring it up."

"Confuse it?" repeated Barclay. "Bullshit. It could *clear* things up. Tell me what you know, and I mean right now. Don't fuck with me, Tim. You're starting to look like a suspect yourself."

"Is that a warning?"

"No, my man, it's a threat, and you'd better take it seriously. You're in enough trouble already with that fraud indictment hanging over your head."

"All right, all right, take it easy. Here's what happened, Jake. Here's what I know . . . The four of us who made up the majority block, along with the mayor, agreed that Sampson was the best choice for police chief. The right experience, the right attitude. That made it a four-to-three vote. But this was all decided the night before at a work session, before the official convening of the council meeting. We couldn't vote during the work session because it was unofficial. Hold on." Richards took a moment to call out to someone that he was on the phone and would be off in a few minutes. "So like I say, we had all decided to give the job to Sampson. We were surprised Jenkins was going along with us."

"Why?"

"A couple of months before the January vote," Richards went on, "in fact, on the night of the election in November, Sampson arrested a friend of the mayor's on a DUI. Jenkins put pressure on Sampson to forget about it, but he went ahead and filed the charges. That's why we thought it odd that this prick-shit mayor was actually being fair for once and giving the job to the guy who had earned it instead of one of his handpicked lackeys. That's what we *thought*. So the next day, at the official city council meeting, I made a motion to hire Sampson as Archville police chief. It was seconded by Eugene Thompson. The motion received three *yes* votes from the majority and three *nos* from the opposition. By municipal code, the mayor was then required to cast a vote to break the tie. What did the son of a bitch do? He double-crossed us and voted *no*."

LEO A. MURRAY

"It was a set up."

"All the way," replied Richards. "Dick Sweeney nominated Jenkins's buddy, Ralph Cerra. Again, the vote was three to three. And again, Jenkins broke the tie with his vote, a *yes* for Cerra."

"Now tell me why Steve Myers was absent for that vote," pressed Barclay. "He hadn't missed a council meeting in nine years."

"That was part of the set up," said Richards. "After the work session, Al Jenkins announced that he had floor seat tickets for the Knicks-Lakers game at the Garden for the next night. Myers snapped them up in a hurry. He's a huge Lakers fan. Floor seats. Since we had all agreed on Sampson anyway, Myers thought it would be no big deal to miss the meeting."

"And Jenkins knew Myers would drool over those tickets. How did Sampson react to losing what was a shoo-in?"

"He didn't make a fuss, if that's what you mean."

"All right," said Barclay. "That's better, Tim. I'm sorry I had to lean on you like that, but Jack Snook is fighting for his life and didn't kill Jenkins. I'm trying to find out who did."

"What's this about *me* being a suspect?"

Barclay chuckled deviously. "When I'm on a case, everybody's a suspect until they're not."

CHAPTER TWENTY-TWO

RIGHT AFTER HE hung up with the nervous ex-councilman, Barclay got a call from Monica. "I'm over here staking out West's office, and we've got some action. Look in your e-mail. I sent some shots of a stocky guy who's paying a visit to West right now. Guy's got government plates on his car, and he's *way* not cute."

"Hold on a second." Barclay stepped over to the dresser and flipped open his running laptop to pull up his Gmail account. The JPEGs opened in a flash, and the image of the stocky man heading into West's building popped out crystal clear. He laughed. "I love it!"

"You recognize him?"

"Sure, it's our Mr. District Attorney Thomas. How long's he been inside?"

"Ten minutes. Wait a sec, here he is. And, Jake, now he's carrying a briefcase."

"I love that too," said Barclay. "Forget the West stakeout. Follow Thomas."

"Could be the same money bag they offered you."

"I wouldn't be surprised, honey. I wouldn't be surprised. Later."

He called Lovello and told him the news.

"That's perfect," said the lawyer. "We've got this guy pegged right, Jake. He's a corrupt, power-grabbing son of a bitch, and he's also a little stupid. Good. I like going up against the stupid of this world."

"Now that you mention it, I do too," said Barclay. "I'm on my way over to see that guy with the surveillance footage. Let's find out who was stupid enough to make that final call to Jenkins."

Ten minutes later, Barclay was pulling out of the hotel parking lot in his Jaguar two-door. As far as he was concerned, it was put-up or shut-up time. Either that, or smash and grab. He was prone to grow impatient when the facts weren't immediately forthcoming. Was that such a bad trait for an investigator? In fact, Barclay knew, impatience breeds strategy.

Down the highway several miles, Barclay reflexively took notice of a dark Volvo sedan that seemed to be following him at a careful distance. He made a routine left and then down a few streets made a right. Sure enough, the Volvo stayed with him. Could it be that Thomas put a tail on him to make sure their paths didn't cross when he visited West?

Damn right it could be.

Monica rang in. "Jake, we're in business." She had followed Thomas's car to a rest area not far from Glenside. There, he'd met a man in a late-model Cadillac. The DA got into the Cadillac and, after five minutes, went back to his car, still carrying the briefcase. "I got pictures galore. Both men, and the Caddy's plate number. I'll run it now."

Barclay glanced in the rearview mirror and saw the Volvo still back there. "I wonder if that's going to come back as registered to Judge Harkins."

"The new judge on the Snook case? Hmm."

"Where is Thomas now?" asked Barclay.

"He's headed toward the courthouse, and I'm headed back to West's office."

*   *   *

In the county chambers of Judge Thomas Mooney, Deputy Attorney General Leonard Carson was making his pitch for wiretap authorizations on Clarence West's office, along with the homes of Dr. Evan Fisher and Elizabeth Jenkins. "There is evidence of serious crimes being perpetrated, Judge," argued Carson.

"I can read," growled Mooney from behind his messy desk. Mooney had only been on the county bench for three years, but he had his sights set on the next primary election for the state supreme court. A wrong decision on the eavesdropping request could blow up in his face and destroy his chances for higher office. "Yes, these *are* serious charges. What are your sources for this evidence?"

"I'm not at liberty to disclose that to the court at the moment, Your Honor. But my office is convinced the charges are well founded, based on solid undercover work."

"Isn't that big-shot private eye out of LA on the Snook case?"

"Yes, sir," said Carson. "Jake Barclay you mean. He's John Lovello's investigator."

The judge had his reading glasses on the tip of his nose and peered at Carson over the top of the frame. "If I recall, Barclay's got a reputation for pushing kind of hard, doesn't he?"

"I have read something to that effect, Judge. I don't know if it's criticism or praise."

That brought a tentative smile from Mooney. "You saw they took me off of the Snook case, and you knew I'd be pissed and ready to hit back. That's why you came to me with this application, Mr. Carson. Isn't that right?"

Carson lowered his head, then looked up with a grin. "I guess so."

"Do you know why they replaced me with Harkins?"

"I'm not privy to the situation, sir."

"And neither am I," replied Mooney. "But I goddamn well want to know what's going on. It's no secret that Judge Harkins has taken hundreds of thousands of dollars from the various trial lawyer groups. Talk about a conflict of interest." He looked back at the wire application. "What about jurisdiction? This alleged bribe money crossed state lines. That'd make it a federal case."

"Yes, Judge, but the cash in the briefcase came *from* and was returned *to* West's office. Isn't that covered under the Place of Commission clause in the Pennsylvania criminal code?"

"Which you probably read up on last night," Mooney cracked.

Carson shrugged. "Well . . ."

The judge took a deep breath. "I may be cutting my own throat, but I'll sign the warrant, Mr. Carson. Good for thirty days, renewal subject to developments. I want to be kept informed on a regular basis as to your progress, or lack of."

*   *   *

After fifteen minutes of bouncing from one street to another, with the dark Volvo keeping on his tail, Barclay was no longer amused. He drove directly to the Walt's Mart in Archville and pulled into its huge parking lot. He took a spot near the entrance to the massive building and shut off the engine. He watched the Volvo enter the lot, circle once, then park two rows behind him. Barclay got out and walked directly toward the car. A middle-aged guy in a cheap suit was behind the wheel watching him approach. The detective tapped on the window, and the driver lowered it.

"Hi there. Just wanted you to know I'll be doing a little shopping now. Need anything? Maybe some Grecian Formula to touch up that gray?"

The man's face fell flat like he'd been caught with his hand in the cookie jar. "Sir, I don't know who you—"

"Save it, pal," snapped Barclay. "I made you ten miles back. Better call your boss and tell him you need to work on your surveillance skills."

As he walked toward the store, the follower reluctantly backed out of the parking spot and headed off.

Stepping into Walt's Mart, Barclay's cell rang. It was Monica.

"Jake, you were wrong. That Cadillac doesn't belong to Judge Harkins. It's registered to a Judge Perry Schneider. Turns out he's the county's 'president judge,' whatever the hell that is."

Barclay skipped a beat, then said, "I didn't see that coming. Do we have a picture of him and Thomas together?"

"They're side views, but very distinguishable."

"Go get some prints made," said Barclay. "I'll call you in a bit."

Barclay stopped an aging door greeter, asked where he could find Ned Jameson, and was directed to the customer service desk. In short order, Jameson was paged.

Within a few minutes, a well-dressed man in his forties appeared. He stuck out his hand to shake. "Jake Barclay, right?"

"Yes, sir. You spoke to Jerry Elias, I believe."

"I sure did," replied Jameson. "Let's go in back."

Behind closed doors in the store's security center, Barclay was given a seat at a sophisticated video console running a couple of dozen high-definition monitors that covered the eighty-thousand square-foot store. Three uniformed security men were busy watching for shoplifters and weirdoes.

"Walt sure doesn't skimp on security, does he?" observed Barclay.

"No, he doesn't. This is all the very latest technology," said Jameson. He lowered his voice and leaned close to Jake. "For your information, a woman came in the other day and requested a look at the same footage you're interested in."

"That's interesting."

"She asked a lot of questions about how long we keep the surveillance footage. When I told her we delete every twenty-one days, unless there's a recorded incident, she seemed kind of happy to hear that."

"A woman?" said Barclay. "Can you describe her?"

"Better than that. She's in the footage you asked to see."

Jameson queued up the video from June 20 and pointed at a monitor. "Here you go."

Barclay watched the time counter at the bottom of the screen. At 11:18 p.m., the suspect appeared in the checkout line with a prepaid cell phone.

Jameson stopped the video and zoomed in close on the woman. "You know her?"

"I sure do," exclaimed Barclay. "Can you back up to where she entered the store?"

Jameson worked the controls and pushed the start button. The footage unrolled and Barclay watched. The woman could be seen entering the store accompanied by a man. Barclay asked Jameson to freeze the video and zoom in on him. Once again, he recognized the individual. "Can you burn that whole thing for me?"

"Not a problem," said Jameson.

Back in his Jaguar, Barclay called Lovello. "You won't believe this, John," he began.

CHAPTER TWENTY-THREE

O N HIS WAY into the county jail building, John Lovello ran into Gloria and Tommy Snook, along with Sally Powderly. They had just finished visiting Jack, and all three had that thousand-mile stare that jails evoke. "He's pretty depressed," said Gloria, tearing up. "He hasn't slept much since they said they were going for the death penalty."

"I've got a plan in the works that could put a halt to that," said Lovello. "I can't get into it now, Gloria, but keep your fingers crossed."

Sally Powderly looked away from the defense attorney and asked, "Do you have any solid suspect yet?" She appeared to be nervous and disconnected.

"In a criminal investigation, that's not the kind of information I like to reveal," said Lovello, "if you're not connected to the case." She finally made eye contact with the lawyer. "I was just wondering?"

When Jack Snook was brought into the attorney meeting room, he was clearly bushed and beat like he'd just pitched nine innings of high hard ones.

Lovello said, "Jack, I know you're upset and that's a normal reaction. But we've got a lot going for us all a sudden."

A spark of interest flickered in Snook's eyes as he took a seat at the metal table. "What do you mean?"

Lovello paced around the table, started to sit, then stayed on his feet. "We're making progress, but right now, I'm going to play a trump card, and I'll need your approval."

"Anything," said Snook, "if it gets me the hell outta here."

"This is basically a delaying tactic. Upfront, we agreed to waive the preliminary hearing. Well, since the DA's playing games by moving up the trial date, I want to petition the court to let us have our preliminary hearing." He explained that, under the law, the defendant is entitled to such a hearing where evidence is presented to determine if the case has enough merit to be bound over for further court action. "Jack, I have to tell the court you were not, let's say, 'thinking straight' when you decided to waive the original hearing. Is that okay?"

"Why not? It's true. I haven't been thinking straight since I was arrested."

"At the very least we buy time. It's a stall tactic, but there is case law behind it."

"Whatever strategy you think is right for your game plan," the retired ballplayer said.

Now, Lovello pulled out a chair and sat down. "Jack, I'm working on a lot of angles in this thing. Let me ask you . . . I saw Gloria and Tommy on their way out just now. Sally Powderly was with them. How long have you known her?"

"She's been a family friend ever since Tommy got hurt. That was two years ago. Why?"

"It's just one angle I'm working. Do you know anything about Sally's personal life?"

Snook rubbed his face with both hands like he was working to stay awake. "Well, not much. We heard originally she was dating someone for a good while and then I think they broke up. I'm sure Gloria knows more than I do. All I know is we're very thankful for the way she's helped Tommy recover. It's like a miracle."

"Does she have any relatives that you know of?"

Snook said he only knew of a brother in Florida. "I believe her parents passed away some time ago. How does Sally fit into any of this?"

"We might need her as a character witness or something," replied Lovello evasively.

Snook said he thought she'd be a great choice. "She's really a swell lady."

On his way out of the building, Lovello stopped by the guard office to see the friendly Captain Caswell. He was sitting with his feet up on the desk reading a newspaper. "Counselor," he greeted.

"How's it going, Captain," said Lovello, all buddy-buddy. "Say, let me ask you, you've lived in Archville a good while, right?"

"Fifty-nine years," replied the guard.

"Do you know Sally Powderly?"

"I know who she is, but that's all. She was just here with Mrs. Snook and the boy. She's quite a head turner. Sally, I mean."

Lovello looked out into the hall and lowered his voice. "Can we talk in confidence? Just between the two of us?"

Caswell got up and closed the door to the office. "Sure, John, what's up?"

"I realize you don't really know her, but a good-looking gal like Sally, living single in a small town . . . Maybe you've heard some bit of gossip, maybe a rumor."

Caswell looked down and then looked to the right and then finally looked back at Lovello. "I might be able to tell you something as long as I never told you anything."

"Understood."

Caswell drew in a breath. "This is something I was told by a reliable source. This guy's a cop in Archville, a pal of mine. You know him. Joe Sampson."

"Yes, he's the main witness against Jack."

"I know. It's in the paper. A few years back, Joe told me he was on night patrol and happened to catch sight of Mayor Jenkins slithering out of Sally Powderly's house 'bout four in the morning. In fact, Joe said he saw him a couple of other times leave her house late at night."

"They were having an affair," said Lovello. "People must have known about it."

"I never heard anything. None of my business."

Lovello didn't need to hear more. He thanked the captain and rushed off to the courthouse.

It was ten minutes to four when a clerk time-stamped the petition for a preliminary hearing in the matter of *State v. Snook*. Lovello then delivered a copy of the petition to the district attorney's office. He was not required to do so, but it was a courtesy he was only too happy to extend. Only too happy.

*   *   *

Barclay and Monica were waiting at the Lookout when Lovello arrived.

"Let's use the power of the press," the lawyer said. "Get your man Mars on the phone, Jake. I've got an item for him."

When he had Charlie Mars on the line, Barclay handed the phone to Lovello.

"Mr. Mars, John Lovello here. You might like to know that the defense in the Snook case has just filed a petition to hold a preliminary hearing after all. There'll probably be a hearing on the matter before the court en banc."

"Gotcha. Thanks, John. I'll follow up with the DA. I suppose you'll want to hear what he has to say."

"I'd appreciate that," said Lovello. "I'd very much like to hear his reaction."

The three of them sat on the wall while Barclay detailed his findings at Walt's Mart. Monica was more than a little surprised to hear what the two men already knew: Sally Powderly was the one who bought the prepaid cell phone. Barclay explained how she had made a clumsy inquiry into the store's backlog of surveillance footage.

Then Lovello told them about Jenkins and Powderly having an affair.

"That thickens the plot a bit, doesn't it?" observed Barclay.

"So does this," said Monica, handing over a packet from One-Hour Photo. "The pictures from this morning at West's office and at the rest area where Thomas and Schneider had their sneaky little powwow. Speaking of West's office, shouldn't I be getting back over there?"

"Right," said Barclay. "For now, let's keep on him like white on rice."

They silently watched the sexy redhead walk to her car.

"What about Carson?" asked Barclay.

"I haven't heard from him yet. Let's get back to the hotel. We've got that ball game tonight."

As they were getting into their cars, Lovello got the call from Leonard Carson. He spoke for a few moments, then called out to Barclay. "Change of plans, Jake. We're meeting Len at his club."

*　　*　　*

It was one of those gentlemen's clubs with leather armchairs and a reading room. The dining area was filled with men in three-piece suits. Carson was waiting for them in one of the secluded nooks in back. Barclay and Lovello settled in and ordered drinks.

"I've had a fruitful day," announced Carson.

Barclay and Lovello leaned forward.

"First, as you know by now, Rebecca Jenkins is alive. West swears he didn't know about it until two years ago when the IRS audited her mother. They had flagged all those expenditures going to Glenside. West represented her in the audit. At the same time, he admits Mrs. Jenkins fronted him a substantial amount of money when he ran three times for judge."

"She owned him," said Barclay.

"I'm sure of it," replied Carson. "West claims he believed that Rebecca died in 1974, just as it had been reported. Of course, that left Elizabeth Jenkins sole heir to the family fortune, estimated at that time to be in the neighborhood of $55 million dollars. A lot more now. Remember, in 1970,

Archibald Jenkins's will granted everything to Rebecca if he was deceased by the time she turned twenty-five. After the old man found out about Elizabeth's affair with Fisher, he wanted to avoid the spectacle of a family divorce, so in lieu of splitting up, he changed his will in Rebecca's favor, leaving his wife a pittance." He glanced at his watch. "Five thirty. As of a few minutes ago, a detail of detectives from my office, along with the state police and two nurses, are serving a warrant at Glenside Sanitarium. They'll be taking Rebecca Jenkins into protective custody."

"Who signed the wiretap warrant, Mooney?" asked Lovello.

"Who else? Just like we figured, he was good and pissed about being removed from the Snook case."

The waitress came and took their order for steaks and another round.

Carson had more to add from his interview with Clarence West. It seems the day after Rebecca gave birth to little Albert, her mother was making arrangements for the kid to be adopted. "When she told Rebecca, the girl lost it and went into a rage, had a real breakdown. At that point, the old lady developed a conscience and chose to keep her grandson and raise him in the family. West says Mrs. Jenkins always regretted that decision."

Carson was interrupted by the ringing of his cell phone. He listened for a moment, then said, "Did you run into any trouble? Remember, I want a guard posted 24-7. Report back when everything's in place." He closed the phone. "Rebecca Jenkins is out of Glenside and on her way to the hospital for a thorough exam. I'm told she identified herself as Rebecca Jenkins, a sign she's not completely out of her mind."

"That's great to hear," said Lovello. "Now, what about the bribes? What did West say about that little matter?"

"Oh yes, the bribes." Carson said West admitted he tried to bribe Snook's high-power defense team into leaving Archville. When that backfired, Mrs. Jenkins decided to grease other wheels—Thomas and Schneider—to get Snook's trial moved up and quickly disposed of. "West said he gave half million dollars to Thomas this morning. Of course, we have no evidence for that, or that it was shared with Schneider. If they deny it, all we have is West's word."

Barclay cleared his throat. "Would pictures and video of the DA entering West's office empty-handed and leaving with a briefcase help substantiate West's story? And maybe pictures and video of West's meeting with Schneider? Would that help?"

Carson looked at the detective with a grin. "That'd help a lot."

Barclay removed the pack of One-Hour Photo prints and a flashdrive from his pocket and handed them over. "There you go."

Carson quickly shuffled through the pictures. "Jesus, this is fabulous."

"Wait till you see the video," said Barclay. "Wonderful photography, fine acting."

CHAPTER TWENTY-FOUR

BARCLAY AND LOVELLO were in the Jaguar speeding toward the Complex for the 7:30 start of the second game in the all-star series. The traffic was heavy, and Jake made use of the car's pep to get around slow-moving vehicles. "Where the hell are we with this case?" Lovello was saying. "We've got suspects, and we've got motives. But we have to put them together in the right combination like peanut butter and jelly."

Barclay whipped around a bus and into a stretch of open highway. "One thing's clear, there are people with more of a motive to kill Jenkins than Snook ever had."

"Okay, but what motive, Jake? And who? How does Jenkins's death help or hurt anyone? I've a few ideas."

"Me too," said Barclay, "and they all point to the old woman. The family fortune wasn't just Rebecca's. It would eventually go to Albert."

"And she hated him anyway, according to what West said." Lovello nodded. "Sure, I could see her hiring someone to get rid of the inconvenient grandson."

Barclay agreed. "And maybe this hired someone waited for the opportune moment. He waited until it looked like an argument over a little league game was behind the murder, a heat of the moment anger thing."

"Instead of a well-planned murder for hire."

A few blocks from a wide intersection, they caught a glimpse of flashing lights and heard the sirens of several police and EMT vehicles as they sped past. "I wonder what that's all about," said Barclay.

When the Complex came into view, they saw the large crowds. Barclay said parking would be a problem. "Better to find a spot around here and walk over." He turned into a residential street and started looking. His cell phone rang, and he glanced at the caller ID. "Check this out. It's our man West calling."

"I almost expected that," remarked Lovello. "Let's see what story he's peddling."

It rang three times before it was answered. "Barclay."

The voice on the other end was that of a woman in distress, and she was whispering. "Mr. Barclay, this is Bernice Clark, Clarence West's secretary. I only have a moment to speak. The police are in the other room. Mr. West has shot and killed himself."

Barclay pulled to the curb and hit the brakes. "What did you say?"

"Mr. West committed suicide several hours ago," she related in a strained murmur. "Now listen. This afternoon he gave me a sealed envelope and made a point of saying I was to hand it to no one but you. Please come by the office and get it before the police find out. They'd probably confiscate it, and I promised I'd give it to you. I'll meet you outside."

"Do they know about the letter or that you're contacting me?" asked Barclay.

"No, I didn't tell them about the letter. Right now, I'm in the back room, and they're all out front and in Mr. West's office. They've been here a while."

"Just keep calm," Barclay told her. "I'll be there shortly. I'm driving a blue Jaguar. Look for it." He put the phone down and shook his head. "Here go already."

Lovello looked at him, mouth agape.

"West killed himself."

The lawyer did a double take. "For god's sake. *Killed* himself?"

Barclay swung the car back into the street and stepped on it. "He left a letter for me, and the secretary wants me to take it before the cops do." He shot the Jaguar back onto the main road and turned away from the Complex traffic. "I hate to miss a good ball game, but . . ."

*   *   *

By the time they arrived in the area, the police and medical people were finishing up. There was a modest crowd gathered on the other side of the street from West's building. Barclay parked a distance up the block, and they watched as a body bag on a wheeled stretcher was loaded into an ambulance. A few cops were milling about in front of the building, talking and filling out reports.

"See that uniformed guy in the doorway?" said Barclay. "That's Joe Sampson."

Lovello peered through the windshield. "Yeah, he's the DA's big stick against Snook. He's also the guy who saw the 'When Albert Met Sally' movie."

They got out of the car and walked slowly toward the still gathering crowd. As they got closer, a slender, middle-aged woman in a business suit left the onlookers and came toward them.

"That must be Bernice Clark," said Barclay.

"She looks scared."

They stopped and let her walk up to them. Clark looked over her shoulder once and pulled from inside her sleeve a thick, letter-size envelope. "Mr. Barclay, please take this and go."

"Thanks, Ms. Clark. Much appreciated. We're very, very sorry to hear about Mr. West."

The secretary was bathed in sadness. Again, she looked back at the crowd and the police presence around the office building. "He was really quite a decent man at heart. Oh god, and now the others too."

"What others?" asked Lovello.

She was dabbing a tissue at her wet eyes. "You don't know? It's on the news. Mrs. Jenkins and Dr. Fisher were found dead at the Jenkins house about an hour ago." She quickly turned and walked away toward the crowd.

"I'll be a son of a bitch!" muttered Lovello.

Barclay scratched his head. "A suicide pact? I don't really get that."

They made it back to the car, and Barclay opened the short letter, which they read together.

Dear Mr. Barclay:

Congratulations, you found the secrets. I suspected you would. Elizabeth, Evan, and I are very sorry for what we have done. Money really is the root of all evil. As I write this note, I know, if I had become a judge using Elizabeth's money, it would have been *me* accepting a bribe to play games with a murder trial, instead of Judge Schneider. You probably know by now that I have talked to the state's attorney and provided him with answers to many questions.

Lastly, Mr. Barclay, I want you to know that Dr. Fisher's son, Seth, had nothing to do with Rebecca. Her care was always under Evan's complete control. Seth has done nothing regarding this matter. The two other documents in this envelope relate to the Jenkins Estate and where the money is located. It belongs to Rebecca now, and God knows, she is deserving. Please tell her Elizabeth is deeply sorry for what she has done. However, she neither asks for nor deserves Rebecca's forgiveness.

Were it not for you, Mr. Barclay, who knows how much longer I would have lived this lie. I admire yours and John Lovello's ethics. Believe it or not, I once had the same ethics, until I was seduced by the money.

Sincerely,
Clarence West, Esq.

Barclay sat silently looking at the letter. "It's almost an attempt to make me feel bad."

"West was drawn to the money, and now he's paid the price," stated Lovello. "Talk about your biblical prophecies. Live by the sword and die by the sword, it says."

Barclay shook his head sadly. "But there's also 'vengeance is mine, sayeth the Lord'. I need a drink. Let's hit Marty's."

*　　*　　*

Midway through a second Dewar's, Lovello remembered he hadn't listened to the voice mail left by Thomas. He dialed up the mailbox, and Barclay listened in on the recording.

The district attorney didn't bother with niceties but bellowed out his words. "I don't know what you're up to filing for a late prelim, Mr. Lovello. However, you can be certain that I'll have the president judge dismiss your petition first thing in the morning. Good day."

Lovello clicked the phone off. "Well, well. The poor guy's all upset."

"The time stamp doesn't tell us if he already knew about the suicides," noted Barclay.

Lovello thought a moment. "I bet he knew, Jake. He's thinking that, with the major players out of the way, no one will ever know he and his asshole buddy Schneider got that money. That would mean West never told him about Carson's visit and that he'd ratted them all out."

"He kept Thomas and the judge out of the loop on purpose," said Barclay. "Because he obviously talked to Fisher and the Jenkins woman."

"Let's rattle his cage a bit and see what he thinks we don't know." He called up a number on the speed dial, and Thomas answered after a few rings. "Got your message, Mr. Thomas. Tell you what, I'll bet you a quarter-million dollars the petition will be granted and we'll receive a preliminary hearing."

The pause on Thomas's end was conspicuously lengthy.

"I hear you can afford a big bet," pressed Lovello. "I hear you had a heavy briefcase with you earlier today. That's what I hear. Are you still there?"

Thomas made a kind of disgusted, pig-grunt sound, exclaimed, "You're nuts!" and disconnected.

Lovello put the phone away and rested his elbows on the bar. "I hope *he* doesn't kill himself too. I want to see 'em lower the boom on that tubby little tyrant." He cranked up his voice and regurgitated Thomas's own words. "'I can do things like that. *I'm* the DA in these parts.' Ha!"

Word of the three suicides had crept into the background murmur around the bar, but they ignored it and kept to themselves. After a while, fans who had been at the ball game began filtering in with shouts of victory. The Archville team had won; indeed, it was a shutout, 5-0.

Not in a celebratory mood, Barclay and Lovello slipped outside unnoticed.

As they walked to the car, they quickly decided on a strategy for the next forty-eight hours.

Barclay got Monica on the phone. "You've heard, I guess."

"Of course. It's all over the television, Jake. All three a suicide? Something's fishy about that, I'd say."

"It doesn't sound right, does it?" said Barclay. "Has there been any mention of Rebecca Jenkins in the news?"

"They haven't said anything about her at all. I don't think anyone knows yet, or that'd be part of the story."

"Okay, here's the plan. I need you to do a double surveillance."

"Oh sure, you mean where I'm at two places at once?"

"That's one of your skills, darling," he reminded. "I want a tail on both Sally Powderly and on that cop Joe Sampson. Divide your time between those two."

"This thing's getting a little freaky, Jake."

"And a little deadly."

CHAPTER TWENTY-FIVE

ARLY WEDNESDAY MORNING, Barclay rapped lightly on Fred Saunders's door. It was opened by a haggard man grown older and still holding his habitual Styrofoam cup of coffee. The last resident on Desolation Row. "C'mon in, Jake. Glad you stopped by."

Barclay accepted a foam cup of the black coffee and stood in the kitchen with Saunders.

"Why did they do it?" asked Saunders. "All three of 'em."

"I'm not completely sure how things fit together, but the rough outline indicates they were all implicated in keeping Rebecca locked away for three and a half decades and couldn't face the music when they were exposed."

Saunders refilled his cup from the pot. "I'm worried about her, Jake."

"Don't be. She's safe. Last night, the authorities executed a warrant and removed Rebecca from Glenside. She's at a state hospital for observation. I've only had a tentative report, but it was all good. She's in reasonable shape, Fred, I mean considering. She's not out of her mind or anything."

"And to think all those years . . ." Saunders reached over the sink and tore off a paper towel, which he used to wipe his eyes. "If I didn't have to be to work soon, I'd visit Old Granddad. Jake, why did they keep her hidden like that? Was it really just the money?"

"Basically. The way it started," explained Barclay, "was when Rebecca gave birth to your son and Mrs. Jenkins wanted to put the baby up for adoption. Rebecca had something of a nervous breakdown over it. Since she was set to inherit the entire Jenkins estate, her mother apparently used the breakdown as an excuse to keep Rebecca secretly institutionalized, leaving Mrs. Jenkins in control of the money. I'm not sure how the story was concocted that Rebecca was dead."

"The paper just had a little item about not surviving the birth." Saunders wasn't drinking the coffee but staring into it. "Elizabeth had help from those bastards at Glenside. Even a dumbass like me can see that."

"Dr. Fisher and Elizabeth Jenkins were involved in an affair. Who knows? Maybe he was the one who came up with the idea to hide Rebecca as a way to have his girlfriend hold on to the family fortune. We'll probably never know. As a doctor, Fisher certainly facilitated the whole thing. Whatever. The fact is, they orchestrated the most depraved act of cruelty I've seen since becoming a private eye. And I've seen a few things."

A single tear rolled down Saunders's cheek, and he used the paper towel to wipe it away. "Do you think . . . do you think . . . they'd ever let me see her? I guess not, huh?"

Barclay put a hand on the janitor's shoulder. "My friend, I'm working on that. It'll be up to her doctors. Right now, the State of Pennsylvania is investigating the whole mess, and they'll have a say-so. Eventually, however, Rebecca will be free to see anyone she wants." He gave Saunders's shoulder a squeeze. "I bet the first person she wants to see is you, Fred."

"I wonder if she'll even remember me." Now Saunders straightened up and looked determined and tough. The tears were gone. "Who killed my son?" he asked.

"That's the sixty-four-thousand-dollar question," said Barclay. "But it *will* be answered. And shortly."

*   *   *

"There's no way Jake Barclay could possibly know about the cash," said Morgan Thomas. "I don't give a good goddamn how terrific a gumshoe he is. I had my chief detective shadowing him all morning. He was miles away from West's office when I was there."

Judge Perry Schneider took it all in and nodded. "And what if he had someone else watching West's building while this Barclay fellow was out giving your detective a driving lesson."

They were in a noisy diner in quiet Luzerne County, sitting at a booth where they could have a sandwich and talk without being noticed.

"All right, let's say Barclay has an assistant," conceded Thomas. "Let's say he was watching West's building and saw me there. So what? I'm an official, acting in an official capacity. I meet with lawyers and judges and law enforcement people all the time. Part of my job as DA. The most they could come up with was I had paid a visit to a man who, hours later, killed himself. Again, so what?"

"The briefcase," reminded Schneider.

Thomas waved a hand at him. "That's another 'so what.' Lawyers always carry a briefcase. Part of the uniform. In fact, the term 'briefcase' is itself a legalism. If anyone saw me and I'm asked what I had in the briefcase, what will I say? Of course I'm going to say I had some court documents in there. No one can prove differently. End of story."

"This so-called assistant detective could have followed you right to my car."

"And what will they be able to do with that information?" asked Thomas. "Nothing."

The judge toyed with the french fries on his plate. "If they have no evidence of anything on us, how did Lovello come up with this line about betting a quarter million? That wasn't any lucky guess, Morgan. He knows something, and you're full of wishful thinking."

Thomas looked pained. "I still say they can't prove anything. The only people who could hurt us are now deceased."

"What about these 'new suspects' the media's been playing up?"

"That's more of Lovello's smoke and mirrors. That's his style."

"You're sure about that?" asked Schneider. "You're convinced Snook killed the mayor?

"Put it this way, Perry, I've got a strong case, and that's all I care about."

The judge took a bite of his sandwich, chewed, and swallowed it. "Tell me about Lovello's petition."

Thomas took a one-page document from inside his suit jacket and went over the points with Schneider. "It's just a delaying move," he maintained. "Lovello's known for bullshit like that."

Schneider continued to eat and think.

"Maybe we should do this," said Thomas. "Go ahead and grant his petition. Let him have his little victory. Lovello will see at the prelim that we've got the goods on his client and we're ready to proceed with murder in the first—and the death penalty."

"So Lovello will be looking for a deal, maybe like the one his client turned down."

"Exactly," said Schneider. "Lovello won't risk Snook's neck by going to the mat with this thing. Sure, there'll be a little noise for a while, but then pretty soon, it'll be off the front page and forgotten. If they try bringing in some alleged money changing hands, it won't work. Snook's on trial, not me or you. All that stuff will be inadmissible."

"Will Judge Harkins go along with that?"

Thomas smiled as he lifted his glass of iced tea. "What do you think?"

LEO A. MURRAY

*　　*　　*

While the two corrupt officials were miles away making their corrupt plans, Monica was sitting in the rental car on a quiet residential side street in Archville. Her mini binoculars were trained on a two-story colonial several blocks away. Sally Powderly kept a modest but neat and trim house, with her newish Ford Edge in the driveway. Monica had a rock station on the radio but a commercial for a funeral home made her turn it off. "I've had enough of the dead for a while, thank you," she muttered.

She got bored with the binoculars, put them on the passenger seat, and opened up a package of Twinkies. Keeping a bare eye on the street, she munched on the treat as she checked out her camera. While she was about to eat the second Twinkie, she suddenly brought the video unit up to her eye.

A sleek Mazda sedan was pulling into Powderly's driveway to park behind the Ford. A man in a golf shirt and jeans got out of the car, and Monica zoomed in to see it was the cop Sampson. He walked up the porch steps and into the house without knocking. She kept watch for the next fifteen minutes, and then Sampson and Powderly came out carrying a picnic basket. He put the basket in the trunk of the Mazda. The couple shared a quick smooch, got into the car, and drove off.

She kept rolling as the Mazda headed down the street. Quickly, she put the camera aside, started the car, and moved out.

*　　*　　*

Lovello was at the hotel pulling himself together for the day when his cell went off. He saw it was the district attorney calling and clicked on. "Well, well, *Mr.* Thomas," he said, "have you decided to take me up on the bet?"

"You're an asshole, John. Are you aware of that? Anyway, Judge Schneider has decided to go ahead and let you hang yourself."

"In other words, you lost the bet."

"I never agreed to any bet," said Thomas. "What I agreed to do is to put your murdering client in the death chamber. But for now, Judge Schneider has decided you can have your preliminary hearing. For whatever good that'll do you."

"I love working with small-town hillbillies like you, Thomas. Because I always win."

Thomas gave out an unconvincing laugh. "We'll see who's small town. The hearing is scheduled for Friday morning at ten o'clock in Central Court. Not much notice, is it? Have fun." He did his pig grunt and hung up.

Lovello sprang into action, with no time to lose. He contacted the hotel's events manager and booked a conference room for immediate use. Then he called Barclay. "The preliminary hearing is on for day after tomorrow."

"That was a quick decision and not much notice. I wonder why."

"They're running scared, Jake. Thomas and Schneider are feeling the pressure, and they want to get this over with as soon as possible. I've just rented a 'war room' here in the hotel. Get over here as soon as you can and bring everything you have, including your timeline, the photos, and videos. Everything."

"I'll be there in half an hour," promised Barclay. "I'll call Mars and tell him about the Friday hearing. We need the press on top of this case now more than ever."

*   *   *

Monica had followed Joe Sampson and Sally Powderly to the public beach at Thunder Lake, ten miles outside of Archville. She was able to sit inconspicuously in the lightly crowded parking area, giving her a clear view of the couple. They had spread a blanket a good ways from other sunbathers and were feeding each other snacks from the picnic basket. "Isn't that sweet," cracked Monica. She set the video camera on the dashboard, lined up the shot in the fold-out screen, and let it rip.

She reached over and picked up the remaining Twinkie, watching the couple on screen.

After a while Sampson and Powderly laid back side by side, settling in for a while. The sun was only mildly bright, but they each kept their sunglasses on. Occasionally, Sampson would lean over and kiss her on the ear.

*   *   *

Barclay and Lovello were hunkered down in the hotel conference room, with items spread out on the table, including Jake's homemade timeline. Jackets off, ties loosened, they were getting tired after two hours. Lovello was pacing about, while Barclay sat at the end of the long table, looking through some papers.

"Are you convinced?" asked Lovello.

Tossing aside the documents and leaning back in his chair, Barclay said, "Yeah, you're right. You got 'em nailed."

Lovello looked at his watch. "Monica should be here shortly with the other goodies and we can wrap this case up, Perry Mason style."

"With me playing Colombo, I suppose."

"I was thinking more like Mike Hammer." Lovello picked up a copy of the *Gazette-Times* and tossed it in front of Barclay. "Seen the paper?"

Barclay had already glanced at it but now took the time to read. The lead story, of course, was the triple suicide of three prominent Archville residents. But he was more interested in the companion lead: JENKINS HEIR BELIEVED DEAD 35 YEARS ALIVE. Under Charlie Mars's byline, the piece detailed the astonishing fate and subsequent recovery of Rebecca Jenkins. Mars speculated, pretty safely, on the link between the three suicides and the Jenkins daughter's unexpected reappearance. "Certainly," Mars ended his article, "there's a mystery here that must be unraveled."

While Barclay perused the newspaper, Lovello took a call from Len Carson, who wanted to meet. "Same place? Say four o'clock?"

"We'll be there. You heard about the hearing?"

"Yeah," said Carson. "I saw it on the docket. I'm not sure what you've got up your sleeve for Friday morning, but you have my support."

Monica came in a few minutes later wearing a Madonna T-shirt and a shit-eating grin. She put her camera bag on the table, took a seat, and said, "I just left the happy lovers at her house. From the looks of that foreplay at the beach, I don't think they'll be going out anytime soon. We ready to roll here?"

"One final chore, dear," said Lovello. "Take your Sampson-Powderly video, along with all of your other stuff, Thomas and Schneider and all that, including what Jake got from Walt's Mart, and transfer it all to a single disc.

"Not a problem," replied Monica. "There's a Kinko's up the street. I'll just transfer the files right off my camera. How many copies?"

"Three will be sufficient."

Monica stood, picked up her camera bag, and looked at the two men. "You guys are up to something for this Friday hearing, aren't you?"

Barclay fixed her with his own shit-eating grin. "You might say that since we now know who killed Jenkins—and why."

"I think I do too," she said and headed out. "I'll be back in less than an hour."

Lovello was sitting at the conference table writing on a pad. He tore off the note and handed it to Barclay. "Get this for Friday morning."

Barclay read it and slipped the paper inside his pocket. "It's hardball time," he mumbled.

CHAPTER TWENTY-SIX

A T LEN CARSON'S private club, it was the early hour, and only a few retired members were in the dining room. He showed Lovello to a side table by the terrace doors. A waitress appeared, and he ordered a round of gin and tonic. When the drinks came, Carson lifted his glass. "To a job well done, John. Well done."

"Without your help, I might still be up a dark alley."

"Jake and Monica really got the goods on those clowns," said Carson. "I hate to sound like the Lone Ranger, but I don't like crooks—and I really don't like crooks in a position of power over our citizens. No sir, not at all."

Lovello grinned. "Well said, Kemasabi. What's the next move? The grand jury?"

"You bet. With West's recorded confession, obtained under warrant, along with the various pictures and videos of Thomas with his satchel of greenleaf coming out of West's office, then immediately skedaddling off for a sneak meet with Schneider . . . ha! You damn right we'll be taking it before the grand jury."

"What about Rebecca Jenkins?" asked Lovello.

Carson drank as he gathered his words. "She's part and parcel of the whole deal. I can get indictments on Seth Fisher and the administrators at Glenside. For starters, I've got 'em on false imprisonment and kidnapping. Let the grand jury determine just who knew or should have known what was really going on with their patient Gail Harding." Carson leaned forward. "I don't care what West said about Dr. Fisher's son. Seth Fisher had to have known what was going on. We'll be looking into the deep background. Who in the past may have been party to the crime, or rather, crimes."

"How's Rebecca's mental state?" inquired Lovello.

"Surprisingly good, considering the drugs and everything they've kept her on. I've got two psychologists working with her, both experienced crime victim specialists. They tell me she's responding and talking and remembers a lot. In fact, I've got a bit of news that might shock you."

Lovello leaned back in his chair, a hand on his glass. "I'm listening."

"You told me Rebecca had been taken to the cemetery for Albert's funeral, right? Well, that's not exactly precise. A little backstory. When Rebecca was in the hospital giving birth to Albert and Mrs. Jenkins found out the father was a lowly janitor, she not only tried to have the baby adopted out but told Rebecca that—get this—that Fred had *died* in a car accident."

"*What?*" reacted Lovello.

"All this time, Rebecca has been living with the thought that her beloved was dead. Now, here's what really happened at the funeral. They'd fed her a story that Fred's grave had to be moved and reburied. What reason they gave I'm not sure. So when Rebecca was driven to the cemetery where her son was in fact being buried, she was under the false impression it was *Fred Saunders* who was in the casket. Apparently, she'd never been told about Albert's murder."

Lovello shook his head. "Jesus, talk about the evil shit people do. Has she been told Fred's alive?"

"Not yet. The doctors want some time with her before bringing up any disturbing memories." Carson glanced at his watch. "I've gotta go soon. But I wanted you to hear the latest."

"Are you going to be at the hearing Friday?" said Lovello.

"Sure, I like a little entertainment now and then."

"By the way, I'm throwing a dinner tomorrow night at Russel's. Just a little celebration for a bunch of the people who're close to Jack Snook. Come on by."

"Thursday night? No, I can't make that, John. My boss is giving a party, and I definitely have to be there. Of course, the real party will be Friday morning." Carson turned somber, serious as sin. "That I won't miss."

Out in the parking lot, they shook hands on parting.

Carson said, "The murder in Archville really opened up a can of worms all around, didn't it? I'm very pleased you were on the case, Johnny. Truth, justice, and the American way. There I go again sounding like the Lone Ranger."

"Actually, that line belongs to Superman," corrected Lovello. "Which ain't too shabby either."

Back at the wheel of his Chrysler rental headed toward the outskirts of Archville, Lovello rang Barclay and told him about Rebecca's slow recovery and the 'dead' Fred Saunders hoax Mrs. Jenkins had engineered.

"That *horrible* old bitch!" erupted Barclay.

"And she got just what she deserved. Listen, change of strategy. You know under the criminal code out here I have to disclose to the DA whatever evidence I plan to present at the hearing. Fine. Have Monica put together another disc. One *without* any of the Thomas and Schneider footage. And make sure on the other one we have the Thomas-Schneider stuff in front. Follow?"

"Yes, you'll accidentally leave the wrong disc with the DA."

"I can't help it, I got mixed up," cried the lawyer. "I'm an old man. I get confused."

Barclay's chuckle had a sinister edge. "The son of bitch'll freak when he sees that footage. I'm finishing up with the dinner invites. I assume you're off to see Gloria Snook."

"She's expecting me. I won't give anything away of course. I just want her to know things are going to work out for Jack."

*　*　*

It was just before six when Lovello parked his car in front of the Snook residence. As he walked up to the porch, he saw Gloria Snook sitting there in a rattan rocking chair. She was clasping a rosary and may even have been praying. "Evening, Mr. Lovello."

"Gloria." He looked around, saw they were quite alone, pulled the companion rocking chair over next to her, and sat down. "I've got some good news."

"I could use a little good news," she remarked. She may also have been crying.

He kept his voice low but made himself clear. "Before I say anything, you have to give me your absolute word you won't mention this to anyone. I mean *anyone*. Not friends, not family. Not even Tommy or Sally or whoever. I know if you give me your word, you'll keep it."

She perked up, suddenly alive to the vibes. She nodded humbly. "Of course, if you say to keep it to myself, that's exactly what I'll do. You have my word."

"Thank you. When I first took on this case, Gloria, I knew your husband wasn't the kind of man who'd kill anyone, even a bad-news character like Albert Jenkins. He doesn't have it in him. In my line, I know the killer mentality pretty well." He looked her in the eye. "I know who the real killer is and I can prove it. At the moment, I can't tell you more than that, but I wanted you to know as soon as possible."

Tears swelled up quickly and ran down her cheek. "That means Jack . . ."

"Will be coming home. Most likely Friday."

She was dabbing at her tears with a tissue, sniffling.

He reached out and touched her shoulder. "I know it's been a nightmare, but it'll be over soon."

From a distance, the sound of boys chattering broke in on them, and she finished drying her eyes. Tommy and his teammate Vince Anders came running across the lawn and up onto the porch. "Look what Mr. Wetzel got us!" shouted Vince.

"Our own baseball cards!" added Tommy. "The whole all-star team got 'em!"

The boys left a few cards with the grown-ups and hurried inside to watch TV.

Lovello saw these were professionally photographed and printed baseball cards, just like the major leaguers have. "Wow," said Lovello, "these are great." On the back of each card, it read: Compliments of Charlie Wetzel's Used Cars. "I'm impressed."

"Mr. Wetzel's a nice man," said Gloria. "Going to all that trouble and expense for the kids, especially after paying Jack's legal fees."

"I'm certainly glad he brought me in on this case. Nobody likes to see an innocent man accused of a terrible crime. But a long-standing defense attorney like me *hates* to see it."

She actually smiled, something he had not seen her do before. "Thanks for all your work, Mr. Lovello. And thanks for telling me about . . . you know." She put an index finger to her lips.

*　　*　　*

Back in the Chrysler, headed toward downtown, Lovello again checked in with Barclay.

"We're all set for your shindig at Russel's," reported the detective. "I invited Cortino and McCracken and their wives. Mars is coming. I think he's got a girlfriend. I told Monica we want her there too, out in the open finally. What about Carson?"

"He can't make it. I'm stopping by now to see Wetzel and I'll invite him. After all, he's the man who signs the checks."

"By all means, don't leave him out," stressed Barclay.

Wetzel's huge car lot was packed with gleaming late-model used vehicles. Here and there, a salesman could be seen working on a customer. Lovello parked by the office and went inside. A secretary summoned Wetzel, and he stuck his head out from the hallway. "Come on back, John. Good to see you."

"I just stopped in to give you a quick update."

"Much appreciated," said Wetzel, showing the lawyer into his plain but well-kept office. "Sit down, stay a while." Wetzel slid in behind his desk. "What's cookin'?"

Lovello eased into a leather armchair. "I was just over at the Snooks' house. Saw those baseball cards you had made for the all-star team. That was a very classy thing to do, Charlie."

Wetzel shrugged modestly. "After the uniforms, I figured why not go all the way and give 'em a special treat. My ad agency guy handled the whole thing. It's good promotion for the lot."

Lovello shifted in his seat, all business suddenly. "Can you keep a secret for a couple of days?"

"I'm pretty good at keeping my mouth shut, especially when it's something important."

"This is important. Don't say anything until late Friday, but we found out who killed the mayor. I've got the evidence."

Wetzel slapped the edge of his desk. "*Thank you*! They say you're one of the best, and by god, they're right."

"And I thank you, Charlie, for allowing me to do my work without interference."

"I believe in letting professionals do their job and staying out of their way. It's the amateurs you gotta keep an eye on."

"We've won a preliminary hearing for Friday morning," explained Lovello. "We'll be doing a dog and pony show and unmasking the real perpetrators."

"Are you saying there's more than one?"

"I can't tell you who right now, but there are two people involved. One of them actually carried out the killing and the other was a coconspirator. When we present our evidence, Jack Snook will be freed. I hope you'll be there. Festivities start at nine a.m."

"Oh, yes. I'll be there, all right. Damn, that's great, John! Congratulations."

"Thanks. And tomorrow night, over at Russel's, I'm having a dinner for a few people concerned with Jack's case. I'd like you to be there too."

Wetzel was choosing a couple of cigars from a box humidor. He said he'd definitely make the dinner. "When I hired you, I told you Jack was innocent."

"How did you know? On the surface, he looked suspicious."

The car dealer clipped the end of a fine OpusX and handed it to Lovello. "Here, light up this cigar. How'd I know he didn't do it? Because he worked for me and I knew the guy better than most people in town. He was a brawler when he was in the majors, sure. But that was before Gloria came along, then Tommy. Jack Snook is a tried and true family man. Taking a baseball bat and using it to repeatedly clobber someone over the head until their brains run out, that takes a kind of man that Jack isn't. There's no killer instinct in him."

CHAPTER TWENTY-SEVEN

THURSDAY MORNING, JAKE Barclay pulled his Jaguar into the parking lot of a strip mall and immediately spotted Lovello standing next to the Chrysler. He parked nearby and got out with a small package in hand. "As promised, the discs of doom."

Lovello took the manila package, glanced inside, and nodded.

"Remember, disc number one has the Thomas-Schneider stuff in first place. You headed over there now?"

"Uh-huh, I want to catch Thomas and the judge early," said Lovello, "so they've got all day to fret and worry."

"How very thoughtful, John. I spoke with the security guy over at Walt's Mart. He confirmed he'll be at the hearing. I'm still on the other chore you gave me."

"We're getting there, Jake. Later."

Lovello got into his car and drove the few blocks to the courthouse.

He found Thomas sitting at his desk like a man who knows his business and has plenty of it to attend to.

Lovello opened the package. "I am officially delivering the required discovery material." He pulled out a DVD in a paper sleeve, placed it on the desk, then took a folded sheet from inside his suit jacket. "And here's the witness list."

Thomas kept hard eyes on Lovello as he unfolded the paper. He glanced over the list of names for a few moments. "And just who are Ned Jameson and Monica Thompson?"

"Jameson is the security boss at the local Walt's Mart. As for Thompson, she's on Jake Barclay's staff. You know Jake, the pushy PI who handles my investigations. I'm sure you've read about him."

"Yeah," sourly replied the DA, "the pushy guy. Why are those two witnesses?"

"To authenticate certain items of evidence."

Thomas looked up from the list. "Just out of full disclosure, how long has this sidekick of Barclay's been on the case? This Monica."

Lovello shrugged. "I'm not sure. I'll have to get back to you on that."

The district attorney's heavy-caliber stare was almost lethal. Lovello made a quick getaway. He used the stairs as opposed to waiting for the elevator. His next stop was the prison for a quick visit with his client.

The DA closed his door and put the disc in a player. He was horrified at what he saw. There he was, going into the office of Clarence West and exiting carrying a briefcase he did not have when he went in. Next on the disc were several still pictures and still more video showing the DA getting into a car with President Judge Schneider. He stopped the video.

Thomas was literally shaking when he fumbled with the numbers on the phone, trying to buzz Judge Schneider's extension. He finally punched in the right numbers only to find out the judge had not arrived yet.

The district attorney was in a panic. He called Lovello's cell phone. It rang enough times to send the call to voice mail. Thomas wasn't altogether stupid. He was not going to leave any message regarding the video. "John, this is the district attorney. Please call me at your earliest convenience."

Lovello was sitting in the prison parking lot laughing his ass off. "The fuse is lit," he thought to himself as he deleted the message.

A guard accompanied Lovello to the prisoner meeting room. He could not wait to break the good news to Snook.

"Tomorrow, you will be a free man," he burst as jack Snook trudged into the room. Noticing Snook's glum look of shock, he continued, "I am truly sorry for what you and your family have had to endure. From everything I know right now, you're damn fortunate to have Charlie Wetzel in your corner. If he had not hired me to represent you, it's an odds-on bet you would have been convicted."

Snook looked like a man who had been beaten down. He had circles under his eyes and hadn't shaved in several days. Lovello thought no one would recognize the three-time Cy Young Award-winning pitcher.

"Can you tell me who did it?" Snook rasped.

Lovello quickly debated the question with himself before answering. "You will find out tomorrow, Jack. You waited this long, what's a few more hours going to do? Take comfort in the fact that you did not kill Al Jenkins and we can prove it."

It was clear he did not have any spunk left, for Snook reluctantly folded his hands and told his lawyer he would wait. "Are Gloria, Tommy, and Sally going to be there?

Snook was assured by his lawyer they would be there. He then reached into his pocket and gave Snook the baseball card signed by Tommy. "I think it will be a collector's card," he said.

Snook was so moved, he started to weep. Big tears ran down his cheeks as he thought what a great addition the baseball card would be to the downstairs recreation room in the Snook home.

"It will all be over tomorrow, Jack," Lovello promised, and he hugged his weeping client.

Satisfied that he did not have to tell Snook who killed Al Jenkins, Lovello returned to his car. To his surprise, there were no new messages waiting.

*   *   *

Hands in pockets, Morgan Thomas paced nervously around Judge Schneider's chambers. "Yeah, that's it. Blame it on me, Perry. Remember, we're in this together."

Schneider was slumped at his desk, breathing heavy. "I warned you! Lovello and his people zeroed in on Clarence West from the start."

"I still say we can buy him off."

"Oh, *do* wake up." The judge shook his head in disgust. "Lovello and Barclay already turned down a half million. Jesus, for an empty brain box, you've gone far in life."

Thomas took out a pack of Winstons and a Bic lighter.

"There's no smoking in the building," snapped Schneider.

"Oh, shut up." Thomas lit the cigarette, hand shaking. "Let me think."

The judge rubbed his face with both hands. "What's there to think about? They've got us on film. The question is, is that *all* they've got?"

"They've got *nothing*." Thomas looked out the window distractedly. "Like I said before, so what? I was photographed with a briefcase and meeting my old friend the judge. What the hell's it prove? Who's gonna say there was money in that briefcase, huh? Besides, what's it got to do with the Snook case?"

"To hell with the Snook case," barked Schneider. "They're going for something else. You and me. Get Lovello on the phone. Find out how much he knows. Do it *now*."

Thomas tapped his cigarette into a coffee cup, took out his cell, and pushed buttons. "I'm telling you, there's nothing they can prove."

Lovello answered after a couple of rings. "What can I do for you, Mr. District Attorney?"

"Stop the crap, John. What's this stuff on the video?"

"What do you mean?"

"What I mean is, you've got this pointless video of me out doing my job. Why?"

"What are you talking about?" demanded Lovello.

"Like you didn't know!"

"Damn. You weren't suppose to see that," insisted Barclay. "I gave you the wrong disc."

"Look, what are you after? What do you want?"

Lovello said, "What do I want? How about truth, justice, and the American way? That's what I want. Don't you, Mr. DA?"

"Talk English." Thomas leaned down with the phone next to Schneider so they both could hear.

"Okay, I'll spell it out for you. It's like this, you and Judge Schneider have been exposed. West made a recorded confession a few hours before he killed himself. We've got it all on tape. We know what you two have been doing, and we know about the money in that briefcase. The attorney general's office has the evidence. I made sure of that."

Judge Schneider slumped back in his chair. Thomas's mouth was moving, but no words were coming out.

"Are you still there?" asked Lovello.

Suddenly, Schneider erupted, grabbing the cell phone and hurling it across the room, where it hit the wall and clattered to the floor. "Son of a *bitch*!"

Thomas retrieved the broken cell phone and stood looking at it like a kid with a broken toy.

"Get out of my sight!" bellowed Schneider.

"We better-uh . . ."

Schneider was up in a flash and grabbed Thomas by the shirt. "*You*! I should have you skinned alive, you incompetent fool."

Thomas broke away from the judge. "If I go down, *you* go down!" he screamed.

Schneider, sweaty and tense, stumbled back and fell into his chair. The two looked at each other, sailors on a sinking ship.

"What are you going to do?" asked Thomas.

Schneider gritted his teeth. "*Do*? You stupid ass, what the fuck can either of us do but resign!"

Thomas put the broken cell phone in his pocket. He slumped to an armchair, started to say something, then fell silent.

CHAPTER TWENTY-EIGHT

SOME HOURS LATER, an editorial clerk at the *Gazette-Times* was scanning the newspaper's inbound e-mails. One message popped out vividly—Judge Perry Schneider's resignation. It was immediately forwarded to Charlie Mars and the managing editor.

Mars jumped on it. He called Schneider's office but only got his voicemail. He tried another number and got Judge Mooney on the line.

"Are you kidding me?" spouted Mooney. "Resigned? Who sent the e-mail?"

"Margaret Benson, Schneider's secretary."

"Holy shit," mumbled Mooney. "Thanks for the heads-up, Charlie. I've got some calls to make."

In the newsroom, Mars threw together a few paragraphs about the sudden resignation and put them on the Breaking News section of the paper's website. Next, he grabbed his address book and found Margaret Benson's home phone number, which she'd given him three years ago when Schneider was running in a retention campaign. She answered with a soft, sad voice.

"Margaret, it's Charles Mars over at the *Gazette-Times*. I just got your e-mail. What's going on?"

"To be honest, I don't know. He came out of a meeting with the district attorney and was not in a good mood, to put it mildly. He gave me a letter of resignation and told me to send it out. Other than that, Charlie, I don't know anything. Maybe you can tell me."

"I'm in the dark too Margaret."

"I'm just a lowly secretary," said Benson, "who looked after the judge for the last ten years. That's all. I'm not important enough to be told anything."

Next, Mars called Morgan Thomas's office, only to find he had left for the day to prepare for the Snook hearing on Friday. He called Lovello's cell phone.

"John, are you aware that Judge Perry Schneider has resigned?" asked Mars.

"That was quick. Yes, I expected it."

"I don't get it."

"You will," said Lovello. "Meet me and Jake at the bar at the Holiday Inn at seven. We'll give you an earful."

* * *

Lovello arrived at the bar to find Charlie Mars sipping a bourbon. He invited the reporter to join him in a booth so they could talk.

Mars told Lovello the advance story on the next day's hearing was complete. However, he said the story about Judge Schneider's abrupt resignation would probably be the lead story on Friday.

"Listen, Charlie," said Lovello, "Judge Schneider and DA Thomas soon will be receiving target letters from an investigative grand jury in Harrisburg. Those two are dirty. This morning, I purposely tipped my hand for Thomas. I am certain Schneider resigned after Thomas showed him some of the evidence I kind of let slip 'accidentally'. Follow?"

"I think so." Mars listened intently as Lovello filled in the blanks about the bribe money from old lady Jenkins, with Clarence West as the middleman. "I would have thought Thomas would have resigned, given the evidence."

The reporter said he had spent the afternoon trying to track down the DA. "Is he still going to prosecute the Snook case tomorrow?"

"As far as I know," said Lovello. He took out a slip of paper and jotted a few words on it, then gave it to Mars. "Here you go. But you can't talk about this or print anything until after the hearing tomorrow.

Mars looked at the slip of paper and went bug eyed. "Are you serious?"

"Be at the hearing tomorrow and you'll see how serious," said Lovello.

Shortly, they left together and headed for Russell's and the celebration dinner.

* * *

Naturally, the big buzz was about the mysterious resignation of Judge Schneider. Indeed, it was fodder for discussion with most of the area's political players. All seemed to agree: the county's legal system was a powder keg with a burning fuse.

When Monica arrived, Charlie Mars took careful note. She was something of a knockout in heels, short skirt and a tight-fitting top. Quite

LEO A. MURRAY

a cutie. When Mars made room for her at the table, she sat down next to him. "So, you're Jake's secret agent," quipped Mars.

"Sure," she cracked, "I'm a regular Jane Bond."

While the other dinner guests were laughing and talking, Mars started interviewing her for the sidebar he would be running alongside the hearing coverage.

The dinner turned out to be more like a game of Clue, with everyone guessing who killed the bastard mayor. With a couple of drinks in him, Coach Sam Cortino came up with a goofy line, "It was clearly a suicide." That got some laughs. Bob McCracken drew chuckles when he declared, "I've got it! It was Colonel Mustard—in the jar!"

Even Jake Barclay got silly. "No, no! It was a shooter on the grassy knoll, with a backup in the Texas Schoolbook 'suppository'."

Later, Coach Cortino asked if the trio would be staying around for the Saturday game between Archville and Tri-Valley.

"You don't think for a minute we would miss a game when Jack Snook is going to be in attendance, do you?" asked Barclay. He received a rousing cheer from all.

The party finally broke up with Monica, Lovello, and Barclay huddling for a few minutes to go over plans for the hearing.

They then retired for the night.

CHAPTER TWENTY-NINE

B ARCLAY, LOVELLO, AND Monica arrived at the courthouse just after 8:30 to find Central Court filled with the concerned, the curious, and the plain nosey. "Scandal can be such fun," Barclay pointed out. Monica took a seat in back, while Lovello and the detective moved to the defense table. Morgan Thomas was officiously shifting papers as he stood at the prosecution table looking very self-important.

Barclay said, "I didn't really expect him to show up."

"Oh, he's going to take this to the mat," replied Lovello. "He doesn't have Schneider's common sense."

"Or any sense at all."

The district attorney glanced in their direction.

"Here he comes," mumbled Barclay.

There was a manufactured confidence in Thomas's demeanor as he sidled up next to Lovello in his wide-cut gabardine suit and silver tie. "One last time, John," he whispered. "Take the plea and keep your client off death row."

Lovello shook his head sadly. "That's big talk for a man who's about to be unemployed."

"You've got *nothing* that'll stand up in court."

Lovello grinned. "You and Schneider are going to wind up behind bars, while Jack walks."

Thomas leaned close. "I'll bury you, you Hollywood faggot." He eyed Jake. "*And* you."

"Shut up, fat boy," snapped Barclay. "The only thing you'll be burying is your future. I suggest you retain counsel, *counselor*."

Thomas muttered something vicious under his breath and turned away, barely able to contain himself.

"Hope he doesn't have a heart attack," said Barclay. "Of course, that'd save the state a lot of trouble."

Shortly, Jack Snook was brought in by a deputy, and he took his seat at the defense table. He was in civilian clothes and looked more rested and fit this morning. The lawyer put a hand on the accused's shoulder. "Don't worry about anything, Jack, we've got you covered."

Snook made a half-assed attempt to smile.

"I'll have you out of here very soon."

Snook nodded. "Thank you, both of you." He looked over his shoulder and winked at his wife in the first row, mouthing the words "I love you." Gloria Snook smiled weakly.

A minute later, Magistrate Maureen Smith, rotund and proud of it, entered the courtroom and swept onto her high place in the seat of judgment. "Are we ready to proceed?"

Lovello and Thomas each answered in the affirmative.

The magistrate then explained that these proceedings were being held to determine if there was enough evidence to warrant a trial on a charge of murder in the first degree. "Guilt or innocence will not be determined here. That's for a jury trial to decide. Mr. Thomas, call your first witness."

Thomas boldly announced, "The prosecution calls Robert McCracken."

The coach got up from his front-row seat and took the oath, then eased into the witness chair. He spelled his name for the record, looking oddly out of place.

The district attorney removed his glasses and held them in his right hand, still the big man with the big authority. "Mr. McCracken, were you in attendance the night the Archville little league officials voted on the makeup of their all-star team?"

"Yes, sir."

"Do you have personal knowledge that Mayor Jenkins blackballed the defendant's son from being chosen for that team? By 'blackballed' I mean, of course, that the mayor prevented the boy from being elected to the all-stars."

"Yes, I know about that."

"Please tell the court what you know. I remind you that you're under oath, sir."

McCracken was clearly nervous, glancing toward Snook, then away. "Jenkins went out of his way to manipulate the voting."

"Please explain."

"There were contracts that the city gave out," related McCracken, "and if you went along with Jenkins on different matters, not just the Snook kid, you'd get one of those contracts. By giving him my vote for the all-star roster, I got the contract for new sirens for the police, medical, and fire units. I know it was wrong, but it was impossible to do business in Archville without kicking something over to the mayor."

Thomas glanced toward the defense table. "Why was Mayor Jenkins so set on keeping young Snook off the team? The boy had the best pitching record in the city's little league."

"It wasn't about the boy." McCracken nodded at Jack Snook. "It was his father, that was who he wanted to hurt."

"Why? What did Mayor Jenkins have against the defendant?"

McCracken shook his head, shrugged. "I think it had to do with the fact that Jack almost beat him in an election back a few years ago."

"So he had it in for Mr. Snook."

"You could say that," offered McCracken.

"Thank you. No further questions."

The magistrate looked at Lovello. "Your witness."

Lovello stood, said he had no questions, and sat back down.

Barclay leaned in close and casually whispered, "I wish there was a White Castle nearby. I could eat a dozen of 'em right now."

Lovello stifled a grin, used to Barclay's advanced case of pranksterism.

Next to be called was Fred Saunders, who sat very uneasily in the witness chair. Even his Sunday best suit seemed ill-fitting.

"Mr. Saunders," began Thomas, "please tell the court what you found inside the Archville Municipal Building on the morning of June twentieth this year."

"I came to work as usual, six thirty, and found Mayor Jenkins in his office on the floor. There was a pool of blood next to him."

Thomas leaned toward the witness, prompting, "Was there anything else on the floor?"

"Yes, a baseball bat," answered Saunders with distaste. "It had blood all over it."

"A *baseball bat*, I see. And what did you do, Mr. Saunders?"

"I left the office, didn't touch anything, and went down the hall to another office and called the police."

"No further questions, Your Honor," said Thomas.

Lovello stood. "I have no questions for Mr. Saunders at this time. However, if it pleases the court, I reserve the right to recall this witness later."

"Granted," responded the magistrate.

Saunders returned to his front-row seat as the DA called his next witness, County Coroner Paul Winters.

"Your Honor," said Lovello, "the defense will stipulate to the coroner's testimony if his report is placed into evidence."

Thomas had no objections and called his next and final witness, Officer Joseph Sampson.

Once Sampson was sworn in and seated, Lovello rose again. "Your Honor, at this time, the defense will exercise its right under the General Sequester Rule. We ask that the court sequester the witnesses Fred Saunders and Sally Powderly."

"Request granted," the magistrate said perfunctorily. She gave instructions for Saunders and Powderly to leave the courtroom and wait outside in the hall until they were called.

If Thomas was curious about Lovello's strategy, he made sure he didn't show it as he turned his full attention to his lead witness. "Officer Sampson, you are employed as a police officer in the municipality of Archville, Pennsylvania. Is that correct?"

"Yes, sir." Sampson was all-polished cop, with a couple of medals on his pressed uniform.

"Do you recognize the defendant sitting at that table?"

"I do. It's Jack Snook."

"I direct your attention to the evening of June nineteenth this year," said Thomas. "Did you on that evening have a conversation with the defendant? And if so, what was said?"

Sampson was deadpan in his delivery, with little enthusiasm for his own words. "I was at Dunkin' Donuts out on the highway. Jack Snook was there, and we got to talking. That's when he told me he thought the mayor was responsible for keeping his son Tommy off the all-star team."

Thomas paced to the left, then right back to where he'd been standing. He raised his voice for good measure. "And what *else* did the defendant say on that occasion?"

Sampson licked at dry lips. "He said he was mad enough to kill Jenkins."

"Mad enough *to kill the mayor*," repeated the DA loudly. "You're sure that's what he said?"

The witness looked down. "Yes, sir."

A rumble of whispers rolled through the crowd, and Magistrate Smith pounded her gavel sharply. "Settle down or I'll have the bailiff clear the room." She broke into a toothy smile. "You wouldn't like that, would you, folks. Mr. Thomas, proceed with your witness."

"Now, Officer Sampson, after you heard that Albert Jenkins had been beaten to death, you must have instantly recalled the conversation with the defendant Snook just the evening before. Am I right?"

"Yes."

"Did you voluntarily come forward with that information?"

"I did."

"No further questions, Your Honor."

Now, the witness was turned over to the defense for cross-examination.

Lovello stepped up with notepad in hand. "Mr. Sampson, your testimony is that Jack Snook told you he was so mad over the all-star team passing up his son he could kill Mayor Jenkins. Is that correct?"

"Yes, that's what I just said."

"Well, you're a police officer. You know the laws. Didn't you feel compelled to arrest Snook right there at Dunkin' Donuts for making a terroristic threat?"

"No, I did not."

"Did you warn the mayor of Snook's anger?"

"No, sir."

"Why not?" pressed Lovello.

Sampson shrugged. "I thought Snook was only letting off steam over his son not making the all-star team."

"In other words, you didn't feel he was serious about killing Jenkins. Is that your testimony?"

Sampson's face was reddening ever so slightly. "That is correct," he said.

Lovello took his time as he flipped through the notepad; no one could see the pages were blank or filled with doodles, just one of his little courtroom gimmicks. "Tell me, Officer Sampson, what does '10-7' mean in police jargon?"

"It means 'out of service', taking a break."

Lovello turned to nod at Barclay. The detective brought forward some papers, handing one each to the DA, the magistrate, and Sampson.

"I'd like to enter this document into evidence, Your Honor."

"So ordered."

"Now, Officer, please tell the court what this document is."

Suddenly, Sampson didn't seem all that coplike, more like a simple man backed into a complex corner. After looking at the paper a long moment, he said, "It's my duty log for June nineteenth and twentieth, the night the mayor was killed."

"According to the sheet, Officer Sampson, you were 10-7, or out of service, at the municipal building on June twentieth at twelve ten a.m. and again at four a.m. Is that correct?"

"I guess so."

"You guess so?" Lovello raised his voice. "Either you were or you were not off duty at those times on the official record."

"Yes!" blurted Sampson impatiently. "I was out of service during those times."

Lovello reminded the witness that the coroner had fixed the mayor's time of death as occurring between midnight and 1:30 a.m. "You didn't notice anything unusual on the two occasions you were at the municipal building?"

Sampson shook his head and said he had not noticed anything out of the ordinary.

"Did you use the main entrance to the building when you were 10-7?"

Sampson said that he had, in fact, used the main entrance because the police entrance was closed for renovations.

"Do you have a key to the main entrance?" continued Lovello.

"All police officers have a key."

"Did you use your key both times you were 10-7?"

Sampson was getting redder in the face. "Yes, of course, I used my key."

Thomas stood with an objection. "Enough with the key, Your Honor. Can't we move on to something more substantive?"

"Overruled," responded the magistrate.

"Your Honor," said Lovello, "I will now exercise my option to hold this witness over and to recall Fred Saunders."

Again, Thomas objected. "This is a hearing, judge, not a trial. Saunders has already testified."

"Overruled. Mr. Lovello has received the court's permission to recall the witness."

Thomas sat back down with a slow, old man's unsteadiness. Saunders was brought in from the hall, and the magistrate reminded him he was still under oath.

"Yes, ma'am."

Lovello went over to the railing around the witness box. "Mr. Saunders, did you find anything suspicious with respect to keys on the morning you found the mayor in his office?"

"Yes, I did."

"Please tell the court what you found."

Saunders drew in a deep breath, ready to plunge. "I found the mayor's key had been left in the entrance door lock."

"How did you know they were the mayor's keys?"

"From the tag on the key ring. It says 'Mayor' on it."

"Thank you, Mr. Saunders, I have no further questions." Lovello looked at the DA. "Your witness."

Slyly, Thomas declined to question Saunders.

Now, Lovello had Sampson recalled to the stand.

"You have just heard Mr. Saunders's statement that the mayor's keys were in the building's front entrance at six thirty a.m. on the morning of the twentieth, did you not?"

"I heard the testimony," said Sampson, tight-faced and pulled in.

"Well now, if the mayor was killed between midnight and one thirty, that means the keys should have been in the door both times—or at least one time—when you went 10-7 at the municipal building. Yet, you have testified that you used your own key and that you saw nothing 'out of the ordinary'."

Sampson was showing signs of unraveling but piped up loud and firmly. "Those keys were *not* in the door when I went to the building."

"How do you account for Mr. Saunders's testimony that the keys *were* in the door that morning?"

"Objection!" blasted Thomas. "He's asking the witness to assign motive."

Magistrate Smith consulted something on her computer screen. "Sustained. The defense will rephrase the question."

"Your Honor, the matter of that key is critical to my client's proof of innocence." Lovello looked over at the DA. "However, I shall rephrase as the court wishes." He squared off at the cop on the stand. "Mr. Sampson, did you happen to notice—when you were twice 10-7 at the municipal building in the early hours of the twentieth—did you happen to notice anything belonging to Mayor Jenkins anywhere near the front entrance? Perhaps even something left on the steps?"

Sampson was scared but doing a reasonable job of hiding it. "No. I didn't see anything, including keys that belonged to the mayor. Look, Saunders is mistaken. He's been known to take a drink or two. I don't know what he saw, but I know what I saw. There were no keys in that door when I went to the building."

"That's your absolute last word on the subject?"

Thomas got to his feet. "Your Honor, defense is badgering the witness."

"Overruled. You may answer the question."

"My last word," grumbled the witness, "is that I saw nothing belonging to Jenkins, including his keys, in the door or the front entrance area."

Lovello nodded slowly, methodically, letting the wheels slow. He did some more page-turning in his blank notepad, "reading" a page carefully before turning to the next; it really was a cute act and never failed to intimidate, intimidation being just one item in the toolbox. The crowd was literally "hushed," leaning forward in their seats. Once his minimalist theatrics had sucked in all attention, Lovello looked up from the notepad and went on to casually ask, "Officer Sampson, how long have you been romantically involved with Sally Powderly?"

A low buzz erupted from the crowd, the gavel went down hard, and Thomas leapt up, a note of hysteria in his voice. "Objection! Your Honor, Officer Sampson's romantic life is not at issue here."

The magistrate paused, thinking, then nodded. "Under the circumstances, I'll allow it. But please do not wander too far, Mr. Lovello."

"I repeat," said Lovello, "how long have you been romantically involved with Sally Powderly?"

Sampson was apparently on the verge of losing it and was trying his damnedest to keep control. "I am not involved in a relationship with her."

"You're sure of that?"

"Objection!" barked Thomas. "The witness has answered the question."

"Sustained."

Lovello went back to his notepad for just a moment. "All right, you say you are not in a relationship, a romantic relationship, with Ms. Powderly."

"That's what I said," sneered Sampson.

Lovello went back to the defense table. Jack Snook watched with great interest as the attorney picked up a DVD disc. "At this time, Your Honor, I'd like to enter a short video into evidence."

"So ordered. Bailiff, assist defense with the equipment."

The player was set up on the defense table and the large liquid-crystal screen to the left of the bench was turned on. When the lights in the courtroom were dimmed, Barclay stepped over and inserted the DVD. "Ready, Your Honor," he said.

"All right, let's see the evidence."

The screen popped on with a static shot of a residential street, with Powderly's trim, blue-and-white house centered in the shot. Her Ford

Edge could be seen in the driveway, as well as the stylish Mazda parked behind the Ford. "For the record," stated Lovello, "I point out that the time stamp on the screen is showing that this footage was captured yesterday morning."

"So noted," responded the magistrate.

On screen, a man in sunglasses, jeans, and a golf shirt, who looked exactly like Joe Sampson, could be seen coming out of the front door with Sally Powderly, who wore shorts and a T-shirt. The image zoomed in close on them. The man had a picnic basket in one hand and an arm around her waist. After the basket was placed in the trunk of the Mazda, the couple shared a brief kiss, then got into the car.

"Jake," said Lovello, and the video was paused.

When the lights were brought back up Sampson became the focus of all eyes. He was not squirming or moving around but remained rigid and unmoved, in the way many men face a firing squad. He was still and licking dry lips.

"Mr. Sampson," said Lovello, "I can play more of the footage from yesterday for you if you like. Or you can save the court's time and patience by answering truthfully. How long have you and Ms. Powderly been romantically involved?"

CHAPTER THIRTY

S AMPSON SPRANG OUT of the witness chair with a raised fist. "You *re*tard! This has nothing to do with Snook killing the mayor!"

"On the contrary, it has *everything* to do with it," yelled Lovello. "Because *you* killed Albert Jenkins!"

For a full beat, the silence was as complete as the vacuum of space, then the courtroom exploded in a cascade of noise and confusion, a storm sweeping up all in its path. Jack Snook rose from his seat, agog. "What in the—?"

The magistrate sat stunned for several moments before banging the gavel. "Quiet! Quiet down!" It had little effect until she stood and screamed like she was trying to close down a rock concert. "Shut *up*!" The crowd noise faded quickly. "*Thank* you!" she cracked without a hint of gratitude. She looked at the witness and growled, "Sit *down*, Officer!"

Sampson sank back into the chair. "Judge, I won't *dignify* his crap with a response!"

"Because you know I can prove it!" responded Lovello.

"Objection!" sputtered Thomas lamely, confused and ignored.

"Objection overruled!" Smith shot a glance toward a low murmur from the back rows, which ceased instantly.

Barclay leaned back in his seat and folded his arms like he was waiting for instructions on who to punch.

"Now that we have everyone's *attention*, defense may continue. Officer Sampson, please answer counsel's question."

"The hell I will! I'm taking the Fifth with this creep!"

"Fine, that is your right," she replied. "You may step down and resume your seat."

"No thanks!" the cop said as he left the stand. "I'm out of here."

"I'm about to find you in contempt, Mister. *Resume* your seat."

Sampson gave her a tough-guy look. "You don't have anywhere near the authority to keep me here." He started toward the aisle but was blocked by a deputy sheriff.

"You'll see what authority I have. Deputy, escort the witness to his seat. Make sure he's nice and comfortable." That drew a low-ball snicker from somewhere, but the judge ignored it.

Joe Sampson stood firmly in front of the deputy, then apparently thought better of whatever he was thinking of doing, and allowed himself, snarling, to be shown to the front row.

The magistrate nodded at Lovello. "Call your next witness."

"Thank you, Judge. I now call Sally Powderly."

A deputy summoned her from the hallway. She came into the courtroom looking sedately feminine in a simple skirt and blouse, blonde hair neatly coiffed. Powderly was sworn in, and she took the stand.

Lovello flipped through a couple of pages in his trick notepad and that seemed to bother the witness. Good. "Ms. Powderly, do you sometimes shop at the local Walt's Mart?"

Her voice was firm and direct, though cautious, leery of a trap. "Of course, everyone does around here."

"I understand. At this time, I'm going to show you a video clip and will ask you to tell the court what you see." Lovello nodded toward one of the deputies, who dimmed the lights. "Okay, Jake, clip number 6, please."

The surveillance footage unrolled with a close angle on the busy checkout counter at the popular big-box store. In the center of the frame was a woman with blond hair wearing a long-sleeve top.

"Freeze it right there, Jake."

The witness glared at the static image on the screen.

"Ms. Powderly, do you recognize this customer at the cash register?"

"No, sir."

"Look closely."

"Objection!" asserted the DA. "The witness has answered the question."

The judge was eyeing the video with interest. "Overruled."

"But, Your Honor—"

"Overruled."

Morgan Thomas sank back into his chair, a bloated, half-defeated creature.

"Ms. Powderly, that's you in that video buying a prepaid cell phone, isn't it? Don't you recall?"

Now, her easy feminine grace began to peel off like cheap varnish. "I do not."

"You've said that you sometimes shop at Walt's Mart. Do you ever wear a wig when you go there?"

Powderly opened her mouth, but nothing came out.

"I remind you," said Lovello, "you've sworn to tell the truth. Perjury is a serious crime. I ask you again, is that you buying that cell phone on the night of June nineteenth?"

She bit her lip, looked toward Sampson, then away. "It might be. I told you I shop there sometimes like everyone in Archville."

"Why the blond wig?"

She offered a half-ass smile. "Yes, I wear a wig when I don't have time to fix my hair. That's not a crime. A lot of women do that."

"I see." Lovello made it sound like he didn't see at all. "So, you admit that's you buying the cell phone?"

Thomas stood. "Objection! Your Honor, we have no idea if this video is authentic or in some way doctored. That's easy to do these days."

"Judge," interjected Lovello, "I have here in the courtroom the security chief from Walt's Mart who will testify to the genuineness of the evidence and the item that was purchased by this witness. We have available the original time-stamped receipts."

"Objection overruled. Proceed, Mr. Lovello."

Now Lovello moved closer to the witness stand. "You bought that cell phone, didn't you?"

Powderly came apart so quickly it was shocking. She gasped and looked toward Sampson.

"This is all *bullshit*!" yelled the cop.

"Quiet!" shouted the judge. She looked at the witness. "Answer the question."

"Don't tell 'em a goddamn thing!" shouted Sampson.

Magistrate Smith banged her gavel. "You are now in contempt of court, sir. Deputy, take Mr. Sampson into custody. Put him in the holding cell until further notice."

The deputy came forward and put his hands on Sampson, who shoved him off. "You don't have the authority!" The deputy grabbed Sampson by the hair, bent his head down, and brought his knee up sharply into the cop's face. Sampson was slammed back in the seat, then bounced forward into the deputy's arms, dazed and bleeding from the nose. "Come along quietly," warned the deputy, "or I'll cuff you right here in front of everyone." Two other deputies moved up next to Sampson and jerked him out of his seat. He was led away sputtering and cursing.

The magistrate turned her attention back to the witness. "Answer counsel's question or you too will be held in contempt."

Powderly did not have much fight left. "What was the question?"

Lovello was losing patience but enjoying it. "You know very well what I'm asking. Did you buy a prepaid cell phone at Walt's Mart on the night of the nineteenth? A simple yes or no will suffice, young lady."

"Objection," said Thomas. "Counsel is badgering the witness."

"Overruled." Smith looked at Powderly. "This is your last chance. Did you buy the phone or not?"

Powderly's voice was so low she could barely be heard. "Yes."

Lovello was pacing in front of the defense table, lining up his guns. "All right, we've established that you're the person in this video. Now, how many calls did you make on that Samsung phone?"

The witness wasn't looking at anyone but had taken a great interest in her lap. "I don't remember."

"Then let me refresh your memory," said Lovello. "AT&T records I will introduce into evidence show that the phone was used for just one call, one call, and that call was to Mayor Albert Jenkins's cell phone. Does that help you remember?"

"No, it doesn't," declared Powderly.

Lovello went back to flipping pages in his intimidating notepad. "You don't remember. Is that your testimony?"

"I just said that."

"All right, let's take this one step further. According to Walt's Mart's security supervisor, who is right here in the courtroom, you went in a few days ago to inquire about the store's surveillance system and how long the footage was kept before being erased. Do you deny that?"

Powderly threw up her hands. "I was just curious, that's all."

"But why?" pressed Lovello.

"I *said* I was just curious. That's why."

Lovello moved directly in front of the witness stand. "How long have you been romantically involved with Joe Sampson?"

"Who said I was . . . We're just friends," started Powderly, before trailing off into silence.

"Jake, roll video. Clip 3, please."

This time the footage showed Sampson and Powderly lying on a blanket at the beach, kissing and hugging like teenagers.

The witness was in tears and used a tissue to dab at her eyes. She was no longer looking at the screen.

The district attorney stood, blathering, "*Your* Honor, this witness is obviously distressed. Mr. Lovello has a reputation for—"

"Sit down, Mr. Thomas. You begin to bore me with your poorly conceived objections. I'm not interested in Mr. Lovello's reputation. A man was murdered in this jurisdiction. The people demand justice. And that's what they're going to get." The magistrate turned to the witness. "I suggest you answer counsel's questions without further dissembling." When Powderly looked confused, the judge added, "*Dissembling*, that means *lying*."

The courtroom was absolutely silent. Powderly was a train wreck heaped on a chair.

"Proceed, Mr. Lovello."

The defense lawyer said, "You and Joe Sampson were lovers—we can see that on the surveillance video captured by a member of my staff. Do you deny it? Or, are you going to continue to lie and get into more trouble than you're in already?"

Powderly was wiping her tears away with a tissue. "Yes," she finally eked out.

"Yes *what*?"

The witness glanced around the courtroom like she was looking for an escape hatch.

"Answer the question, and *truthfully*," the judge scolded.

"Yes, yes, yes!" blurted out Powderly. "We are a couple! So what?"

Lovello let that sink in before going on. "That's better. Now, my next question, and you really need to tell the truth, young lady."

"Objection!" called out Thomas. "He's prejudging her testimony."

"Sustained. Defense will refrain from leading the witness."

"Yes, Your Honor," said Lovello. "Ms. Powderly, you've admitted, reluctantly, a romantic relationship with Joe Sampson. But what about Mayor Jenkins? Were you ever involved romantically with him too?"

It was all coming apart now, and Powderly was like a lost child trying to find her way back home. "We dated," she said quietly.

"Okay, you were involved with Albert Jenkins. What happened to that relationship? I suggest he dumped you. Isn't that true?"

"That's ridiculous!" she snapped.

"Isn't it true, Ms. Powderly, that you had a grudge against the mayor because he jilted you? Perhaps even made certain promises he never kept?"

"Objection," said Thomas without enthusiasm. "Counsel is still leading the witness."

"Sustained."

Lovello paced, stopped, paced some more. "All right. We've established, haven't we, that you were in a relationship with Joe Sampson *and* before that with Jenkins. Now I ask you, did Sampson tell you that he hated Jenkins because he kept him from getting the job as Archeville police chief? Isn't that true?"

"I never heard him say that."

"Did you help Sampson beat the brains out of Mayor Jenkins?"

"Of *course* not!"

"Why did you use that cell phone you bought to call the mayor just an hour or so before he was killed? Was it to set him up for murder?"

"No, it was just a social call to test the phone," responded Powderly.

"A social call at midnight. I see. A former boyfriend you called at midnight. Which of you killed the mayor? Was it both of you or just you or just Joe?"

"Objection, Your Honor!" barked Thomas from his seat. "He is again leading the witness."

Magistrate Smith looked at her computer screen and thought for a moment. "As I said in my opening remarks and the prosecution has itself pointed out, this is *not* a trial. This is a *hearing* to determine if there is enough evidence to try Mr. Snook for capital murder. Any evidentiary material that tends to prove someone else did the killing is within the purview of this hearing. Objection overruled."

Lovello wasted no time hitting the mark. "Sally Powderly, I ask you again, while you're under oath in a court of law, whose idea was it to kill the mayor? Yours, because he jilted you, or Sampson's because Jenkins kept him from getting the job as police chief?"

There was no sound at all coming from the spectators. All eyes and ears were on Powderly. She sat there looking destroyed and distraught.

"Ms. Powderly," prompted the judge.

And now it all came out in a rush of emotion and guilt. "It was Joe," she said mechanically. "I had nothing to do with it. Yes, I was mad at Albert after we broke up. We were supposed to get married, but he lied and tricked me. Albert was only interested in sex and his own self-importance. A hideous man! He was so goddamn high on himself. He had the Jenkins name and thought he ruled everyone in Archville. The son of a bitch! I'm glad he's dead, dead, *dead!* Yes, Joe was pissed because he didn't get the police chief's job." She wiped at her eyes with a tissue, make-up smeared, no longer an attractive young woman, but a grotesque thing that talked. "It was Joe's idea to use Mr. Snook's anger over the all-star roster as a cover for . . . for what he did."

"You made that late-night call to set up Jenkins, didn't you?" stated Lovello.

"Yes. Joe wanted him in his office when no one was around."

"Where did the baseball bat come from?"

"I don't know," said Powderly. "But he wanted to make it look like it had something to do with the all-star thing. The whole thing hinged on Jack Snook saying he wanted to kill Albert."

"And you were there when he . . . killed the mayor?"

"Yes!" she shouted. "And I was so goddamn happy to see Albert like that, begging for his goddamn life. He was such a coward!"

*   *   *

Lovello looked at the magistrate and suggested that someone should read Ms. Powderly her Miranda rights.

"It's a little bit late for that, Mr. Lovello," the magistrate said.

Jack Snook was shaking in his seat. After hearing Sally's confession, he desperately wanted to hold his dear wife and their lad. Jack had never figured there would be an outcome like this. He was getting tense.

Finally, the defense attorney asked for his client's immediate release. "So ordered," said the magistrate. She also ordered the deputies to take Ms. Powderly into custody.

Tears of sorrow and joy were streaming from Gloria's eyes as she made her way to the defense table. "This has been such a nightmare," she said as she embraced Jack with a hug and a kiss. Tommy was right behind her. The three of them turned to John Lovello and offered their thanks. The tears were flowing as the trio told Lovello he had performed a miracle. Jack hugged his attorney. "God bless you, John Lovello," he said. "You got my life back for me. How can I ever repay you?"

"I don't think it amounted to a miracle," he said. "And I am sorry about Sally. I know she was your good friend. We just went where the evidence took us."

"Apparently not that good," said Gloria, still wiping tears from her eyes and holding on to Jack and Tommy like she would never let go. "I can't believe that *fucking bitch* stayed so close to me and Tommy knowing Sampson killed Jenkins and she watched it," said Gloria.

"That was the only way they could keep tabs on what was going on," explained Lovello.

"That is why I could not reveal the names to you when we spoke yesterday."

The elder Snook seized the moment to tell his son that while Sally Powderly had greatly assisted in his hand injury recovery, she had gone "bad." "Please, son, do not be afraid to put your trust in people," he said. "Most people are good and worthy of your trust."

Meanwhile, DA Thomas was packing up his papers at the prosecutor's table. He walked over to Lovello and offered his hand to shake. Lovello decided to be a gentleman about it and shook Thomas's hand.

"You know, John, I'm going to need a really good lawyer."

"Stop right there," said Lovello. "I only represent the innocent."

Thomas was livid. He slammed his briefcase closed and practically ran from the courtroom.

"What's the matter with him?" asked Jack Snook.

"I think he has a legal problem," said Lovello.

Snook was using his hand to wipe the tears of joy from his tired eyes. Well-wishers had pushed their way to the front of the courtroom to congratulate Snook and Lovello. Jack literally pulled his attorney to the side so he could talk to him. Lovello offered him his handkerchief.

Snook once again embraced him in a big bear hug. "John," said the teary-eyed Snook, "I want to pay you for your services."

Lovello waved his hand back and forth. "My fee has already been paid by Charlie Wetzel," Lovell said.

"No," said Snook. "That's not what I mean." The ex-baseball player then told his attorney he wanted to give him one of his championship rings as a reward for his work.

Lovello was stunned. He told Snook he could not, and would not, take the ring. "You earned those rings, Jack. You deserve them. Someday, they will be Tommy's. And I would guess, at this point, Tommy will be adding to the Snook treasures."

Snook hugged his attorney one last time. "You're a good man, John Lovello."

CHAPTER THIRTY-ONE

L OVELLO WANTED TO get his client out of the courthouse as quickly as possible. Avoiding the press, however, was going to be difficult. After all, it was nearing noon, and all three affiliate television stations had live broadcasts scheduled. He conferred with Monica and Barclay.

The two detectives suggested to Lovello that it might be better to have a controlled environment for a press conference. The defense attorney agreed. "But where?"

Barclay suggested the Snook home for 5:30. "We can manage it from the front porch and make the six o'clock news. When it's done, we take Jack inside and leave no opportunity for questions afterward."

Lovello said he liked the idea.

"I'll handle the announcement outside," said Barclay. He instructed Monica to escort the Snooks to Gloria's car. "If you run into any reporters, tell them to be at the Snook house for 5:30."

With little trouble, Monica managed to get the Snooks to the car. She returned to the courthouse to find Lovello and Barclay talking with Deputy State Attorney General Carson.

Arrangements were being made, she learned, for Fred Saunders to see Rebecca Jenkins Saturday morning at ten.

Barclay told the attorney he would bring the janitor to the hospital. "It will be interesting to see how it turns out," he added.

During the conversation, Carson also told the trio that he had sent "target" letters to Judge Schneider and DA Thomas, informing them that they were the targets of a grand jury investigation.

"Can you believe it?" asked Lovello. "Thomas actually approached me to represent him."

They all enjoyed a laugh.

Barclay then called Charlie Mars. "We're going to that Irish-themed pub up the street from the courthouse if you're interested," said Barclay. Mars said he had already filed his hearing story and would meet them there.

On the walk up the street, Lovello asked Jake and Monica what they thought about telling Mars about the "target" letters being sent out.

"We owe the guy," said Barclay. "He's been a tremendous asset."

It was decided to give the information to the reporter. "However," said Lovello, "it cannot be attributed to us."

Monica and Jake agreed.

While the trio waited for Mars, Lovello admitted he didn't feel one bit sorry for DA Thomas and Judge Schneider. "They took money to play games with a trial that could have cost a man his life. They were owned lock, stock, and barrel by old lady Jenkins. They'll get what they deserve."

However, when Mars arrived, he already knew about the letters being mailed. Monica, Jake, and John were not surprised. "I have a good source in the state attorney's office," he explained. Mars's friends marveled how seriously Charlie Mars took his work.

What Mars didn't know, however, was the magnitude of the bribes. Lovello gladly filled in the blanks for him.

Barclay excused himself. "I have to see Fred Saunders to inform him about the reunion tomorrow."

Mars inquired about the "reunion" and asked if he could be there.

However, Lovello advised against it. "There will be plenty of time for stories later on. I think it should be a one-on-one meeting. After all, it has been thirty-five years."

Nothing more had to be said.

On the way to Archville, Barclay once again reminded himself of the Grateful Dead song, "Truckin'": "What a long, strange trip it's been."

Saunders had taken the day off from work for the hearing, but Barclay was not surprised when he did not answer the knock at the door. The detective knew where to find him.

Barclay walked up to the American Legion. He found the janitor enjoying his beer and Old Granddad. "I have good news for you, Fred. Arrangements have been made for you to see Rebecca tomorrow morning at ten."

Saunders took a deep breath and released it slowly. Then he ordered another Granddad.

"I have doubts," he said. "You can't just make things right after thirty-five years."

The detective admitted to Saunders it was only natural—and right—that he have doubts.

Pointing at the shot glass on the bar, Barclay told his friend, "There would be no answers found in there."

Barclay ordered a Yuengling. "It's been thirty-five years for Rebecca too," he said. "You owe it to yourself and to Rebecca to at least meet."

Saunders, near tears, said he was afraid she might reject him. "I thought about her night and day. If I only had known she was alive, I could have rescued her myself."

Barclay dismissed the statement. "Listen, Fred. Rebecca is the victim here. The victim of a cruel old woman who put money above everything else most people hold dear—family, love, and friendship."

Saunders could not hold back his tears. He lifted his shot and was shaking so bad he nearly spilled it. "I'm trying to pull it together," said Saunders. "But I can't."

Barclay told Saunders they were both very alike. The janitor raised his eyebrows. "That's right, Fred. We survived a war in a country where the host population wanted us dead. I don't know about you, but each time I think about my survival, I get stronger."

The detective insisted that his new friend look at the positive side of things. "Just meet with her," he said. "I realize that one meeting is not going to replace thirty-five years and erase all of her bad memories, but it will be a start."

Saunders agreed with Barclay's assessment. "Now that you said it," said Saunders, "I do feel new strength when I think about my survival."

Barclay breathed a sigh of relief. "I'll pick you up at nine a.m.," he said. "And don't drink too many more of those things," Barclay said, pointing once again at the shot glass.

Barclay looked at his watch. He had just enough time to go back to the hotel and change before the press conference at the Snook house.

Meanwhile, Jack Snook was home and feeling comfortable with his freedom when there was a knock at the door. Snook pulled the door open to find Charlie Wetzel standing on his porch.

"I know grown men do not usually do this," said Snook, "but I'm going to do it anyway."

The big former major league pitcher put his arms around Wetzel and hugged him. "Thanks for everything, Charlie. I don't know how I'll ever repay you."

Wetzel insisted there would be no discussion of repayment. "I did what I did because I believed in you, Jack." However, the used-car dealer told Snook he would like a VIP pass when he was inducted into the Baseball Hall of Fame.

"The sportswriters passed on me once already," said Snook. "What makes you think I'll be inducted now?"

Wetzel told him not to worry. "I'm sure you'll be nominated next year."

Just then, three vans from a catering company pulled up in front of the Snook house. Jack was curious.

"Oh yeah," said Wetzel. "I was banking on you getting released today, so I ordered enough food for a party." He went into great detail about how disappointed he was when the last one was cancelled on the night Tommy was blackballed.

"Charlie, you've done enough," said Snook. "Let me pay for this."

Wetzel would have no part of Snook coming up with any money. However, the used-car salesman also knew the media would be there soon for the press conference, and it was likely that his generosity would be mentioned and he would be able to write the impromptu party off on his taxes.

As the caterers went about setting up the tables and chairs, Gloria looked outside. She hadn't planned on a party that night, but she knew her son deserved a celebration after what had happened to the original one; they all did. She quickly learned it was Wetzel who was behind the event.

Gloria Snook found Wetzel talking to Charlie Mars. "Jack and I very much appreciate all you have done, Charlie Wetzel."

He smiled warmly. "It was my pleasure, Gloria. It's justice for good people."

At that, Gloria Snook walked over to Wetzel and gave him a big kiss on the cheek. "I don't know why there are so many jokes about used-car salesmen," she said. "The one I know is an angel."

Wetzel chuckled at the notion of being an angel. "Don't say that too loud or I might get a bolt of lightning from the Big Guy upstairs."

As the media began assembling and readying cameras and microphones, Lovello and Barclay briefed Jack Snook on what he should and shouldn't say.

"Right now it's the KISS plan: Keep It Simple, Stupid," said Lovello.

It was time to face the reporters. Three cars pulled up on the opposite side of the street.

The cameras shifted and started rolling. The all-stars had just returned from their final practice before the big game with Tri-Valley on Saturday.

Naturally, the all-star team had become darlings of the media. Much to the amusement of Snook and Lovello, the cameras turned onto the team first. Only after enough video of the team's arrival had been obtained did the press conference begin. Jack Snook stood on the front porch with Gloria beside him. John Lovello announced that there would be a brief statement and time for only a few questions.

"I don't know where to begin," said the ex-ballplayer. "I know I'm glad to be back with my family, and I owe a great deal of thanks to the people who believed in me."

The man who had accomplished so much in the baseball world choked up, and tears rolled down his cheeks. He pulled Gloria close to him and kissed her. "Let me see you put that on the news," he said.

Jack "Snuff" Snook, the hulking ex-baseball player, was crying on national television, showing the major league world that he was really human. "I can't go on with this," he said.

"Give me a few days to adjust, and I will answer all of your questions."

As Gloria and Snook embraced once more, they looked around for Tommy.

"He should be here with us," said Gloria.

"I'm sure he wouldn't want to miss a 'Kodak moment' like this," said Snook, and everyone laughed.

However, Three Fingers and the rest of the team were huddled under the oak tree in the front yard. They were devouring a tray of porketta sandwiches that had been taken from one of the tables in the yard.

"You'd think they haven't eaten in weeks," said Gloria.

The news media refocused their attention to the team. Jack Snook asked Lovello and Barclay to come into the house with him. He led the two men down to the recreation room.

"I can't begin to find the words to thank both of you for the tremendous job you did to find the real killer." He began to fiddle with the glass case holding two World Series rings.

"As a small token of my appreciation, gentlemen, I want each of you to take a ring. They are just symbols of years gone by. I want you to have them."

Lovello was the first to speak. "What did I tell you earlier? Put those damn rings right back where they belong, Jack. You owe us nothing. This whole matter was a rewarding experience for me and Jake. Undoubtedly, it will end up in our memoirs some day."

Barclay chimed in, "By the time Tommy is done, there's likely to be even more rings in that case."

They shared a hearty laugh, but there was no one who could deny the possibility of additional rings being added to the collection.

Outside, Coach McCracken told his team members, all of whom were still devouring the sandwiches, that he wanted them in bed early. "Tri-Valley is a very good team. We will have to bring our A game if we expect to win the state final."

McCracken then announced that a final team meeting would take place at 10:00 a.m. at the Complex. "That will leave you a few hours to recoup before game time, which is seven o'clock."

The party broke up at about 10:30 p.m. Charlie Wetzel was the last to leave. "Too bad we can't buy stock in baseball players. The kids on that all-star team are going to set the world on fire," he chuckled.

Gloria said she would clean up in the morning. Then she turned to her husband, glad to finally have a minute alone with him. "It's good to have you home, Jack," she said.

He embraced her. "Pinch me so I know I'm not dreaming."

CHAPTER THIRTY-TWO

VINCE ANDERS WAS the first one to get sick. He called his mother to his room at about 5:00 a.m. He was throwing up and complained of strong pains in his stomach.

A few blocks away, Danny Fitzgerald had the same symptoms. In the Snook home, Tommy was heaving in the bathroom and had bad diarrhea.

Almost simultaneously, the parents of each ballplayer decided to go to the emergency room at the local hospital. Concerned parents and retching boys bumped into each other in the hospital's parking lot. Eventually all twelve players were seated in the ER, slumped over and green at the gills. The symptoms were the same. The common denominator: salmonella poisoning. The doctors named the pork sandwiches as the culprit after obtaining a history.

Inside the hospital, the doctors started IVs one by one. "The sooner we start the fluids, the better," said Dr. Thomas Renella. "These boys are going to be sick for a couple of days."

While concern for the boys was foremost, all the parents began wondering about the game, now just twelve hours away. Jack Snook called Sam Cortino to deliver the bad news.

"I'll see if we can get a postponement," Cortino said, half asleep, and quickly terminated the call.

* * *

In Drewmore, Jake Barclay was sipping coffee and browsing the day's newspaper. As he read about the scheduled reunion of Rebecca Jenkins and the man known affectionately as Crossing Guard Fred, he wondered what the future held for them. His daydreaming was interrupted by the ringing of his cell phone.

It was Sam Cortino, delivering the bad news about the team. "The boys seem to have been the only ones who consumed the pork," he said. "It had to be the pork."

Cortino went on to tell the detective that he had made a call to the league's district commissioner to ask for a postponement. Cortino said he was not overly optimistic because of the league's tight schedule.

"We better pray for rain," Barclay said.

"That's the only circumstances under which we probably can get a postponement," said Cortino. "I'll keep in touch throughout the day."

Barclay noticed the time and hurriedly showered and left the hotel. He had one stop to make before he went to get Fred Saunders for the meeting with Rebecca. He estimated Fred's size and stopped at Walt's Mart to buy a few things.

Meanwhile, Fred Saunders awoke from what little sleep he'd managed to get and put the coffee on. His mind was reeling as he thought of the various scenarios awaiting him at the hospital. He worried about being rejected by his only love. Much time had passed, he thought, and sometimes people change. "Could she totally recover from such an ordeal?" he asked himself. Questions bombarded the janitor. However, he managed to refocus and prepare to see the woman he still loved after thirty-five years.

Barclay interrupted Saunders's disturbed reveries, knocking on his door at 7:45 sharp. He found Saunders wearing clothes that had been in style when the crossing guard first met Rebecca.

"Here, Fred, put these on," said Barclay as he handed him the bags from Walt's Mart.

"I really don't need your charity," said Saunders, shoving the bags back toward the detective.

"Look at it as a gift," the detective said, "not charity. You really should look nice when you meet Rebecca. It's almost like a first impression. A second first impression."

"Meeting someone again for the first time, that's a good one," Saunders said and cracked a half smile as he accepted the bag. "You drive a hard bargain, Mr. Detective."

To Barclay's utter surprise, Fred Saunders emerged from the bedroom in his new clothes looking clean cut and even handsome. "You clean up nice, Fred," said the detective.

Fred just grumbled. "I'll pay you for these clothes."

Saunders and the detective got into the Jag and left Archville.

*   *   *

At the hospital, the parents of fourteen boys were presenting their insurance ID cards to the billing people. The doctors had released the boys under the conditions that they rest for seventy-two hours and drink plenty of liquids. It now appeared as though the dream of a World Championship was starting to fade.

"In the summer heat," said Dr. Renella, "you'll get run down in a hurry if you don't rest."

Jack Snook stepped away from the group and called Sam Cortino on his cell phone. "Any news yet?" asked Snook.

Cortino reported that the league would have a decision by noon. "I wouldn't hold too much hope for a postponement," said Cortino. "Saw the weather too," he added. "Not a drop of rain in sight."

Cortino had called a meeting of all the league coaches to fill them in on recent events and warn them of the possibility that the all-stars, who had brought much pride to the community, may have to forfeit the game with Tri-Valley.

Midway through the meeting, Cortino's cell phone rang. It was the deputy commissioner for the league. The words he spoke deflated Cortino.

"There will be no postponement of the scheduled game between Archville and Tri-Valley." The deputy commissioner continued, "If Archville does not field a team for the game, they must forfeit."

Cortino told the deputy commissioner that the team could not play because of illnesses.

The league official then told Cortino he would advise the Tri-Valley coaching staff that the game was forfeited and thus save the team from traveling to Archville.

*   *   *

Nearing the hospital with Fred Saunders, Barclay's phone rang. It was Cortino. "Today's game has been forfeited."

Barclay was lost for words. But he knew also that the team could not play up to the caliber they were capable of while battling the illness. "Tough break, Sam. I don't know what to say."

The detective couldn't believe the dream was over for the kids just like that. He told Saunders what had transpired. Saunders too was speechless.

Barclay steered the Jag into the hospital's parking garage. He noticed right away that they were going to have to deal with a problem.

There were at least a dozen photographers swarming outside the hospital. "Probably from the sleazy tabloids," he muttered.

Barclay was just pulling into a parking space when he noticed that Deputy Attorney General Carson was parking a few spots down. He motioned to Carson to come to his car. Both men commented on the mob scene, while Fred sat sweating in discomfort and anxiety in the passenger seat.

Then Barclay had an idea. "Got your handcuffs?" he asked Carson.

Carson asked what the detective had in mind.

"It's likely that these vultures don't know us or Fred. Let's walk him in as a prisoner being taken for medical treatment."

Carson smirked. "You are downright devious, my friend. That plan just might work."

Fred Saunders felt uncomfortable about the cuffs, but the horde of reporters waiting to pounce made him even more nervous, and he let himself be handcuffed and led toward the waiting cameras.

One of the photographers yelled to the men and asked if any of them was Fred Saunders.

"No," said Barclay. "This man is a fugitive felon we are taking to the emergency room."

The plan worked, and the trio entered the hospital without incident.

"That was easy," said Carson. "Got any tricks up your sleeve for when we leave?"

"I make these moves up on a minute-by-minute basis," Barclay said, and all three enjoyed a chuckle.

*   *   *

In Archville word was spreading fast that the game had been forfeited. The coaches had assembled at the Complex. It was obvious they were deeply saddened by the team's illness.

Barney Clarkson was the first to chime in. "I think these kids are deserving of a tribute of some kind when they are better."

"Perhaps the parents should find a lawyer and sue the catering company," said Ed Gardener.

"You obviously watch too many ambulance chasers' television ads," said Clarkson.

"Let's give them a parade when they get better," said Coach McCracken. "We can get the high school band and the fire companies to participate and maybe host a picnic afterwards."

All the coaches were in favor of a parade for the team. They were all thinking it, but it was Coach McCracken who announced, "This isn't the end. In fact, it's only the very beginning. We have these kids next year in teen league and don't forget high school and American Legion ball. They're only going to get better."

* * *

Meanwhile, the charge nurse at the hospital was making sure the visitors' room was empty in preparation for Fred and Rebecca. Nurse Anne Marinelli and the other nurses had been talking all morning about the reunion of the two lovers after thirty-five years. "I think it would make a great movie," she said.

Saunders was brought into the room first, his knees about to buckle from the anxiety.

"You must be Fred," Nurse Marinelli greeted him warmly and extended both of her hands for a clutching handshake. "I cannot imagine what you are feeling right now. Please sit down and let me know if there is anything I can do to make you more at ease."

Saunders's legs trembled as he sat down and waited mutely for Nurse Marinelli to bring Rebecca in.

Minutes later, the door opened, and Rebecca took soft, hesitant steps inside the room. Rebecca and Fred Saunders exchanged their first glance in three and a half decades. Neither one spoke. They just eyed each other, afraid to speak.

Saunders's head flooded with memories of their past, so full of love that they were blind to the world outside each other. He remembered the photo-booth pictures and the Friday-night ice-cream sodas. He could feel himself tearing up, but he held back so Rebecca would not see him crying.

With his voice cracking from nerves, Fred broke the silence. "I think we have much to talk about. The world is a much different place now, and I don't know how we will fit in."

For the next two hours, the pair just talked. Rebecca told Fred in vivid detail how she was whisked away on the night their baby was born. She explained the confusion and devastation she suffered for three and a half decades. And Fred, as best he could, told Rebecca what she had missed and described what the world was like now.

"You and I had a lot taken away from us," he said. "But I hope we can make up for lost time now."

Rebecca readily agreed. "I am going to be very afraid for a while, and I will need someone I trust to be by my side."

"Boy am I relieved we got that out of the way," Saunders said. As he relaxed, wave after wave of emotion washed over him. "Hardly a day went by that I didn't miss you, Rebecca. I feel like I've been caught up in some kind of a nightmare."

"Me too," she said. "We have really. I'll never get those years back. Neither will you."

Nurse Marinelli knocked on the door and told the couple the visit was over. "You can come back at six p.m. if you like, Mr. Saunders."

Fred embraced Rebecca and told her that he still loved her. "I never saw anyone else," he added.

"Me either," she said with a devilish smile.

Fred knew inside that he and Rebecca were going to spend the rest of their lives together.

The crossing guard had some pep in his step as he met Carson and Barclay in the hospital cafeteria.

The two men stared at him in greedy anticipation.

"We still have feelings for each other," Saunders blurted out. "It will take some time, but I know it will work out. I can feel it."

Barclay was relieved that the visit went well. "Never mind a book, this case might make a good movie," he said as they walked toward the exit.

Barclay called Lovello and Monica and filled them in on the visit. They too were relieved. The detective then told them to check out of their hotels and meet him at Marty's in Archville.

Next, he called Coach McCracken and asked him to invite the coaches to Marty's for a farewell drink.

Jack Snook was his final call as he drove Fred back to Archville. "How's Tommy?"

"Still sick, but nothing like this morning. God, I feel so bad for those kids."

"Me too," said Barclay. "But I feel there is a great future for those boys, especially Tommy."

"I think you're right," Snook said.

"John Lovello, me and Monica are going to meet the coaches at Marty's for a farewell cocktail if you'd care to join us," said Barclay.

"I'll be there, but only to say good-bye to you three."

LEO A. MURRAY

As they arrived in Archville, Fred Saunders said he would like to say farewell too. "I'm not in any mood to drink, but I owe you and John Lovello my sincerest gratitude for what you did."

"We were doing our job," said Barclay. "We just happen to be good at it." They shared another laugh.

At Marty's, Barclay first asked for the back room, and secondly, he asked Marty to start a tab.

"Sure thing," said Marty. "What's the occasion?"

"A good-bye party," was the reply.

The new friends trickled in one by one. It was more like a wake than anything else. Barclay told his friends that John Lovello and Monica Thompson were on their way. "I'll wait until they get here. Meanwhile, I have an open tab, get whatever you want."

"I'll take a case of Dewar's," said McCracken with a smile. His wit was just the thing to break the ice and generate some laughter. Everyone had been feeling down in the dumps with the team getting sick and exhausted after everything they had been through.

McCracken told his coaches that the team may not have gotten by Drewmore if it wasn't for Barclay's efforts with the birth certificate of Vinny Benito. "The guy's a genius," said McCracken.

Just as Monica and John Lovello stepped into the back room at Marty's, the coaches and Jack Snook gave them a standing ovation. They were truly humbled by the thunderous roar they received from people, who ten weeks earlier, they did not know.

When the applause stopped, Lovello cleared his throat and began to speak. "This has been one of the most bizarre cases I have ever worked on. There's no reason to go into detail because you all know what has transpired over the past few weeks, period.

"One thing is for certain: We will never forget you guys. You owe yourselves a round of applause for all you give back to your community through what you do for the kids."

Sam Cortino almost let a tear run down his cheek.

"Come on," said Lovello. "Give yourselves a clap."

The back room roared.

The exit party was just what the doctor ordered, Barclay thought. He was thinking that it would be nice if Charlie Mars were there. He hadn't finished the thought when Mars came through the door.

Barclay fixed his fingers on his lips and blew a loud whistle. He began acknowledging each person whom he came to know during the investigation.

Of course, there were McCracken and Cortino. But the defense attorney wanted to especially acknowledge Charlie Mars.

He called Mars up to where he was standing and put his arms around the reporter, practically squeezing the breath out of him. "Ladies and gentlemen, until I worked this case in Pennsylvania, I had no use for reporters." He went on to say that Charlie Mars changed that.

"The people of this area are fortunate to have a guy like Charlie Mars standing guard over the First Amendment for them. He is indeed a warrior when he goes after a story."

Mars was humbled by the gratitude from the detective. "Can I quote you on that, Jake?" His remark drew a well-deserved laugh.

But the time of departure was at hand. Handshakes and hugs were the order of the day before the California trio exited Marty's. Everyone in the room knew the two detectives would be long remembered when anyone ever spoke of the year Archville broke the twenty-year jinx in the tournament.

Outside, Lovello said he was returning to California. Monica and Jake, the new partners, were going to take a few days in Upstate New York to relax.

"Don't do anything I wouldn't do," said Lovello as he flashed a grin.

"Is that some kind of sexist remark, Mr. Attorney?" asked Monica. "We're business partners," she said with a big smile. "And really good friends."

As they drove out of Archville, Barclay looked into his rearview mirror, first out of habit and secondly to wonder if he would ever return.

The End

Edwards Brothers, Inc.
Thorofare, NJ USA
January 30, 2012